WESTCOTT HIGH 2

SARAH MELLO

—

I dedicate this book to my sister, Lauren, for listening to me talk about Westcott so much, we both started to believe we live there.

First Printing, 2020
United States of America
ISBN: 978-1-7331743-1-2 (paperback)

Author: Sarah Mello
Editor: Andrea Reimers
Book Cover Design: Olivia Heyward

CONTENTS

1 TEN LESSONS

Leaving the frigid wind behind me on the empty sidewalk, I pulled open the heavy door of Laurel's Bakery. The wreath hanging center smacked against the glass as the door shut behind me, and the bell attached to the wreath rang loudly. It was an old-school way of alerting the cashier a customer had entered their establishment, and I appreciated the vintage touch. The hour hand on the clock, which hung on top of crimson floral wallpaper, hadn't yet landed on the seven that Saturday morning, so with the exception of an older gentleman who sat alone reading the paper in a mustard wool sweater, the shop was still. I wiped my Converses against the welcome mat, wrapped myself into my long-sleeved flannel shirt, and walked to the counter.

"What can I get for you?" asked the barista.

“I’ll have ten black coffees.”

He gave me a strange look, then punched the numbers on the register and finished ringing me up. “I’ll have that right out for you.”

After taking a moment to admire the rows of cinnamon buns and colorful pastries lined in the glass dome below me, I dragged my feet and empty stomach to the big window in the corner of the bakery and set up camp at an unstained wood table with a mix of metal and fabric chairs surrounding it. Within minutes, the barista brought the coffees to the table via two serving trays, along with a few silver canisters of creamer and multiple packs of sugar. We exchanged a forced smile, and then he headed back to the counter. I grabbed a coffee, and with heavy eyes, gazed out the window and took a sip; my freezing fingers wrapped tightly around the warm paper cup.

Cliff was the first one to walk by the window that morning. As the wreath bounced off the glass, he stepped through the threshold and removed his hood. For the first *real* time in three weeks, our eyes met. As always, Cliff oozed privilege, from his Tag Heuer Monaco watch to his designer sneakers. The only thing whiter than his shoes were his perfect teeth, gifted to him by his parents’ impeccable genes. Most kids would kill to be Cliff. But his kind of bloodline could also be a curse, and no one knew this better than him.

He walked over to the table and sat at the head; I expected nothing less. Staring absently through the window, he leaned back in the fabric chair, neither of us saying a word. I grabbed another coffee and extended it toward him. He took the cup, reached into his back pocket to pull out his wallet, and handed me a five-dollar bill.

Cliff taught me about money. In eighth grade, when my mom's money was tight, I had the crazy idea that I could put a dent in her debt by tutoring. I was too timid to charge what I was worth, so I accepted IOUs and ten bucks an hour for doing someone else's homework. That was until Cliff and his friends walked into Laurel's Bakery one afternoon. I don't know if it was the ten dollars that caused him to cringe or the way the sophomore tossed it on the table and patted my head on his way out, but Cliff walked straight up to me, still sweating from football practice, and said something I'll never forget: "You could make four times that money in half the time if you make that prick bring three friends next week."

After my embarrassed look, he continued. "If you're charging ten bucks a session, make it two-on-two. You'll get more bang for your buck that way. They get to work with friends—more fun for them, less work for you. Plus, they'll finish in half the time with double the brains per team. You'll just be an overseer." He laid a fifty-dollar bill on the table. "Just a suggestion." As I attempted to give the cash back, his next words were final. "If someone gives you money, you take it."

I couldn't help but think an eighth grader shouldn't be giving out financial advice and fifty-dollar bills in lieu of ordering baked goods with his friends at the front of the line, but money was imbedded in Cliff's psyche, and he couldn't let a teachable moment slip through his fingers.

It wasn't normal. But then again, *neither was Cliff.*

The bell on the door rang again and in walked Norah. Modeling a magenta faux-shearling coat and a high ponytail, she walked over to the table and pulled out a chair next to Cliff. She then reached for her coffee and grabbed a creamer canister with frail, paint-stained fingers—her usual look.

Norah taught me how to be tough. One afternoon in ninth grade, as I was waiting on Lana to finish cheer practice, I heard a combination of sniffling, grunts, and thuds coming from the art room. When I walked in, Norah was smashing her paint brush against a canvas in the dark. The word around school was she'd entered her painting into a showcase and received critical feedback. And to Norah, who relied on painting as an emotional crutch ever since her dad took off, news like that was devastating.

"Maybe you should start over," I'd suggested from the doorframe.

She continued beating the brush against the board, never looking behind her. "Painting is like life, Sonny. You don't start over. You just try to make the shitty things better."

Two months later, she placed that same painting into an art exhibit and sold it for a hefty sticker price.

It was admirable—and although I really hated to admit it—*so was Norah.*

Next to arrive was Winston—dressed in his trusty jean jacket and a dark-gray cashmere scarf. His face was a little paler than normal, and his eyes drooped. He sat down next to me, grabbed a cup, then added sugar to his coffee and chugged it.

Winston taught me humor. When I met him in tenth grade, he was being bullied, and I fancied myself his rescuer. Little did I know, he'd go on to help me more than I ever could aid him. He dismissed everything with sarcasm—a talent I envied. Perhaps things did affect him, like the times his dad would trash his *Vogue* magazines because boys supposedly weren't allowed to enjoy fashion, but Winston never showed it. And when I suffered through bad breakups or slutty-sister scandals, Winston was right there with his witty one-liners to cheer me right up.

He was my humor, *even when my world wasn't so funny.*

A gust of cold air rushed into the shop. This time, Ari appeared wearing a black sweater, ripped black jeans, no makeup, and no jewelry. She looked bare, and beautiful. Arms folded across her chest, she hurried over to the table, collapsing into the seat next to Norah.

Once upon a time, Ari taught me what confidence looked like. When the Cobalts came to Westcott, most of them scattered through the hallways like nervous new kids on their first day of school, but not Ari Ziegler. While standing at her locker in black combat boots and hole-filled skinny jeans, she'd belted out musical riffs like the hallway was her personal stage.

"What do you think sounds better?" she asked me, followed by thirty seconds of singing.

Taken aback by her boldness, I stared at her in complete silence, and once she realized she had asked the wrong person, she gave me a quizzical smile and walked away.

I didn't know at the time that her song was about Cliff, and as she sunk lower into her metal chair in the bakery that morning, *I couldn't help but think just how much her tune had changed.*

Buckets was next to walk by the window, his camera dangling from his neck. As he opened the bakery door, everyone looked up. The sleeves of his hunter-green jacket hung long around his fingertips, and unlike Cliff, he kept his hood on. After sitting down next to Winston, he removed his camera and placed it beside him on the table, then slowly reached for a coffee.

Buckets taught me about pictures, and not the ones he'd take on his camera. Back in tenth grade, I was assigned Buckets as a science-project partner. Up until that day, I thought he had it all together. But as I pushed through his small cluttered apartment, stepping over piles of unwashed laundry and moving boxes that had never been unpacked, I realized it was all a facade. Buckets couldn't photoshop the embarrassment on his face, and I couldn't pretend not to notice.

"That's why I take photos," he said with a blank stare. "It reminds me there *are* beautiful things in this world."

It was the first time I had witnessed what Buckets's life was truly like; you'd never know by the picture he painted through his gallery, or by his confident demeanor, *that it was anything but beautiful.*

Piper's wavy honey-colored hair blew in the wind as she walked by the glass window. She stepped inside and removed her tan peacoat, then strode against the polished concrete floor in ballet-slipper shoes. As she sat down in a fabric chair, her eyes cut from side to side, and when she thought no one was looking, she reached for a coffee.

Piper taught me about work ethic; no one worked harder than her. In the ninth grade, she received her first C on a major assignment. You'd have thought someone cut her beautiful honey locks off with scissors or chucked her violin into the ocean. She ran out of the classroom crying, and I followed. After catching up with her in the parking lot, she turned and faced me with a ghostly complexion.

"It's just one grade," I told her. "It's fine."

But to Piper, a C meant more than a bad grade. It meant she had failed herself. It meant the grueling all-nighters she pulled were null and void. She slammed herself into her car and began sobbing uncontrollably. I watched through the windshield, and although I wanted to help, she wasn't the kind of girl who would have accepted it.

Piper was always on top, so when our eyes met that cool fall morning, it was hard to believe *just how far she'd fallen.*

JC came in shortly after, jerking the heavy door open with one strong pull. The abruptness caused us all to stare. He wore a leather jacket and fitted jeans; his Chuck Taylors matched mine. Dropping down beside Buckets, he avoided all eye contact as he reached for his cup.

Ironically, JC taught me patience. I'll never forget the first big fight I had with Dean before our breakup. JC had just finished one of his wrestling practices with my father in our home gym, and on his way out to his car, he passed by me as I sat on the front porch steps in tears. I knew he felt uncomfortable as he listened to my sighs. I knew he was exhausted and just wanted to go home. But rather than bolting toward his car to avoid a two-hour conversation about boy problems—he stayed. I thought by hour one, in true JC fashion, he'd tell me to suck it up and get the hell over it, but surprisingly those words never came. Before I knew it, my face was dry, and he somehow managed to shift the conversation to Led Zeppelin and then the WWE.

I never thanked him for that night or apologized for being so selfish. Luckily for me, *he was used to that.*

Dean, dressed in his customary basketball hoodie and joggers, walked in next—and when his blue eyes met mine, I admittedly felt a bit of relief. He removed his hood and walked to the table, taking his seat next to me. I breathed in the familiar smell of his sheets as he settled into his chair.

Dean taught me what love was, and what it wasn't. Pre-breakup, he was my everything. We didn't just see each other at our best and worst—we *were* each other's best and worst. But after his mother's death and the incident between our dads, he became tormented and conflicted, and I couldn't rid him of either. When he ended things with me, I had run up the stairs while frantically dialing Winston, and then paced my bedroom floor for over an hour in hysterics. Once I couldn't go on any longer, I took a hot shower, changed into pajamas, and walked to the corner of my room to turn off my lamp. Through the sheer curtains, I saw Dean's Audi outside on the curb—still parked in the same spot. As soon as I turned off the light, he started his car and slowly pulled away down my street. It took me a few minutes to realize what that meant, but when I figured it out, it eased my pain.

Because Dean breaking my heart that night wasn't love, but sitting outside in his car until I went to sleep was; and as my head hit the pillow that night, I knew even if I didn't have him anymore, *I had that.*

Kyle walked by the bakery window, and after opening the door and swiping his sneakers against the welcome mat, he walked toward us with both his head and hood down. He took his seat at the other end of the table, never reaching for a coffee, never looking up.

Kyle taught me about goodness. He was a sweet soul, and there was no catch. After one of his heated breakups with Ari, I drove over to his house to keep him company. We talked about things he'd never confess to, shed tears he'd never admit to shedding, and watched movies he'd never acknowledge watching. Before I knew it, it was one in the morning. It wasn't unlikely for me to sleep at his house if I was too tired to drive home, especially in the middle of a storm. After the thunder nearly split the house in two, he loaned me a big T-shirt and I headed to the spare bedroom to crash. Half an hour later, the power went out and I couldn't sleep, so I tiptoed to Kyle's room.

"The power is out and I'm scared," I said as I shined my cell-phone's flashlight in his face.

Without much thought, he pulled the comforter back. "Take my bed," he replied as he grabbed a pillow and throw blanket, and made a pallet for himself on the floor.

He could have told me to go back to the spare bedroom, or home, or to the ground. But he gave up his warm bed for me—on a night when he needed it most.

Because that's who Kyle was. He was good to people,

even people who weren't always good to him.

I grabbed the remaining cup, prepared the coffee for Kyle, and passed it down the table. It had been three weeks since the conversation we all had with Principal Winchester in parking lot C, and we'd hardly spoken a word to one another. As we sat around the table that morning, the ambiance was so tense and heavy, I could feel it pushing against my chest. Relationships were still in shambles and friendships were still broken, and no amount of free coffee or cinnamon-bun aromas could fix that. We all sat in silence, listening to the sound of the old man flipping through the newspaper until finally, someone spoke.

"What are we doing here?" Cliff asked me.

I took a deep breath, reached into my back pocket, and pulled out a small sheet of paper. Everyone leaned forward, and Cliff and Kyle made their way to the center of the table.

"Fourteen sixty-two South Ambrite Street," Buckets read aloud. "What is that?"

Cliff snatched the paper from the table and began lifting it toward his face, but no sooner did Norah pluck it from his clenched fingers. She stared at the paper for a good ten seconds before she came looking for answers.

"It's a note." I wrapped myself tighter into my flannel. "From Jacob."

"I thought his note said something about colors?"

"It did. But there was a second note, tucked underneath

the black pillow the brooch was sitting on."

"Brooch? That rainbow thing sitting on your nightstand is from Jacob?" Winston took the paper from Norah's hands with a napkin. "I thought we were done with Jacob after he betrayed you."

Cliff sighed. "Did we just come here to talk about your relationship problems? Because I can go."

"Well, we can talk about yours if Sonny's don't interest you," Winston replied.

Before I knew it, the silence had turned into our typical banter. After everything we had been through together, most would find our lack of growth disheartening, but it was a small step up from ignoring one another for weeks so I viewed it as progress.

"Jacob gave Norah a black box to give me before he left." I snuck a glance at Dean before continuing. "Inside of it, yes, was a brooch and an apology note—"

"Well, as long as he apologized via note . . ." Winston peered at the crinkled paper.

"But that was tucked underneath it," I continued, rolling my eyes at him. "The address led me to a printing shop outside of town. I went inside and there was an order under my name."

Norah leaned forward, placing her clasped hands and elbows on the table. "What did you find?"

"These." I pulled a stack of photos out of my back pocket.

She took them from me. "Holy shit," she whispered, glancing up at the others. "It's Piper."

Piper lunged across the table, grabbed the photographs from Norah's hands, and hastily flipped through them; her flowery perfume rushed into my nose as everyone crowded around her.

"Kyle and I were in the club's sunroom the day we saw Piper on the golf course." I paused, glancing up at Kyle. "But before that, I was having lunch with Jacob. When I saw Kyle walk into the club, I left Jacob in the café. He must have seen Piper and Principal Winchester exchange the manila envelope on the way back to his car and snapped these pictures. Maybe he thought it was odd. Maybe he planned on showing the photos to his dad."

"Did you confirm that with him?" Buckets asked.

My fingers tightened around the fistful of flannel in my palms as everyone walked back to their seats. "I'm not exactly speaking to Jacob after what he did."

"Don't you mean what *your dad* did?" Ari questioned.

Learning Mr. Ballinger had hired Ron Harrison to investigate the odd financial happenings at the sporting-goods store was surprising. And finding out *that* was the hush-hush case Ron had been working on was a shock. But my dad's arrest and admission to embezzlement took the cake. No one understood why he stole the money from his company and framed Dean's dad, but like most shoddy businessmen in Westcott, he got off with a slap on the wrist, a large fine, and a slightly bent reputation.

"Jacob knew why they moved here," Winston retorted. "And he knew about his dad's case. He lied to her."

"He withheld the truth," Ari corrected.

Winston's lips slowly protruded in a condescending pout. "You'd know all about that, wouldn't you?"

"Don't you get it?" I grabbed the photos and held them out in front of me like a hand of cards. "Principal Winchester said we have no proof, but now we do. These, along with the Princeton profile, are enough to turn him in."

The silence that followed was so freakishly quiet I thought I had convinced everyone off the bat. I watched as their eyes made a few rounds, eagerly waiting for someone's reply.

Buckets chimed in. "Not to be the buzzkill, but I'm not exactly willing to continue this charade. Winchester has us on camera admitting to breaking the SCC . . . admitting to breaking into Piper's house . . . the safe. He made himself clear—we drop it, he drops it." He looked side to side, then leaned forward in his chair. "Look, I'm a Cobalt, Sonny. I need this school. Maybe you, Kyle, and Cliff—and every other Violet here—can take these kinds of risks, but I can't get kicked out of Westcott over some stupid ploy to take down our principal. My parents would kill me."

"And JC doesn't even go to Westcott anymore," Ari

argued. "So what does it matter?"

JC transferred to Jefferson High a week after the parking lot C conversation. Some people assumed he left so he could wrestle again. Others thought he took off because he couldn't take the public shame of stealing the answer key. And if you didn't know him, either of the two would be logical assumptions. But for those of us who did, we knew the reason he left was sitting across from him at the table that morning. Because everyone knew JC loved to wrestle—but not more than he loved Piper. And losing her? Well, I guess he couldn't bear it.

I glanced over at JC. He sat there, motionless. He and Piper hadn't spoken since their fiery conversation in parking lot C, and they certainly hadn't discussed Piper's betrayal or their broken relationship. I knew her presence was making him uncomfortable; she had a funny way of doing that to everyone.

"This isn't just about JC anymore," I replied, peeling my eyes off him. "The Bella View kids come on Monday morning." I glanced at the Violets. "You know that'll be nothing but trouble for all of us. But if we get rid of the head, we kill the body."

"Hold on. You want to get rid of Winchester?" Cliff asked. "Completely?"

"Don't you?" We locked eyes. "You saw what he did to JC. He was able to convince his *girlfriend* to turn on him.

What makes you think he won't stand by and allow these Bella View kids to ruin us?"

"Sonny's right." Norah's bleak eyes floated around the circle in a catatonic state. "He has to go."

We all stared at one another, unquestionably terrified.

"There's one problem," Kyle said. "There's nothing *we* about this group. I can't trust half the people in it."

"Agreed." Cliff tapped the table with his knuckle; his combative voice stood up nicely to Kyle's. "Someone in this circle could have leaked the video of me and Ari. How do I know I can trust any of you?"

"Coming from the guy who leaked the video of Lana." Winston took a swig of his overly sweetened coffee. "You're the one nobody can trust."

Cliff puffed out his chest. "I didn't leak that."

"Yeah right."

"I told you I didn't," he confidently replied, glancing up at a customer while they passed by our table.

Winston was unbothered. "Who else could it have been?"

"Maybe it was you, Winston," Norah suggested. "Your lips are looser than Lana's standards."

"I'll let you know what yours are like when you pull them off Cliff's ass," he replied. "We all know it was Cliff."

Buckets rolled up the sleeves on his jacket and shifted in his seat. His eyes moved around the room, and he must have swallowed five or six times.

Grinning slightly, Cliff grabbed his lips and let out a quick breath, then focused his attention on Winston. "What makes you think you know anything about my relationship with Lana?"

"Maybe I don't. But I know a lot about you."

"You don't know shit about me," Cliff retorted. "You've known me for a year."

"One year too many."

Buckets shifted in his seat again, picking up and putting down his camera for no apparent reason.

"Think what you want." Cliff stood to his feet and yanked his hood over his head. "I didn't give Buckets the damn video."

"Then who did?" Winston asked as Cliff walked toward the door.

"It was Lana!" Buckets's voice struck me like lightning; his words nearly knocked me out of my chair.

Cliff stopped, made a U-turn, and walked back toward the group.

"Lana?" I muttered, my stomach churning at the thought. "What are you talking about?"

Buckets shrugged his shoulders. "It's true. She gave me the video. She asked me to leak it."

"Why would she do that?"

We all followed his eyes as they slowly traveled toward Cliff's; Cliff stared back into his. "Jesus, Poland. Talk!"

"She didn't want to go to Columbia," Buckets quickly replied. "Leaking the video was her attempt at ruining her reputation so she wouldn't get in. It was all on purpose. Mr. Hill. The parking lot B situation. Everything. She planned it all. Once the video was debunked and she got into Columbia, I'm assuming she just made the tough decision to go to New York anyway."

Through his sweatshirt, I could see Cliff's chest pumping up and down as his breathing quickened. The thought of Lana making a mistake and cheating on him with a teacher had already been a big pill for him to swallow. But perhaps knowing she chose to by orchestrating this charade was a pill not even Cliff Reynolds himself was able to digest.

"Why would Principal Winchester debunk a video that Lana herself admitted was real?" Ari asked. "Has anyone ever wondered that?"

"Same reason he just let Coach Dirk go," Buckets answered. "Westcott is the last of the Crescent. The school can't afford any bad publicity—that includes back-seat hookups with temps and keeping coaches who dabble in embezzlement."

"Wow." Norah glanced at me. "You must be so proud."

When I looked at Cliff again, his mind had already commuted back to Buckets's announcement. "Lana would have told me," he said, shaking his head as if that'd make everything untrue. "Why the hell didn't she tell me?"

"She didn't want anyone to know," Buckets replied. "Especially you. And I swore I wouldn't tell a soul." His eyes left Cliff's and met mine. "You can't tell her, Sonny."

I took a moment to collect myself. Flashbacks of sideways glances and indirect sly comments flooded my mind. I couldn't understand why she didn't confide in me. Or in Cliff. Or in anyone. I couldn't wrap my mind around why Lana felt ruining her life was the only way to save it. But maybe that was what Westcott had come to—*and maybe she was just smart enough to do it*.

"There's one more problem," Piper said, her voice shattering the stillness of the room. "You don't have the Princeton profile." She gave the photos one last look before tossing them on the table. "I do." Aggressively, she slid back into her peacoat. "And I'm not willing to get involved."

"Wait, what? Piper—"

"I'm sure you remember what he said, Sonny," she interrupted, shuffling to collect herself. "He doesn't want to hear another word about any of this. If we stay silent, so will he."

Winston huffed. "Just when I thought Judas was turning a corner."

"You really believe that?" I asked, my eyes moving back and forth between her and JC. "It'll only get worse and you know it!"

She dug for her keys.

"Say something, JC!"

The two engaged in quick, agonizing eye contact. Agonizing not only for them, but for everyone at the table who once believed they were the power couple amongst us.

"Like what?" JC stared down at his lap, almost in a state of surrender. "All I wanted to do was wrestle, Sonny. And I'm doing that now." He slowly lifted his head and looked at Piper. "I don't need anything from you."

The room was so cold it almost had a blue tint to it, and our faces were frozen as we awaited her reply.

But while we all thought she'd come back with a sappy "sorry," silence took over instead. Piper stood up, walked to the door, and placed her hand on the glass. "You know what, Sonny?" Turning on the balls of her feet, she twisted back around and glared at me. "If you're looking for your next mystery to solve, why don't you focus on Casey?"

"Why would I do that?"

"Nobody wondered why she's not here this morning?"

"She's babysitting her brothers," I replied.

"You sure about that?" Piper reached into the deep pocket on her peacoat and walked back to the table. She took out her cell phone, scrolled for a second or two, then shoved it into my hand; everyone piled up behind me.

"What the hell . . . ," Kyle whispered.

My eyes left the screen and found hers.

"You aren't the only one with suspicious photos." With a

raised brow, Piper snatched her cell phone from my hands and rushed to the door.

There are nine lessons my friends taught me. Nine specific things I could remember while they were cheating on my best friend, or framing another, or dumping me on my front porch steps. Because life gets the best of us sometimes, and in a school like Westcott, where the stakes were so high, we didn't always know how to treat each other. Sometimes we shocked the people we loved the most—our friends. And more importantly, sometimes they shocked us.

Because while the nine of them had all taught me something valuable, it was Casey who taught me the biggest lesson. And that was learning that despite what we thought we knew about her, *none of us really knew her at all.*

2 SMOKE

Smoke. Most of us wouldn't define it as the visible vapor and gases given off by a burning substance. Nor would one describe it as the gaseous products of burning materials made visible by the presence of small particles of carbon. Smoke means fire. . . . Everyone knows that. Because it doesn't take a genius to figure out when there's a visible suspension of carbon in the air, there's a fire nearby. And by the end of that day . . . one of us would prove it.

"So this is Jefferson High?" I fanned my hand in front of my face as I walked by a group of smokers. Lana's silk black dress, the one I snatched from her suitcase before she went back to New York, grazed the top of my knees as it blew in the wind. Travel plans stood in her way of coming home for Thanksgiving, so she'd come to town to visit—leaving a few hours before JC picked me up for his homecoming dance. Truthfully, I couldn't say I was upset about it. After everything I learned about the video leak at the bakery that morning, being around her wasn't as easy as it used to be.

JC loosened his matching black tie. "It's no Westcott," he said as we walked toward the filthy gymnasium doors. "And by that, I mean there's no blackmail, corruption, or psychotic principals who are out to ruin your life."

"As far as you know," I replied, shamelessly gawking at the herds of high school students passing by. "Everyone here looks so—"

"Normal?"

"Normal sums it up." I followed JC into the gym. The music was blaring and the strobe lights seemed to be on a mission to blind everyone in sight. "Do you like it here so far?"

JC pushed through the crowd and the crowd pushed back. "I like being the best wrestler on the team."

"You had that at Westcott."

"Yeah." He plopped down on a metal folding chair against the wall. "Minus the whole being on the team part."

I joined him, taking my seat in the metal chair next to his. It was a far cry from the white velvet couches at Westcott dances, but for Jefferson, it somehow fit perfectly. "I still can't believe you go to public school now. . . . It's kind of cool in a way."

"Cool?"

"Yes, cool." I cautiously leaned back in my wobbly chair and crossed my legs. "There's something about the unknown that truly fascinates me."

JC shifted in his seat. "Jesus, Sonny. It's public education, not the Voynich Manuscript."

"I'm just shocked your parents let you leave Westcott is all."

"Yeah, well, Jefferson has the second-best wrestling team in the state. That's the only reason I was able to convince my dad to let me transfer."

Dragging my eyes to the right, I gave JC a little push on the leg. "Well, we miss you at Westcott. You, and all of your cutting one-liners."

"I doubt I'm missed."

"What are you talking about? We miss you."

"*You* miss me. You don't count."

I quickly dropped my head, then focused my attention on the dance floor. It was hard to look at JC when his mind was on Piper, so somehow staring out into a pack of strangers seemed easier. "I can't believe she walked out on us this morning."

"Did you really expect her to help?"

"Why wouldn't I?"

"Sonny." JC leaned back in his chair and put his arm around mine. "It took me weeks to get Piper's attention, and once I had it, it took a few more for her to even consider going on a date with me. The girl isn't exactly known for her quick decision making. You put her on the spot."

"You're making excuses for her."

"I'm just saying I'm not shocked," he replied. "Piper's driven by success. Sure, maybe back in ninth grade she fell for an idiot like me. Maybe once upon a time, I could make her laugh and forget her worries. But the older we get—I don't know—we realize there's less shit to laugh about. Responsibilities pile up, and it no longer matters what dude you dated in high school. It matters where you're going when you're out. Maybe Piper's just smart enough to know what none of us are willing to admit. That none of this shit matters, and it definitely isn't worth risking the rest of our lives for."

"So you're okay with what she did to you?"

"I never said I was okay . . . but Piper can't fix that."

"Then who can?"

"Me." JC's brown eyes scanned my right cheek. "By accepting what happened and doing what I can to move forward. Why do you think I'm here in this shithole?"

My chin dipped to my chest. I couldn't help but feel overwhelmed by the unfairness that was his life. How did a Violet like JC end up in a school where the best thing there was him? How could such a promising story turn so vile? It was hard to conceptualize. I wanted to hug him. I needed to cry. It was the first time JC took a loss of any kind, and I felt at fault . . . *and maybe I was.*

Taking a shallow breath, I changed the subject. “Well, look on the bright side. . . . At least you have less homework now.”

“That’s the bright side?” He paused. “Wow. Jefferson’s more of a shithole than I thought.”

I raised my right finger. “Lest you forget what it’s like to be us. After we left Laurel’s this morning, I spent eight hours working on my paper for the Westcott Awards, and a whopping twelve minutes on myself before you picked me up. Anything’s brighter than that.”

“That’s right. . . . Your first draft is due in a couple of weeks. Are you done yet?”

“I’m sitting semi-pretty at the halfway mark.”

JC tossed his hands behind his head in a stretch. “You know . . . it’s almost undoable.”

“What is?”

“Being a Westcott student,” he replied. “There’s so much pressure to be the best athlete, the smartest kid—don’t get me started on the number of extracurricular activities and service hours you have to log to even get noticed around there.” He dropped his arms. “It’s like you tiptoe the line of mental exasperation, and *right before* you’re about to snap, they throw you a party with velvet couches and chocolate fountains and rope you back in.”

I ran my finger over the side of my chair, lifting it to my eyes to find a streak of black soot. "You know, I've never appreciated those couches until now."

"Well, have fun on them. If you need me, I'll be here on my cheap metal folding chair with a horrible reputation and no homework."

"People will find out the truth," I told him. "Believe me. With or without Piper's admission . . . one way or another . . . everyone will eventually find out you didn't steal the answer key."

"Yeah," he replied. "Maybe."

A few minutes of silence blew over us. JC watched his new classmates engage in cheerful conversations and dance battles. I watched the clock. Eventually, when I couldn't stand the silence any longer, I spoke. "You know, the last time we were in this setting you were scolding me about *my* relationship."

Curiosity took him over.

"Dean," I continued. "You told me to be careful. Don't you remember?"

"Ah. I remember. And I see you didn't listen."

"We're just friends," I said, exaggerating each word.

"Is that why his hand was on your leg underneath the table this morning?"

Contrary to popular belief, specifically JC's, Dean and I weren't back together. We were working on rebuilding our friendship. Taking things slow. And occasionally placing our hands on each other's thighs when our friends weren't looking.

"He's not as bad for me as you think," I mumbled.

"Whoa. Your confidence is shaking the gym."

"Really? I thought that was the judgment in your voice."

"No." JC's voice heightened. "No, I'm pretty sure it was your confidence."

"I really don't want to hear your opinion on it." My eyes narrowed. "And you know, what exactly do you have against Dean anyway?"

"The same thing everyone else does."

I raised my hands, then dropped them on my lap. "If I can forgive him for breaking up with me and dating Norah, I'd like to think my friends can too."

"Look, I'm just concerned." He ironed his navy slacks with flat fingers. "I get it. You've loved Dean for as long as I've loved Piper. You two have history. But I think getting back together with him so quickly may be a mistake. Especially if you still like Jacob."

The crowd around us seemed to grow, or perhaps I was shrinking. I hadn't given Jacob much thought since he left Westcott, or at least that's what I pretended when my friends brought him up. But in every sense of the word, I was avoiding doing so.

"And on that note." I stood to my feet. "What do you say

we go dance?"

JC turned his nose up at the idea. "I don't dance."

"No, *I* don't dance—making this the perfect opportunity for us to completely humiliate ourselves in front of a ton of people we don't know." I cracked my knuckles and stared at the dance floor, then looked at JC with raised brows. "You coming?"

The next hour involved body convulsions, the robot, jumping around in circles, tae kwon do, and some incredibly twisted version of the Irish treble jig. I hadn't seen JC let loose and have that much fun since our eighth-grade dance, and for a split second, I realized I hadn't been that happy in nearly a year. Song after song, belly-aching laugh after laugh, we danced our way out of our darkness.

The music eventually shifted when the DJ put on a slow song, while simultaneously putting everyone else out of their misery.

"Bathroom break!" JC leaned his sweaty forehead toward mine. "I'll be right back!"

He took off, and I found myself at the food and drink table. Standing off to the side, I grabbed the ponytail from my wrist and tossed my hair into a wretchedly messy bun. It wasn't long before I noticed the eyes on me. Jefferson girls passed by the table, delivering scathing stares that were so long I thought they'd never end. Feeling self-conscious, I pulled my hair back down and tried to straighten it out with my clammy fingers.

"Bet you never thought we'd be so nice," a raspy voice seeped into my right ear.

I turned and was face-to-face with the homecoming queen. The sparkling chrome crown sat on top of her medium-length hair. Her dark brown roots were showing, which somehow only made her more likable. She wore a figure-hugging red dress that hit the floor and wore it with ease. I stared into her mysterious eyes, instantly connecting with her. She was captivating, breathtaking . . . everything a queen was—and everything I wasn't.

"Yeah, I guess not."

"School pride is a big bitch," she said. "But they're all harmless."

I nodded. "Guess I forgot I was on their turf when I was out there—"

"Tearing up the dance floor?" Her pearly-white teeth appeared. "Where'd you learn all those moves?"

"Um . . . JC."

"Ah." Her plump lips wrapped around the top of her punch cup as she took a sip. "You're a Westcotter."

"Sonny. Hey, congratulations . . .?"

"Brystol." Her thin tanned arm reached for a brownie. "But most people call me BC."

Suddenly, JC appeared on the other side of me, causing me to jump a little. "What's up, BC?"

"Hey, JC."

"So many acronyms in one circle." My bad joke went unnoticed as my eyes swayed between them. "Do you, uh, do you two know each other?"

He shrugged, staring her up and down slowly. "Sort of."

"I gave JC the official Jefferson tour on his first day, which in retrospect is odd being it's my first year here."

"And you're homecoming queen? That was fast."

She washed down the brownie with the punch, her eyes staying locked in with mine the entire duration of the swig.

"What brings you to Jefferson?" I asked.

"The need for a fresh start." She shivered. "I just wanted to get out of my old town."

"Any reason why?"

"Lots," she replied, reaching for another brownie. "But you'd have to move there to understand."

"Well, I'm glad you're here." JC's eyes strayed; they wandered around Brystol's body.

"Thanks, JC." She took one last sip of punch, then straightened her crown. "I should probably go pretend to like people." She smiled at him, then winked at me before strutting back into the crowd; JC watched.

After a good ten seconds, I snapped my fingers in front of his face. "Geez, what is it with red dresses?"

"What?" JC rolled his shoulders back. "I'm single." He admired her figure once more, then looked at me. "You wanna get out of here?"

After multiple drive-throughs later, we pulled into my dad's driveway with full stomachs and lighter souls.

"You're so wrong." JC slammed one last pile of Wendy's fries into his mouth. "You put In-N-Out and Cook Out into the ring, and In-N-Out walks out every time."

I grabbed the passenger-side handlebar. "That's a whole lot of *outs* in one sentence, and I'm officially in a food coma and can no longer hold this conversation."

"So I win?" JC looked at me while he took a sip of soda.

"Do you need me to say it?"

"Come on. It's me. You know I live for victories."

I rolled my eyes. "Fine. You win."

He raised his brows, wiped his lips on the back of his hand, and opened his car door; I met him on the other side.

"What's your dad doing for money now that he and his business partner from the store split?"

"Probably living off investments until he opens another business." I paused. "Why don't you come in and ask him yourself?"

"Yeah right. He won't even look at me."

"I think you'd be surprised at the levels he's willing to stoop," I replied, stepping onto the walkway. "Just ask Mr. Ballinger."

JC dragged his Ferragamos against the bricks. "Coach

must have needed the money for something urgent. Otherwise, he wouldn't have done something like that. There's no way."

"Why do you stick up for my dad so much? He literally jerked you up by your shirt and kicked you off his team."

"If he truly thought I stole the answer key, he should have."

I crossed my arms and climbed the porch steps. "Do you really think he had a reason for taking the money?"

"I do." He nodded. "And I think had Mr. Ballinger not blown the whistle, he would have replaced it."

I began thinking harder about JC's statement but quickly shook my head to rid my mind of the thought. "My dad tried apologizing to me . . . told me I wouldn't understand . . . but that he's sorry for the damage he caused *my boyfriend*." I let out a short breath. "He didn't even know Dean and I aren't dating anymore. That's how close we are." I paused, my eyes watering. "That's how bad things are."

As we approached the top of the stairs, JC gave me a nudge to the ribs. "It'll get better," he said, offering me what little hope he had left.

But just as he uttered those three words, my black heels landed on the porch—and things actually took a turn for the worse. My eyes were instantly pulled to the welcome mat, where a *very* folded-up piece of paper lay. JC saw it too. The small talk subsided and all I could hear was the distant sound of whatever football game my dad was watching in the living room. We stood there, firmly positioned in place, staring down at the paper.

JC walked forward and bent down to pick it up; I stayed behind, too afraid to move.

Meet me in parking lot C at midnight.

We need to talk.

JC dropped his hand by his side. He looked around my ill-lit yard, then at me. “Who the hell is this from?”

I walked forward and took the note from his fingers. “We need to talk? What does this mean?”

His eyes made zigzags above my head. “Could this be from Jacob?”

“Jacob?” The suggestion caused my pulse to race. “But Jacob’s in Long Beach.”

“He could have made the drive.”

“I don’t know.” I peered at the paper with a pit in my stomach. “This is typed. Jacob’s left me a note before, and he didn’t take the time to type it. Why would he type this one?”

“Maybe he’s trying to impress you.”

“I’m a writer with an old soul.” My hand dropped. “If you’re trying to impress me, it wouldn’t involve a printer.”

“Why don’t you just call him and ask what he wants?”

My mind traveled back to the multiple unanswered messages I'd sent Jacob on the day he left. When he finally replied, our text thread was a compilation of apologies and beautiful words only he could say. But I didn't know how to respond, so I never did. "Because I haven't spoken to him, and I'm not sure I should."

"Why not?"

"I don't know." But I did. "I'm hurt. I'm hurt he never told me about my dad . . . his dad . . . the truth."

"So you don't want to go?"

"No . . . yes . . . I don't know."

JC hopped down my porch steps, one Ferragamo at a time. "I'll drive."

I chased behind him, reaching for his back. "Wait! Maybe I shouldn't! Maybe this is a bad idea! I'm not even sure what I'd say!"

"I'll be in the car, and if the conversation goes left, we can leave. But I'm definitely not letting you go alone." He shrugged. "Just hear him out."

"But—"

"Look, I know what he did. He didn't just lie to you; he technically lied to everyone. All the times we shot hoops together, Jacob never mentioned the case to me. Believe me, if he would have, I would've warned you. And I can't understand why he didn't, but maybe he had a good reason, and if anyone would be willing to hear him out . . . it'd be you."

I took stock, knowing I was feet away from walking inside, taking off my heels, and crashing into my warm bed with a good book and hot tea. I yearned for it, and bounced up and down on my tippy-toes while trying to make a final decision. And although I could have sworn I picked the tea, minutes later I was back inside JC's Mustang, kicking fast-food bags away with my heels. I shifted in my seat the entire drive, squirming with anxiety.

Something wasn't right.

Quicker than we should have, we made it to the entrance of the school. JC pulled onto the street and crept down the road. An eerie sensation rushed through me.

"This place is even more hellish at midnight," he muttered.

I nodded, and the closer we got, the faster my head moved. "I . . . I think this might be a bad idea."

Thankfully, *someone else thought so too.*

"SHIT!" JC slammed on the brakes, almost sending me through the windshield, seat belt, and all.

Cliff jumped out of his car after cutting us off; JC did the same. I thought seriously about scooting into the driver's seat and leaving him there, but I imagined it's frowned upon to ditch your date, and supposedly stealing vehicles isn't respectable either.

I stepped outside just in time to catch their argument.

"What the hell are you doing here?" JC asked.

"I'm saving your ass," Cliff whispered, his voice filled with anger. "What makes you think you should go anywhere near that parking lot after everything that happened? It's laced with cameras. You two find some stupid note and decide to do exactly what it tells you?"

"How do you know about the note?" I asked.

Suddenly, a line of cars pulled up behind JC's. Within a matter of seconds, the entire gang was crowded around us—minus Piper, plus Casey, and unfortunately for me, Dean came too.

Winston walked toward me wearing a fake Gucci robe and a face that said it all.

"Are you kidding me, Winston?" I whispered, instantly regretting my decision to fill him in via text. "You told everyone?!"

"I told Casey." His suede house slippers came to a halt. "I can't be held responsible for how it got around the group after that."

"I only told Buckets," Casey mumbled.

Once I knew Buckets was informed, it was easy to trace how the evening's event trickled up the totem pole and reached Cliff.

"Are you insane?" Kyle grilled me, capturing my full attention. "What the hell are you thinking coming here?"

JC stepped forward. "It's my fault. I wasn't thinking

about the cameras."

"Really?" Winston tightened his robe. "One would think you'd remember those."

"Sonny's weeks away from entering her piece into the awards, JC! She can't be caught doing anything shady!"

"Okay, Winchester! Jesus!" JC rolled his shoulders back. "I didn't think a conversation in a parking lot was shady."

"Everything we do from this point on is shady," Kyle replied. "Don't you get that? What would my dad think if he saw Sonny here with *you* at midnight?"

Norah held her chin high. "Real stupid, Sonny. I'd actually like to beat you at the awards, and I can't do that if you aren't there."

"I think she gets it, guys," Casey said.

Cliff turned to the side, and once his eyes met Casey's, he beelined it toward her. "And what the hell is up with you?"

Casey sent her glasses back up her nose, but they couldn't shield her frightened eyes; her voice cowered. "What do you mean?"

"Cut the shit, Langdon. We saw you with Sawyer. Piper showed us a picture of you and him having dinner."

Sawyer Ellington. A Royal Blue from Bella View. A Chosen Ten. A famed quarterback with enviable genes and an attractive bloodline. Cliff's reflection . . . and his direct competition.

Casey squirmed in her soft-pink sweatshirt. I wasn't sure

if it was Cliff's towering stature or her guilty conscience that caused it, but she squirmed nonetheless.

"What are you doing with a Bella View kid?" Cliff asked. "What did you say to him?"

Norah took a step forward. "You didn't give him any information on us or what happened three weeks ago, did you? Anything you tell Sawyer will get back to the rest of them."

"They all come here on Monday," Kyle said, taking advantage of the opportunity to stare Casey up and down. "They'll use it against us."

The two of them locked eyes. They hadn't spoken since he dropped her off in the friend zone, and their feelings for each other were still spilled out in parking lot B where they left them.

She looked the other way. "Look, I wanted to tell you guys but I didn't think anyone would care."

"But you *do* think we care to hear all about the Enhanced Fujita scale on which tornadoes are classified?" Winston asked.

I scrunched my nose. "Are you talking to him?"

"Forget that." Norah placed her bony hand on my shoulder and moved me to the side. "Are you talking to him about us?"

"No! I wouldn't do that! He's been assigned to my brothers in the Westcott Big Brother program."

Ari called her on it. "That program comes with candle-lit dinners?"

"It was innocent." Casey chewed on her lip. "We were only talking about my brothers. And Sawyer's not that bad; he's pretty genuine."

"Genuine." Kyle grabbed the back of his neck and squeezed hard. "I know Sawyer, Casey. There's nothing genuine about him."

"And he definitely wouldn't be taking you to dinner," Cliff said. "He's up to something."

"What's that supposed to mean?" she asked.

Kyle sighed. "It means he's not the type of guy who would—"

"What?"

"He wouldn't—"

"Be seen with trash like me?" Casey looked at him, jaw clenched. She turned around and walked toward her car.

Kyle grabbed her arm before she got too far. "Why would you even say that?"

"It's what you're thinking, Kyle. Sawyer wouldn't be talking to me because I'm a Cobalt with a messed-up family, and he's a rich kid from Bella View."

Confusion crossed his face.

"You think I don't know what Cliff and all your football buddies say about me? You think I don't know what everyone at school is thinking? That I don't deserve to be there . . . that I'm not like the rest of you . . ."

"That's not what I think!"

"You don't get it, Kyle." But that certainly didn't stop her from explaining it. "You have no idea what it feels like to be a mother to your siblings at sixteen. To cook meals for your brothers because they're too young to use the stove, while you pretend you aren't hungry when the food is gone because your aunt forgot to get groceries. You have no idea what it feels like to have a junkie dad who doesn't care that you exist, and a mother who cares more about finishing a bottle of vodka than helping her kids finish their homework." She tossed her hands in front of her. "God! You just hop in your Range Rover every morning, without thought, and cruise to school—never fearing it won't crank or that you'll run out of gas with no money to fill the tank. Your head hits your pillow at night without a real care in the world while I'm up until three in the morning studying, praying to God I can keep up with my grades so I don't get kicked out of the very school that doesn't even want me there. And the real kicker? There isn't a thing I can do about my life, or where I am, or where I live. I'm not trash because I want to be, Kyle. I'm trash because it's all I *can* be."

"Stop." Kyle cut his eyes to the side and stepped forward some more, attempting to exclude the rest of us from their next conversation. "Look, I don't let anyone say that shit to me, including you. You're not trash, Casey. Your dad's an idiot, and your mom needs help, and none of that is your fault."

"You don't get it," she said again, shaking her head and backing away. It was clear by her body language that she wasn't ready to talk to him.

"Then help me get it. Help me understand."

"You're a Violet, Kyle." Casey shrugged, tears forming. "You'll never understand."

One would assume that was the part of the conversation where he grabbed her. Kissed her. Told her everything he likely said to his shower wall for three weeks. But you have to understand something about Kyle Winchester: he didn't always live up to what he *should* do. He had the genetic makeup of an exotic model but didn't see it. He was privy to the finer things in life but didn't care. He was amongst a whole group of Violets who could date a plethora of bombshells at Westcott, but he didn't have eyes for them. Kyle wasn't a superficial guy looking for arm candy. Kyle was good, even to those who weren't always good to him. People like his ex-girlfriend. So maybe he should have reached for Casey, maybe that's what he wanted to do. But Kyle did what he always did. . . . He did good by Ari, dug his hands into his pockets, and buried the urge to console her.

Everyone watched Casey get into her beater car and drive away. As I stood there, standing in an arid cloud of black muffler smoke, I realized no one knew her—not in the way we thought we did. Because while we were aware she had been dealt crummy cards, not a single one of us knew just how miserable her life really was.

I checked the time on my cell phone. "Let's just go home."

"Hang on a minute." Dean lifted his head. "We don't *know* the note was from Jacob. It could be from anyone."

"Like who?" Ari asked.

"Don't you all want to find out?" He glanced at me, but clearly too slighted by my decision to meet up with Jacob, he quickly looked away. "Someone dropped a typed letter on Sonny's porch. Let's make sure we know who it's from before we just call it a night."

It was obvious Dean didn't want to admit that Jacob could've been in town for the weekend, trying to get in touch with me. It was even clearer by the eagerness in his voice that he *really* hoped he wasn't. A wave of silence rolled over the circle. We stood there, staring at one another, waiting for someone to make a move. To no one's surprise—Cliff was the first one to do so.

"I told you—we're not going into the parking lot."

"We won't," Dean replied, brushing by Cliff's shoulder. "Just follow me."

Reluctantly, we piled back into our vehicles and followed Dean down a side street just outside of school grounds. He pulled his Audi onto the curb, starting what was going to be a long line of cars. The shadowy street lay in the middle of two wooded lots, and if you walked through the left lot, you'd run straight into parking lot C.

Dean climbed the small grassy hill beside the woods, then looked back at the rest of us. "Put your phones on silent."

We reached into our pockets, everyone likely wondering when we promoted Dean. Together, we stepped into the woods; the moonlight and cell-phone flashlights lit the way. For the next five minutes, all I could hear was the crunching noise our shoes made against the sticks while we walked in the direction of the left wing; and all I could think about was Casey.

"Big Brother program?" Winston whispered as he walked closely by my side. "Why wouldn't she tell us about that?"

"I have a feeling she doesn't tell us a lot," I replied, my mind revisiting her speech. "I didn't know all that stuff about her home life, did you?"

"Not exactly." Winston fished for a pack of Skittles in his robe and opened the bag. "But I also didn't know she's been going on dates with a Tella Blue kid."

"Bella View."

"Look, we've got to do something." He poured a pile of Skittles into his mouth. "As much as I'd rather dip my tongue into battery acid than admit Cliff is right, I think he may be right about this one. There's something off about this Sawyer thing."

"Even so, I am *not* getting involved in her love life anymore. If she's enjoying Sawyer's company, well, then maybe we should just let her."

"She's enjoying his company all right—until he pours pig's blood on her at the Christmas Gala."

The annual Westcott High Christmas Gala, an event to remember. It's supposed to be a party thrown in our honor, to celebrate our year-long achievements and to bask in the holiday season with our friends, but it's mostly just an opportunity for us to dress to the nines, for Ari to show off her vocal abilities, and for relationships to fall apart last minute before the New Year.

I gave him a confused look.

"*Carrie*? The movie? The book?! She's lured to the stage to accept the title of prom queen, only so the Sawyers of the school can pull the rope and unleash a bucket of swine juice all over her head."

"Oh, right. I just assumed he's trying to make Kyle jealous, but your theory of gutting pigs and dumping their innards onto Casey's head sounds much more plausible!" My irritated voice heightened. "What's with Kyle anyway? Why didn't he stop Casey from leaving? Because he didn't want to hurt Ari's feelings?"

"Close." Winston tossed more Skittles into his mouth. "He's still in love with her."

I went to disagree, but he stopped me.

"You see the way he stares at her in the halls. Every time she passes by, Janitor Joe has to come mop up the drool."

"You really think he's still in love with Ari? Even after everything she admitted?"

"All things point to yes," he replied. "Besides, it doesn't really matter what Ari did. Doesn't mean Kyle was ready for it to end."

His comment gave me pause.

We finally approached the end of the woods, and with a long wall of thin trees in front of us, we came face-to-face with the left wing. Dean held out his arm to stop everyone from walking forward, then ducked down. We did the same. The building was hard to look at. We knew what it stood for, and what it cost to build. Money aside, the bribery and corruption behind the transaction would forever be embedded in the soil below it.

"I don't see Jacob," Buckets whispered, his eye up to his camera.

"Me either." I peered into the vacant parking lot, and then checked the time. "It's midnight now."

"Well maybe he's not here yet," Norah suggested.

"He's here. Somewhere." Cliff pulled his hood over his head. "He's just waiting for Sonny to walk out."

"Shit!" Winston whispered as he stared down at his cell-phone screen.

“What? What is it?” I asked.

“I just accidentally double tapped a pic on Sawyer’s Instagram from three years ago.”

Everyone sighed in unison.

“Unlike it,” JC suggested.

Winston tapped again.

“No! You can’t unlike it after you’ve already liked it,” Norah schooled him.

He re-liked the picture. “Okay, I’m not one-hundred percent positive, but I’m pretty sure this isn’t the same photo.”

“Oh, God!” I snatched his phone out of his hand and closed the app. “We talked about this! You know you have a heavy thumb! You can’t scroll that deep!”

“What the hell are you doing on his Instagram?” Norah chucked a stick at Winston’s right arm; he lost his balance and fell onto a loud pile of brush. “One stick? That’s all it takes to knock you on your ass?”

“Not everyone needs six Xanax,” he replied, wiping off his sleeve.

“Would you two just shut up?” Kyle stood to his feet. “Look, we shouldn’t be here. If Jacob has something to say to Sonny, he can call her. I’m leaving.”

“Kyle’s right,” Ari said. “This has nothing to do with us. Norah dragged me here.”

“Because Jacob was my friend. I came here to make sure

no one jumps him in the parking lot."

"You two are friends?" Winston asked Norah. "Does he know that?"

"Shh!" Cliff stood up, his eyes glued to the building.

"What?" Buckets adjusted his camera lens. "Do you see someone?"

Cliff's eyes danced across our faces as he breathed in through his nose. "Do you guys smell that?"

We all sniffed.

"I don't smell anything," JC replied.

"It's smoke," he continued. "That's smoke."

We stood there, staring at Cliff, staring at each other, sucking the thick midnight air into our nostrils. The woods were black and our faces were barely visible to one another, but we all sensed the fear in each other's eyes. And although our flashlights hardly lit the way toward the school that night, something much brighter was about to light the way back.

At that moment, we jerked our heads toward the parking lot. Our pupils turned yellow. Our faces lit up. And what we thought was a semi-innocent stroll through the woods was now a middle-of-the-night meeting at a crime scene.

The left wing was on fire.

"Holy . . ." Kyle broke through the group and watched his father's prized possession ignite in flames.

"Shit . . . ," Norah mumbled.

Just as Kyle went to run ahead, Cliff jumped in front of him. “No!” He pushed Kyle backward. “Let’s get the hell out of here!”

We all stared at the building a little longer before realizing we shouldn’t have still been standing there.

“Run!” Buckets whispered loudly, tearing through the woods toward the cars. “Now!”

Smoke. Most wouldn’t define it as much more than a sign of fire, but to the nine of us standing in the woods that night, it would be remembered as the moment we realized our lives would never be the same.

3 LITTLE WHITE LIES

Little white lies. Those harmless mistruths we tell others when we aren't comfortable enough to tell the real truth. Perhaps it's because we're terrified of our thoughts, so we pretend we're not thinking them. Maybe we don't know what we think, so it's easier to recite lies. Or maybe we're scared of what we'll say if we allow ourselves to be forthright, so we mask the truth with a sheer veil of dishonesty. A little white veil—one that's so meek and innocent—it couldn't possibly be harmful. *Right*?

"Sonny!" Kyle ran up behind me as I walked through the jungle-like hallway the following Monday. The theme was high-strung, and it was nearly impossible to relax. "Have you seen all the cops?"

"Have you seen the reporters?" I held my notebook

tightly against my chest as my burning eyes scanned the crowd full of confused students. I had spent my entire Sunday watching the local news with my dad, glued to the TV like some crazed fan. Next to Lana's scandal, the left-wing fire was the biggest thing to happen in that town, and it caused millions of dollars in damage. The building was barely still intact, with over fifty percent of it completely charred by the flames.

"I overheard my dad talking to police yesterday. The fire wasn't accidental."

"I figured as much," I replied, opening my locker with one hand while rubbing my eye with the other. I hadn't slept, I hadn't stopped thinking about the fire, and I hadn't stopped thinking about my note. My typed, anonymous note. Part of me wanted to believe JC and everyone else who thought it was from Jacob. The other part of me couldn't ignore Dean's theory, although I knew his reason for thinking it was heavily influenced by his hope that it wasn't from him. "Do they have any suspects?" I asked, glancing down at my phone. I thought I'd hear from Jacob after I didn't show up to the parking lot. At the very least, I thought he'd ask to reschedule since our meeting place turned into a sea of flames. But I hadn't heard a word. No call. No text. No Jacob.

Kyle leaned against the neighboring locker and tossed on his hood. "No suspects yet. But it's my dad. . . . He'll find out who did this."

I gathered my textbooks. They felt heavier than normal, or maybe my strength had abandoned me. "I can't believe we didn't see this person. I mean, we were right there."

"The fire started by the back door. From where we were standing, we wouldn't have been able to see anyone."

"But still. I can't believe we didn't notice anything."

"I can't believe we were there at the same time," Kyle said. "I've never seen anything like that in my life."

"Never," I added. "Who would be crazy enough to light the left wing on fire?"

"I know, right? Without Principal Winchester inside?" Winston walked by us with a red lollipop in his hand. It perfectly matched his long-sleeved red shirt, and knowing him, that was no coincidence. "They could've at least waited until this morning when he arrived."

I stood in disbelief. "Really, Winston? Candy at seven thirty in the morning?"

He opened his locker and ripped the sucker from his mouth. "What? I got it from Harold."

"Who's Harold?" Kyle asked.

"The bald guy from Channel 6 news." He held it up against his shirt. "Look."

"Tell me you didn't trade an interview for a lollipop." I waited for his reply with a pained look on my face.

"I've done much worse for candy."

Kyle rolled his eyes, then gave me his attention. "Have you talked to Casey?"

"You mean since she stormed off the other night?" I raised my brows. "No. I haven't texted her . . . and she hasn't texted me."

"Why didn't she tell anyone about her living conditions?"

"Like who? You?"

"Anyone," he replied. "I mean, we used to talk for hours every night. Nothing ever came up."

"I told you, Ky, that kind of stuff wouldn't come up. She's—"

"Embarrassed?"

"Wouldn't you be?" I asked. "I'm sure she isn't itching to share her leaking-pipes crisis with her Violet friends."

Hearing a loud slurping noise, we jerked our heads to the right. "I'm a Cobalt," Winston said, gawking at his sucker. "She could've talked to me."

I dropped my chemistry book into my backpack. "Not to hurt your feelings, Wins, but you aren't the greatest person to talk to sometimes."

Kyle co-signed. "You're judgy."

"And you guys make horrible decisions," Winston retorted. "If it weren't for my pessimistic nature, you'd both be drowning in a pit of your own mistakes. I'll have you know I've saved you both from multiple crises."

"Yeah, well, can you save Casey from this one?" Kyle

asked.

Winston turned his head. "Will you please explain this whole rivalry to me? I thought Bella View Day, Archwick, and Westcott were sister schools."

"It started decades ago with our parents," I replied. "The Crescent schools were set up like the perfect trio, but they were just trying to one-up each other in rankings with the Ivy Leagues, sports, academics, money—"

"Power," Kyle added. "It was a trifecta of power-hungry administrators and parents trying to be the best, and the students were all expected to compete against each other."

"Sort of sounds like Westcott," Winston said. "Why is everyone so scared of these kids? You guys are just like them."

"No one's scared," Kyle fired back. "There's just bad blood between us and Sawyer."

"Bad blood?"

"Me, Cliff, Sawyer, and a couple other guys from Archwick were the only freshmen to make varsity for our teams that year—and we all competed in the Crescent College Showcase."

At the mention of the CCS, my heart dropped.

"What the hell is that?" Winston asked him.

"It was a football camp where the best players from each school competed against one another while Ivy League coaches observed for recruitment."

"So what happened?"

"Cliff outplayed him," Kyle replied, shrugging a little. "Sawyer's never let it go."

"That's it?" Winston wasn't convinced. "Sawyer's butt-hurt because Cliff played better than him at some stupid camp?"

Kyle's eyes slowly lifted and found mine.

"Yeah." I swallowed. "Look, Sawyer comes from a competitive family. He's used to winning and getting exactly what he wants. I just find it hard to believe he'd want Casey."

Winston flung his book bag over his shoulder and walked toward us. "Aren't you the one who encouraged *this* competitive little snob to go after Casey?"

Kyle play-punched Winston in the arm; he slapped him.

"It's just unusual." I zipped my book bag and slid my shoulders underneath the straps. "I don't mean anything by it."

"Some would say it's unusual to wear light-washed jeans in November. But what do I know?" Winston looked me up and down while rubbing his arm, then walked away down the hall.

I watched him disappear into the crowd, then ran my hands over my pants. "They're not that light."

"Just promise me you'll keep me posted on Casey," Kyle said, redirecting my focus.

"Why can't you just talk to her yourself?" I slid my hands

into the pockets of my distasteful jeans. "Oh wait, that's right. Because you told her to leave you alone."

"So I wouldn't hurt her," he added. "I told her to leave me alone so I wouldn't hurt her. Look, I was heated that night. I said a lot of things."

"But don't you think that particular thing came a little late? A few days prior, you got back together with Ari. Don't you think that did her in?"

"Yeah, and I'm sorry for that," he replied. "Winston was right to be worried. I wasn't over Ari and I knew there was a chance we'd work things out." He paused and lowered his voice. "I just didn't expect it to be so hard that time."

"What do you mean?"

"I mean I had met Casey," he answered. "Unlike all the other times we got back together, there was someone else."

"But you still did it."

He didn't reply at first. His eyes wandered over my head and his mind left the chat. But he eventually returned—with a sentence I didn't want to hear. "I did. I always do. That's why I said what I said in the parking lot. Casey's too good for me, Sonny, and I'd ruin her if we dated. Maybe it took hurting her to see that."

I reached forward and picked lint off his hoodie. "Are you sure this has nothing to do with you and Ari?"

"What?"

"I know you two ended things after the scrimmage game

but—I don't know—it seems like you're not over her."

"There is no me and Ari," he replied. "And I never said I'm not over her."

"You never said you were."

Just then, I spotted Cliff on the other end of the hall. He was standing in front of his locker with a blank look on his face and a blue sling on his arm.

"I'll be right back," I said, peering over Kyle's shoulder. Without wasting another second, I walked toward Cliff. Once I reached his locker, I lifted my closed fist and knocked on the door.

Cliff jumped and made eye contact with me. He looked like he'd been awake all night . . . and perhaps he had been.

"What the hell, Sonny!" He slammed his locker. "I'm already on edge!"

"Yeah . . . I guess we're all a little on edge."

Cliff began pushing through the mass of students toward the other end of the hall. I wasn't sure if that was his way of ending our conversation or his way of telling me I had to walk and talk, but I chose to follow him. "My dad's been on my ass about this stupid fire—asking me a million questions."

"I think that's less of a mean-father thing and more of a concerned-parent thing." I walked beside him, trying to keep up. "What's with the sling?"

"Not that it's your business, but I hurt my arm."

"How? Running through the woods?"

"SHUT—" Cliff stopped in the middle of the hallway and looked side to side, then lowered his head toward me. "We weren't in any woods. Ever."

"Whoa . . . why are you getting so heated?"

"Heated? Are you trying to be funny?"

"What do you mean?"

He looked at me strangely as if I was the crazy one for not understanding. "Just keep your mouth shut, okay?"

"Keep my mouth shut?" I pulled my shoulders back and pushed my face toward his. "What are you talking about?"

Cliff acknowledged a waving volleyball player before continuing. "Jesus, Sonny. I thought you'd be a little more paranoid. Cops are swarming this place."

"So?"

"So there will be an investigation, and someone is going down for this. No one can know we were in the woods. If anyone, especially Winchester, finds out we were anywhere near the left wing that night, this entire thing could be pinned on us."

"But we didn't do it."

"Yeah?" Cliff nodded. "And JC didn't steal the answer key."

Up until that moment, everything was rumbling at bay. The scattered conversations were all around me, but quiet. The paranoia was present, yet subtle. But Cliff's words set everything into motion, and for the first time since the fire, my skin started to burn.

Cliff weaved in and out of students as he shifted down the hall, taking long strides while I nearly jogged to keep up. "Tell everyone else to keep their mouths shut too," he said, staring ahead.

"Do you think Principal Winchester suspects us?" I asked, sweating at the thought.

"I don't know."

His reply caused me to stop, but I quickly came to and caught up with him again. "Well, maybe you should lose the sling. It may look suspicious."

"I think I'll risk it." He checked his phone, then bobbed his head from side to side as if searching for someone. "This is my throwing arm. Have to keep pressure off it."

"Is it—"

"It's fine," he quickly replied, checking his phone again. "Have you talked to Ari? She isn't answering my calls."

Before I could respond, the double doors abruptly swung open in unison, sucking the air from the hallway and causing everyone to look. The sunlight burst into the building, and in true Bella View fashion, the Royal Blues made their boisterous entrance into Westcott High.

London Vanderbilt, Stella King, Alice Kennedy, Sawyer Ellington, Quinn Myers, and Max Crimson stood underneath the doorframe, nearly stopping to pose as they commanded the attention of the onlookers—me included. Whether it was admiration for their fresh wardrobes, jealousy of their well-rested complexions, or shock that the school made room for the six of them regardless of the burned-down left wing—I couldn't be sure. But everyone stood in awe.

They walked side by side down the hallway, and as they approached me and Cliff, our eyes cut to the right. Sawyer passed by us, almost in slow motion. His brown shaggy hair was styled to perfection; his olive-toned skin complimented his green eyes. He and Cliff exchanged a heavy glare; then Sawyer nodded, gave him a phony smile, and continued walking down the hallway.

At that moment, there was an undeniable shift in the air. But unfortunately, it wasn't *the* shift. I wish it was. I wish the corruption behind the left wing, or the Bella View students invading our school like unwelcomed rodents, were the darkest moments of our junior year. But unbeknownst to us, there was a darker shift coming.

That's for later.

Assistant Principal Clemmons's voice suddenly came over the intercom. "Good morning, staff, and students. Please report to the auditorium for a mandatory rally. Everyone, please report to the auditorium for a mandatory rally. Thank you."

Cliff's eyes slowly left the speaker and met mine. "Look, if you see Ari, tell her I'm looking for her." He repositioned his backpack and walked toward the auditorium, passing by Guy Penn on his way. Guy was leaning against his locker, one sneaker on the tile floor, one propped up behind him on the wall. With bleak eyes, he watched Cliff as he moved through the crowd, then turned around and stared at me.

I waited for a mischievous grin to appear on Guy's face, but he was emotionless . . . detached. . . . He just wasn't present. Maybe it was the fact that the wrestling team he weaseled his way onto was temporarily falling apart without their star coach and athlete. Perhaps he was overcome with sadness seeing half of his grandfather's land turned into a charcoaled pile of rubble. Or maybe it was something else. Something deeper. Something that was eating him alive from the inside out.

That's for later too.

"A Friday-morning rally on a Monday? This must be serious." Winston popped a yellow Starburst into his mouth as we scooted down our normal row. "It's almost as if a criminal is on the loose."

"Not funny," I said to the back of his head. "I just talked to Cliff, by the way. He wants us to keep quiet about the woods."

"What? Why?"

"Because he doesn't want anyone to find out we were there when the fire started."

"Just out of curiosity . . . since when do we listen to Cliff?" Winston descended into his chair.

"Normally we'd never, but if anyone finds out we were in the woods—" I glanced ahead at Principal Winchester as I took my seat. "If he finds out, he could point the finger at us—and do it with a smile on his face." My eyes paced across the Berber carpet, my sentence sinking in. "Just keep your mouth shut," I told him. "Don't mention the woods to anyone."

Winston propped his feet up on the chair in front of him. "I won't."

All of a sudden, Casey dropped down on the opposite side of me, causing me to jump in my seat. "Can I talk to you?"

"Jesus!" I gripped the armrests. "Don't sneak up on me like that!"

"Noted for next time," she replied, her hands up in surrender.

I glanced at Winston. He lifted his hands, allowing me to take on the conversation solo. Standing to my feet, I followed Casey to a shadowy corner of the room. When we got far enough away from the crowd, she waited for a few peers to pass by us, then spilled. "Look . . . I'm sorry for not telling you about Sawyer. But he's not just mentoring my brothers."

"What do you mean?"

"I mean he's . . . he's helping us."

“Helping you how?”

“He’s helping us get fostered.”

I wasn’t sure why, but at that moment, everything about the way she spoke, and every word she said, felt terribly wrong. “*Fostered*?”

“Mr. Ellington has serious connections to a private child-placement agency right here in California. Sawyer talked to him, and then he met with me. He said he could help us.”

A million questions fought to be first. “Hang on. . . . You want to be placed into foster care?”

“Private foster care,” she replied. “He said he’d help us find a family who’s willing to take us until I graduate from Westcott, and then he’d work on getting my brothers adopted.”

“Adopted? What about your aunt?”

“She can’t afford to keep us and that was never the plan. My mom hoped sending us here would work out until I graduate, but she also promised she’d send money every month—neither of which is happening.” Casey removed her glasses and rubbed her eyes. “Look, even if we could make it work until I go off to college, what’s going to happen to my brothers? They’ll be sent back home, and right back into the same situation as before. I can’t let that happen.”

“Speaking of your mom.” I crossed my arms. “What makes you think she’s going to go for this? She never signed over her parental rights.”

"She'll have to. She's unfit and I can prove it." With trembling fingers, Casey scrolled through her cell phone. "I've recorded it all. Every drunk night. Every threatening conversation. Detailed descriptions of every fight." Casey's tired eyes paced across the screen, and then she held it up to my face. "It's all here. I've shown everything to Mr. Ellington and he wants to help."

The word *why* came to mind but I swallowed it.

"Sawyer is the only thing I have going for me right now, and he's a good guy. Please just try to understand that."

I buried the urge to disagree. "Why didn't you tell us how bad things are? There are people who could have helped you before it came to this."

"People like Kyle?" She didn't agree. "This isn't a shattered cell-phone screen, Sonny. This is my life we're talking about. This is different."

"Kyle cares about you," I replied, tossing my decision to not get involved in her love life out the window.

"No. Kyle gave me a hundred bucks and kissed me. He hung out with me a few times and pretended to care while I ranted about tornadoes."

"That's not easy to do!"

She tilted her head. "I'm done, Sonny. Kyle used me. He used me until Ari came back."

"Listen, I know he handled things poorly. And you have every right not to speak to him after what he did. After what he said. But he never meant to hurt you, Casey, and I think a conversation between the two of you is warranted."

"Why's that?"

"Because Kyle's telling himself he did the right thing, but I don't think he really believes that. And I'm not so sure you believe what you're saying either." I shook my head. "Just think about it . . . please?"

Casey's eyes softened, and for a split second I thought she was considering it, but I was wrong. "There's nothing to think about, Sonny." She shrugged. "He made his choice."

"All right, all right, everyone find your seats. Please and thank you." Principal Winchester tapped the mic; his voice startled everyone in the room.

Casey pressed her lips together, and much to my surprise began walking toward a different row. I watched her walk away, then traveled solo back to my seat.

"Where is she going?" Winston asked as I plopped down beside him in defeat.

"Apparently into foster care."

"Now I'm sure you're all aware that our school was targeted in a horrific act of vandalism in the early hours of Sunday morning," Principal Winchester continued. "Sadly, we have very little information at this time. But this is an ongoing investigation, and rest assured, the person or persons responsible for this act will be prosecuted to the highest degree. The horror our community has faced over the last twenty-four hours is something I don't take lightly. This was a loss. We lost a building. We lost money. But more importantly, we lost a symbol of hope. The left wing was a chance to expand. To make room for students on our waiting list, most of which were from our former sister schools. To say that those kids are disappointed is an understatement." He paused, staring out into a swarm of students he resented. His eyes were glazed over with emotion. But not the kind of emotion normal people would feel when faced with such physical and financial ruin. The fire brought forth a blankness about him. He had fallen. He had lost everything he came to Westcott for. Principal Winchester didn't like losing; his gaze told us he never would again—ever. "The Westcott Police Department will have officers in and out of the school all week, so don't be alarmed if you are pulled at random for questioning. Please understand that we aren't talking about photo leaks here. This is a crime. If any of you have information about the fire, you must come forward." A blanket of silence covered the auditorium. No one was speaking—not even our weekly rally regulars who cut up and acted out. "Now, as you all know, we have a handful of new students with us at school today. A vast majority of them were relocated, but we were able to make room for some. More specifically, the six remaining students who made our Chosen Ten this year. Would those six please stand?" A moment of incredibly forced clapping followed as they stood to their feet while Principal Winchester read their names aloud. "Welcome to Westcott, kids," he said proudly. "I know this isn't the welcome you were anticipating, but we're happy to have you."

Before I knew it, I found myself staring down at my sneakers in a trance-like state. Principal Winchester's speech played in the back of my mind like a familiar record; and his voice sounded as if he were standing above water, speaking to me as I was submerged in it. What would happen if he found out about our midnight meeting? What would happen if he suspected we were involved?

"Breathe, Sonny," I whispered, clenching my eyes shut. "You didn't do this. There's no proof you were there."

"You are enough," Winston whispered into my ear.

I opened my eyes and pushed him.

"That brings me to my last bit of information for the day." Principal Winchester coughed into his closed fist, then shifted his navy-and-yellow striped tie. "It will be no easy task to collect information about the fire. We are actively reviewing security camera footage, but it seems as if our system may have been compromised. We can't tell you much, but we can tell you that this will require all hands on deck. With myself, Principal Clemmons, and the police already up to our eyeballs in work, we decided it would be best to bring on some extra help. We've hired an internal investigator who will assist the Westcott Police Department in its efforts to solve this heinous crime. He will also act as a student advisor—someone you can reach out to if your principals aren't available." He placed his stack of papers down on the podium, then motioned toward the side of the stage. "So, everyone please give a warm welcome to our newest staff member—Mr. Ron Harrison."

As my eyes shifted to the right, my heart found its way into my throat. No matter how many times I attempted to take a deep breath—I couldn't—it's like I had forgotten how to. I watched Ron's shiny loafers appear from behind the curtain. I watched as they glided across the stage—with each step sounding more alarming than the last. My fingers clawing the armrests, I watched as the two men exchanged a firm handshake, and then listened as Ron's familiar voice came over the microphone. His lips were moving, but all I could hear was a piercing sound of nothingness, and my eyes began swelling with tears.

"Thank you, Mr. Harrison. And thank you for taking the position on such short notice." Principal Winchester's navy-blue suit warming his arm, he lifted his hand and pointed toward the back of the room. "I'd also like to welcome Jacob back to Westcott."

Winston turned around in his seat. "Holy shit . . ."

I could feel his eyes on me, burning a hole into my back. But if I didn't look, it wouldn't be real, so I sat still.

"I hate to be the bearer of bad news . . . ," Winston mumbled.

"Since when?" Sinking in my seat, I turned around just as the clapping was phasing out; and after scanning the rows, my eyes finally collided with Jacob's. The words he hadn't been able to say to my face were scattered across his. He looked desperate to talk, so desperate I thought he may burst. And just like that . . . my mystery note wasn't so much of a mystery anymore.

"I know your teammates will be very glad to see you," Principal Winchester said as we waited to see who would outstare the other.

I did my best to pull my eyes away, and then swiveled in my chair. "Not all of them."

"What the hell, Coach!" Dean rushed into the gym immediately following the rally. The room was empty, with beams of sunlight piercing through the windows above the bleachers, shining down like a spotlight on the center of the polished wood floor.

I chased behind him as he journeyed across the court, breaking through dust particles floating in the air.

"Ballinger." Coach T lined up basketballs onto a nearby rack. "How can I help you?"

Dean came to a forceful stop and planted himself mere feet from him. "Why is Jacob allowed back on my team?"

"My team? I think you mean *the* team?"

"We've been working our asses off without him! He quits

on us, then comes back and picks up where he left off? How is that fair?"

"Look, son, don't go getting caught up in the semantics of it all. His dad asked that I make an exception, given the circumstances, and so I did."

Dean huffed, looking around the room for someone to feel offended like he did. "I don't want to play with him."

"So this is your resignation, then?"

"What?"

"I'm assuming you're leaving the team?"

"What? No!"

"I see." Coach T tossed a ball at Dean's chest; he caught it. "Then you'll be sharing the court with Harrison—fair or not."

"Coach—"

"I'm not interested in your complaints, Ballinger. I'm interested in winning championships."

"We can do that without him." Dean forcefully chucked the basketball back.

"You can." Coach T placed the ball onto the rack. "But you'll win them alongside Jacob."

"This is bullshit!"

"And you'll do it with a smile on your face." He sauntered closer to Dean. "Do I make myself clear?"

Dean clenched his jaw, engaging in a staring contest with Coach T. It lasted so long I started to think someone had hit pause.

"Do I make myself clear, Ballinger?"

"Yes!" I answered for Dean because I knew he had no plan to. "He understands."

Coach T patted Dean on the shoulder, then turned around and found something else to do. When he was out of sight, I gave Dean a small shove. "Are you insane?!"

He shifted his shoulders and bolted for the exit.

I walked in front of him and shoved a little harder; he stopped in his tracks. "Dean!"

"What, Sonny?"

"You just risked your spot on the team! And for what?! For Jacob?!"

Irritation pricked at him. He swayed side to side. He grabbed a fistful of his messy brown hair, then let it go. It was clear Dean didn't know how to handle the news—not well anyway. "Did you know?"

"Know what?"

"Did you know he was coming back?"

"Of course not, Dean. I haven't spoken to Jacob since he left."

He cracked his neck, still swaying. "I can't stand that guy."

"I know, but—"

"But nothing! He came here like he owned the place. Moving in on you, knowing you and I had history, then dismissed me when I asked him to leave you alone because I knew he was no good. And he wasn't. That entire family is scum."

"Your dad was the one who hired his dad to—"

"Look, this isn't about any of our dads, okay? What happened between them is just that—between them. It has nothing to do with us. But Jacob lied to you, Sonny. He allowed you to be around Ron for weeks, knowing he was just pumping you for information about your father. I mean, was the whole thing just a setup? Offering you the Farrah Klein story in hopes he could get information out of you?"

"I don't know," I replied, my mind recounting my conversations with Ron. "Maybe."

Dean dropped his face into his hands and let his anger out into them. "I can't stand the thought of another guy using you, or hurting you, and it's my fault he was able to get close to you in the first place."

"Dean—"

He lifted his head, his watery eyes barely making the shift. "I don't want to lose you again. I can't lose you, Sonny."

I hadn't seen Dean so tormented since his mother's passing, and I guess I never took seriously just how much Jacob intimidated him. Wrapping my arms around his upper back, I embraced him for a hug. "I know."

He clung to me, pressing his fingertips into my spine. "I

can't lose you."

"You won't," I replied as we stood in the middle of the room.

Dean eventually pulled away, and what I thought was a momentary loss for words was really just a pause so he could build up the courage to ask me what he asked next. "You don't . . . you don't have feelings for him, right?"

"*What*?"

"You went to meet up with him the other night." He reached over and rubbed his left bicep, attempting to act casual. "Why?"

"JC convinced me to go," I answered. "It meant nothing."

"So I'm right? You don't have feelings for him?"

"Dean—"

"Just answer the question."

"No," I quickly replied. "No, I don't have feelings for Jacob."

He gave me a quick once-over. "Promise me you won't talk to him, then."

"Okay." I stared into his glossy blue eyes—blue eyes so magnetic, you would hurt yourself trying to pull away. "I promise."

Little white lies. Sometimes they come in the form of meaningless compliments we hand out to strangers. Sometimes in the form of affirmative one-liners we tell ourselves to get through the day. Other times, in the form of shaky statements we tell our ex-boyfriends in order not to hurt them. And what in the world could be harmful about that?

4 ORANGE

Orange. A combination of the energy of red and the happiness of yellow. The color of fall and harvest—and the tropics, sunshine, and joy. The hue of creativity, enthusiasm, and determination. When I was younger, the orange crayon was always a tiny nub mixed in with the other barely used crayons in the box. It was my first pick—always there to bring a burst of happiness to any dull picture I drew. But before that day was done, the color orange would forever take on a whole new meaning.

"And then, Mrs. Bennett dared to ask me to play keys at the Christmas Gala in front of the whole class." Winston dropped down beside me in the lunchroom the following Tuesday afternoon. "As if I don't have a date."

"You don't have a date."

"Yes, but *she* doesn't know that." He rummaged through his bagged lunch. "You can't assume such things. It's racist."

"You know, for the overly proud founder of the Culture Club, one would think you'd know the definition of that word by now."

He poured a bag of peanut M&M's into his mouth. "Not that I think you should . . . but have you talked to Jacob yet?"

I wanted to tell Winston I'd lain awake all night, processing my conversation with Dean, pacing my room while making pros-and-cons lists, beating my face with my pillow every time Jacob flashed across my mind. I wanted to tell him I mapped out everything I would have said to Jacob had we met in the parking lot, and that after seeing him in the auditorium, I hadn't been able to think straight. But I had made it that far denying my feelings for him, so I decided to play it cool. Which I realized wasn't exactly my forte after the night I had. "Why would I talk to him?"

Winston's tone took quite an aggressive shift. "Gee, Sonny, I don't know. . . . Because he left you a note asking you to meet him in the parking lot and then showed up at Westcott a day later. It's the obese elephant in the room, and you know I hate elephants."

"Nobody hates elephants." I rolled my eyes. "Look, what is there to say? JC was the one who dragged me to the parking lot. I didn't even want to go."

"But you did."

"And I shouldn't have." I turned to face him, raising my brows to ensure he knew I meant business. "I'm trying to work things out with Dean. Jacob can't just come back to town and try to fix things via some stupid note." I slowly turned back toward my lunch. "Besides, if he really wanted to talk to me, he could've knocked."

"Maybe he got wind that you were out with JC, so he left the note on your welcome mat. Maybe Norah told him."

"Don't you think she would have mentioned that in the woods?!"

"*The woods are alive*!" Winston belted out as a few peers passed by our table, staring at them with an exaggerated smile. "Julie Andrews!" he shouted in their direction. "*The Sound of Music*! Great film! Inarguably her best role!" They continued walking by, confused. "Assholes," he mumbled while dropping his head toward me. "Jesus, Sonny! What happened to keeping quiet?!"

"It's hills, not woods. The hills are—" I sighed in frustration, then popped a cracker into my mouth. "Literally everyone knows that."

"These hills are far from alive." He bit into his peanut butter and jelly sandwich—extra jelly. "Everyone in this room looks like they're two shakes of a lamb's tail away from a nervous breakdown."

Winston was right. Principal Winchester's speech hadn't

left us. Neither had the cops. One by one, students were being pulled from classrooms, lunch hours, even after-school activities, to be questioned. Parents were in and out of the building so much they almost felt like faculty. The fire was gone, but the fear of an arsonist at large was hovering over our heads, and I couldn't help but wonder if someone amongst us was involved.

Suddenly, Casey approached our table. "Any room for me?"

Still chewing on my cracker, I stared at her wrinkled blue sweater as she sat down across from us.

"Welcome back," Winston said. "It's been a while."

"It's been a couple of days," Casey replied. "Just needed some time to clear my head."

"Any update on your situation?" I asked.

"Just waiting to hear what my next steps are."

Winston gave his two cents. "Don't you think this is a little risky? Foster homes can be a great holding place, but there's no guarantee you'll like your foster parents. Sure, maybe you'll feel financially more stable, but you could end up bouncing from house to house. You could even end up separated from your brothers."

"And what happens if you're placed into a home that's much worse?" I asked.

She stopped unpacking her lunch, then stared at us through her thick black glasses. "There is nothing worse."

Casey had hard-to-read eyes, ones that demanded to be studied. When you stared into them, you felt connected to and detached from her all at once. Connected because you instantly adopted the urge to protect her; detached because you couldn't understand her or her life—or the lack thereof.

"Then we're happy for you," I said, kicking Winston's leg underneath the table before he could disagree.

Winston grunted. "Yeah! So happy!"

Out of nowhere, Norah slammed her lunch tray down beside Casey and stared at us.

"Are you lost?" Winston pointed to the left. "The rugby team is that way."

"Choke on a Skittle, Winston." She sat, pushed Casey's food away from her tray, then guzzled sparkling water.

"What are you doing here?" he asked. "You can't sit with us."

"Take your overused *Mean Girls* references and shove them up your ass. I'm here to talk to Sonny."

"About what?" I questioned.

Her eyes shot around the room like lasers. "Have you noticed the ripples in the water since the Bella View kids got here? They're already acting like they own the place."

"How so?"

"London's faux-leather-leggings wearing ass was in my seat first period."

"Try saying that ten times," Winston replied.

"She has it out for me," Norah continued. "I can tell."

I glanced over at their table. "I can't believe they were still allowed in."

"Only those six since they're on the Chosen Ten," Casey said. "The other transfers are coming when the left wing is refurbished."

"Maybe you'd like to date one of them too," Norah said, glaring at Casey. "Why don't you switch tables already?"

"Why don't you?" Winston retorted, his voice louder. "For the love of God, please do us the favor."

Casey tossed her hands up to end their argument. "Listen, Norah, I don't know what kind of Crescent rivalry went on between you guys in the past, but Sawyer's a good guy. We're friends."

"Sawyer doesn't have friends," she replied. "He's a complete asswipe."

Winston put his pointer finger in the air. "And that's coming from Norah. Queen Asswipe."

Before I knew it, their banter became background noise, and my eyes had traveled across the lunchroom. They landed on Jacob, who was sitting with a handful of guys from the basketball team. I couldn't believe I was staring at him. I couldn't believe he was back. His head was down, his headphones were in, and he looked lost—in every sense of the word. I wondered what song he was listening to. I wondered what he would have said had we met at midnight.

I wondered when he'd ask for a raincheck. *I wondered why I wanted one.*

"Sonny!" Norah yelled.

I blinked, mentally rejoining the conversation.

"Have you noticed?" Casey asked.

"The ripples?" I suppressed my emotions and reached for my water bottle. "Yeah, I've noticed."

"Not the ripples," she replied. "Ari."

"What about Ari?"

"She's apparently acting weird."

I took a big sip of water, hoping to wash down my internal emotional turmoil. "How weird?"

"She's not responding to my texts," Norah replied. "She came into first period this morning all sweaty and out of breath."

Winston cracked open his soda; drops flew everywhere. "Perhaps she'd been with Cliff?"

"You don't miss an opportunity, do you?"

"It's my talent."

Norah rolled her eyes. "She ran out of class as soon as it ended and I haven't been able to find her since."

Her words began to hit me. "Cliff told me yesterday morning she hasn't responded to his texts either."

"Look, I'm not trying to spread rumors," she said. "But something's not right."

"What a welcome!" Sawyer sat down next to Casey,

leaving Norah's heavy statement dangling in midair. "A closed-down building, hard-ass teachers, and a whole lot of mean teenagers. It's as if I'm back at Bella View." He glanced around the table at us. "Well, minus the whole arson part."

"Too bad your school went under," Norah said. "Or else you'd still be there and not pathetically trying to fit in here."

"Norah Soros, right? The painter?" Sawyer's crooked smile gave me goosebumps. "I vaguely remember you. Can't believe you're one of the Chosen Ten."

Every kid in the Crescent had one goal: *To beat the best, to be the best*. It almost became our mantra. To do that, you had to travel outside of your school. You had to compete against the kids from the other two. Hence the showcase. Hence every other event the schools held. From music competitions, to uppity dance conventions, to fancy art exhibits—everyone had their day. So although we never attended classes together or walked the same halls, in some twisted way, we all knew each other.

"It's almost as shocking as you being a Chosen Ten," Norah replied.

He shrugged, his peach-colored T-shirt hugging his broad shoulders. "I got lucky I guess."

"Luck's got nothing to do with why you're here."

Smiling a little, he brushed off her statement. "Hey, maybe we could collab sometime?"

"Hey, I'd rather eat paint." Norah grabbed her lunch tray, stood to her feet, and headed toward the other side of the cafeteria.

"Is she always that friendly?" Sawyer asked as he watched her strut away.

"Typically only on Mondays," Winston answered. "I'm Winston Banks. I'm sure you remember my good friend, Sonny—"

"Sonny Carter." He stared me up and down, his eyes beaming. "Of course I remember you. Haven't seen you since the showcase."

I dug my fingernails into my palms underneath the table as I stared back.

"That was a crazy day, huh?" Sawyer's perfect white teeth peeked through his full lips as I dug into my palms some more.

"I'll text you later?" He placed his hand on Casey's shoulder, then scooted from underneath our table and made his way toward his own.

"You didn't tell me you went to that showcase," Winston said, glaring at me.

"Yeah. I went to watch Kyle."

"What showcase?" Casey mumbled, her eyes stuck to Sawyer's back.

Suddenly, Cliff stopped by. "Do you think I can borrow you for a minute?"

I jumped, glanced at him, then closed my eyes and grabbed my heart. "Can everyone stop sneaking up on me?!"

"It's important," he replied, sucking me in with his eyes.

I gave everyone around me a curious stare, then pushed myself away from the table and followed Cliff out of the lunchroom. I didn't ask questions. By the confident way he led me, they didn't seem necessary. We made a sharp left turn, then another, and an out-of-breath Ari met us on the other side of the wall.

"What's going on?" I asked, my eyes shifting from Cliff's to hers. "Norah's super worried about you."

Ari put her ring-covered finger over her lips and pulled me into a nearby vacant classroom; Cliff followed.

"What is it?"

"My phone," she said, gnawing on her black fingernail polish. "It's gone."

I closed the door behind us. "What do you mean it's gone?"

"I realized it wasn't in my jacket pocket when I got home the other night." She tucked the strands of hair that had escaped her high ponytail behind her ears. "It must have fallen out when I was running through the woods."

"Well, did you go back and check?"

"First thing this morning," she replied.

"*This morning*? You've been without your phone since Sunday? Why didn't you go back sooner?"

"I didn't exactly want to be spotted by police roaming around a crime scene, searching for my phone in the woods like a *criminal*." Panic rose in her voice. "I let Sunday and Monday pass, and then went back this morning to look for it. I parked on the side street and retraced my steps. It's not there."

"It has to be," I replied. "You must have missed it."

"I don't think so." Cliff shook his head. "I went out there and looked before school started. I couldn't find it either."

"Maybe you both overlooked it."

Ari jerked her hands out in front of her. "We both wouldn't have missed it, Sonny!"

"Have you tried calling it?" I asked.

"It's on silent, remember?" Her forehead glistened as she paced back and forth beside the windows.

"We have to find it before someone else does," Cliff said. "If Winchester gets his hands on it, we'll all be questioned."

The room was noiseless and still in such a way that it made me believe we were the only three in the school. After everything that happened between us and Principal Winchester, our chances of sliding under the radar were slim to none. He was waiting for one of us to slip up so he could punish us for what we knew—things we were never supposed to know. At that moment, I realized it no longer mattered that we had nothing to do with the fire—because if he found that phone, it wouldn't look that way. And in a town like Westcott, with a principal like Winchester, *that's all it really took to be guilty.*

I weaved around the desks in pursuit of Ari. When I reached her, I grabbed her by the arm to put an end to her pacing. "Are you sure you've checked everywhere? Your room? Your car?"

"Yes, I'm sure."

"Did you go anywhere after we left?"

"I . . . I don't think so."

"Ari." I squeezed a little tighter. "How can you not remember?"

"I don't know!" She ripped her arm away from me. "I think I went home."

Cliff pushed himself off the desk and walked toward her. "You *think* you went home? What the hell does that mean?"

"Whatever I want it to mean," she hastily replied. "What do you care?"

"I don't. I care that your phone is found since the screen is filled with multiple texts from *me*—at one in the morning—asking if you made it home okay."

"Yeah? Well, maybe you shouldn't have been texting me in the first place. Since you're so embarrassed by me and all."

Cliff placed his cupped hand around his mouth and dragged it down his lips. "Don't start, Ari."

"Trust me." She darted for the door, ramming her arm

against Cliff's sling on her way out. "I won't."

Cliff tightened his mouth and grabbed his arm; an unpleasant grunt followed. He reached for the nearest desk and dropped.

After watching Ari walk out of the classroom, I shifted my eyes toward Cliff, quickly taking my seat next to him. "Where do you think she went after we left?!"

"Nowhere." He winced. "She's trying to make me think she went to a guy's house."

"What would that matter? I thought you two were done."

"We are." He removed his sling and chucked it across the room. "Stay out of it."

I glanced down at the floor. "Don't you need that?"

"I need to find her phone."

"You also might need to hear this." I stood to my feet, walked toward the front of the classroom, and bent down to pick up his sling. "Sawyer brought up the showcase."

Cliff slowly stood up.

"Not . . . what happened . . . but he sort of referenced the day in conversation."

"What did he say?"

"That it was a *crazy day*." I raised my brows as I shoved the sling against his chest. "But the way he smiled at me—I don't know—I don't have a good feeling about it."

"Shit," he whispered.

"Look, I won't say anything."

"Yeah?" He nodded. "And what about Kyle?"

Just then, I heard the staticky sound of the intercom, followed by a loud beep, and Ms. Pamela's demure voice. "Sonny Carter, please report to Mr. Harrison's office immediately. Sonny Carter to Mr. Harrison's office. Thank you."

My heart sunk. I hadn't spoken to Ron in weeks, nor did I want to, but I knew that conversation was unavoidable. "I have to go," I told Cliff on my way out of the room. "We'll find her phone, but don't go back to those woods."

"Sonny!"

Stopping just underneath the doorframe, I turned back around.

Cliff stood still in the rayless classroom, staring at me with fierceness. "Remember what I told you."

I placed my hand against Ron's office door and absently stared through the frosted glass. His nametag plate hung off to the right, and I could hear his muffled voice through the thick sheet of wood. I turned the cold silver knob and pushed the door away from my face, then stepped inside.

"Yeah." Ron spun around in his chair and looked at me over the side of his phone. He motioned for me to have a seat. "Yeah, I'll get that to you first thing tomorrow morning. Yep. Thank you." He hung up. "Sonny! Come in." His eyes were fixed on me while I nestled into a navy sled-base chair.

"How have you been?"

I raised my shoulders and pushed my palms against my thighs. "Fine."

"Not exactly a good week for small talk, I know." He relaxed into his midback manager chair and twisted a pen around with his fingers. "But how's your paper coming along?"

"Fine."

"Fine." He rocked his head back and forth. "That's good to hear."

"Did you need something?" I asked him, hoping he'd release me back to lunch, or literally anywhere other than his office.

Ron straightened in his seat. He placed the pen on a stack of papers and leaned forward, his clasped hands and elbows resting on top of his dual-sided desk. "Listen, Sonny. I'm very sorry about your father. I hope you understand I was hired to do a job, and it was one I couldn't talk about. Not even with you. It certainly doesn't reflect how I view you as a student."

"I would hope not," I replied. "I'm not my father."

"You're not. But it must've been a blow when you realized what we were doing in Westcott."

"Not as big as the one from yesterday when I realized you were back."

Ron squinted a little. "Well, I hope your dad's case won't

change our trust with one another."

"Trust?"

He sat back in his chair; his voice was deep and almost sluggish. "As the new student advisor, it's important that every student here feels they can talk to me about their problems. Whether academic or personal."

"I see." I traced my finger along the rips in my jeans, staring into Ron's dark brown eyes, striving hard not to see Jacob's in them. How he thought I could trust him after my father's arrest was baffling. Even more confusing was his new role as our *student advisor*. But there was no way that Violet parents would believe their kids were involved in the fire, and Principal Winchester knew they wouldn't be happy knowing their tuition dollars were going toward a private investigator, so he slapped a fancy title on it to ease their minds. "Congrats on the job."

"Thank you, Sonny." He tilted his head back and held his stare with me. "Means a lot."

I nodded, then glanced above my head at the air vents. "It's a little cold in here. Do you always have the temperature down so low?"

"It's been a hot week."

My eyes swiftly locked in with his. "Right . . . I think I should get going."

"Certainly." He stood to his feet and shifted his maroon tie. "It was good to see you. And just know that I'm here if you need to talk . . . or get cool."

"Got it." I stood and felt my way around the chair as I backed up, then turned and walked toward the door.

"Oh, Sonny! One more thing!"

My fingers had barely grazed the doorknob when I had to twist my head back around. "Yes?"

"You wouldn't happen to know anything about the fire, *would you*?"

Within a matter of seconds, the frigid room felt more like a sauna.

"What . . . what makes you think I know anything about that?"

He grabbed the pen off the stack of books and tapped it against his desk, his head down. "You once asked me what you should do if you had incriminating information about someone at your school." He looked up; his body was stiff and taut as a board. "Maybe you knew the fire was going to take place? Maybe you know who's responsible?"

"I don't recall that." My eyes narrowed as my mind raced back to that conversation. "I'm sorry."

"You said there was something you needed to do before talking to me about it. . . . Do you want to tell me what that was?"

"I . . ." My chin hit my chest. "Um . . ."

"Sonny?"

"No," I replied, lifting my head so quickly my neck

could’ve snapped. “I don’t know anything about the fire.”

There was a long pause.

“I see.” He gave the desk a few more taps with his ink pen. “Well. You know where I’ll be if you want to chat about anything. Yes?”

“Yeah.” I took a deep breath. “Thanks.”

As I turned around to open the door, something bright on a nearby bookshelf caught my eye. I stared at the item as a rush of horror tickled my skin. Fear had immobilized me, and my ability to ask logical questions fled.

“Was there something else, Sonny?”

“No.” I opened the office door. “Nothing else.”

What do you think of when you see the color orange? Some may think of citrus or the tangerine sun fading along the horizon. Others may think of the amber edges of leaves when autumn exhales its first cool, calming breath. But as I stared at the bookshelf that afternoon, orange took on a whole new meaning for me. Because if you’re staring at your friend’s missing phone, you think of arson.

5 WIND

Wind. It moves things. It moves you. When I was a little girl, there was no better feeling than prancing barefoot through my backyard and twirling around in circles while gusts of wind blew through my hair. The cool grass underneath me seemed thick . . . safe . . . and the innocent whistling sound blowing by my ear never posed a threat.

But as I grew up, it began to mean something else. When it blew through my hair, it meant a day full of battling tangles. When the chilling breeze beat against my face, it meant watery eyes and frozen bones. And when it whistled, in the same way it did back then, it meant a storm was coming. And unlike before, *I was old enough to know it wasn't innocent.*

"You aren't sticking around for dinner?" Mom plated two

heapings of lasagna. "I made your favorite."

Before the divorce, Darcy Carter was known for her traditional Vietnamese dishes. Like *pho*—a delicious noodle soup, and *bún chả*—grilled pork served over a bed of white-rice noodles and herbs. But post-Dirk, lasagna and chicken nuggets were all Lana and I seemed to get.

"Frozen lasagna is not, and never will be, my favorite anything," I replied as I took a bite out of a day-old dinner roll from the club while putting on my shoe. "And placing something into the oven doesn't exactly mean you made it."

"I made you."

I hopped around the kitchen on one foot as I put my other sneaker on.

"Winston likes my frozen lasagna." Her black hair pulled back into a low ponytail, Mom rolled up the sleeves on her floral purple-and-pink silk robe so they wouldn't touch the sauce.

"Winston has low standards. He'd eat anything."

She picked up her plate and a bottle of Merlot, then headed toward the bar stool. "How's school going? Has everything cooled down?"

"Not funny."

"You know I never liked that school."

I put my jean jacket on. "Is that a confession?"

"Can you imagine?"

"Actually?"

"Your father insisted you go to Westcott. I always wanted you and Lana to go to a normal school as I did."

I grabbed a water bottle out of the fridge. "So we could be normal like you?"

"Hey!" She twisted the cork off the wine. "I'm not crazy yet, so I'm doing all right."

"Debatable."

"Where are you heading off to?" she asked as she sat down and poured a glass.

"I'm meeting up with some friends at the club. I won't be out long."

"Maybe I should give you a curfew. Good moms do that."

"Thank God I settled for mediocre with a slight drinking problem." I took another bite from my roll, then dropped it on her plate.

"You're being nice. It turned to heavy after your dad's arrest."

I grabbed my keys from the green countertop. "And *that* is my cue to leave."

"Be back before midnight," she shouted as I walked through the foyer toward the front door.

"Good moms would have said ten!"

Thirty minutes went by and I was no longer hobbling around the kitchen pretending things were fine. Instead, I was sitting around a large table in the middle of the club's dining room with the group. The crystal chandeliers hung in rows above our heads, pairing nicely with the pearly white tablecloths and white banquet chairs—and after delivering the missing phone news, our white faces too.

"Where do you think he found it?" Norah lowered her voice but was unable to suppress the rising panic. "Do you think a student handed it in? Or maybe the yard guys?"

"I'm not so sure the *groundskeepers* mow in the woods." Winston waved a hand at a server.

"Mr. Harrison said he found it this morning." Ari swallowed excessively. "Near the side street where we parked, dead, lying face down in the grass. He questioned me for a few minutes, and then I left."

Cliff exhaled, clearly relieved they never saw his one-in-the-morning text messages.

"What did you say?" Kyle asked.

"I just told him I was vaping after school yesterday," she replied. "Before I went back inside for my Monday vocal lessons. I told him I didn't want to get caught, so I went outside of school grounds and must have dropped my phone without realizing it."

"Are you still doing that? You swore you'd quit."

"I did. . . ."

Kyle leaned in, holding serious eye contact with her. "You sure?"

She curled her hands into her sweater and nodded.

It wasn't hard to tell Ari found comfort in Kyle's concern, and as I watched Cliff's eyes move back and forth between the two of them, it was easy to see he found it unsettling.

"Did he buy your vaping story?" Norah asked.

"I . . . I don't know." Ari looked off toward the side of the room. "I think so, but he sort of *looked* at me."

Cliff leaned forward. "What do you mean?"

"I mean . . . he looked like he might've not believed me."

"He's a PI." Dean shook his head, mindlessly dragging his finger across the condensation on his glass of ice water. "It's his job to not believe you."

Ari rejoined the conversation. "Look, who cares, right? I got my phone back."

"Try to hang on to it this time, will ya?" JC removed his Jefferson wrestling jacket and dropped it on his lap, while Ari gave him the finger with a mocking smile.

"Guys, put this into perspective here," said Winston. "It's not like Principal Winchester confiscated her phone. Let's not get our panties in a wad over mall-cop Ron."

"But my dad hired him to look into things internally." Kyle looked up in exasperation and sighed, sending a reminder to everyone at the table. No one knew his dad's dark side better than him, and if he was nervous, we all should have been. "This will get back to him."

"Look, everyone calm down," JC demanded. "We didn't do anything. We aren't responsible for the fire."

"But we're associated with Ari," Norah argued, scratching at the yellow paint on her thumb so aggressively I thought she'd draw blood. "We all know what happened between us and Winchester. If he finds out Ari's phone was found anywhere near the left wing, he'll automatically think it was us."

"If he hasn't already found out," Dean added.

"Best case—we never hear another word about the phone. Worst case—they start to suspect all of us." Casey tightened her messy ponytail. "But Winchester will have a hard time proving we were involved, seeing that we weren't. To think he could jump from finding her phone to *actually* accusing us is ridiculous."

"So is assuming he wouldn't jump to that conclusion!" Norah leaned forward as if she had a secret. "Why don't we just head down to the damn station right now and turn ourselves in?!"

"You need to calm the hell down," Cliff replied. "No one is turning anybody in for anything. This isn't about proving our innocence. Unless Harrison, Winchester, or the police start questioning us, we're good."

"And if they do?" Dean asked.

Cliff rolled his head toward him. "Then Ari sticks to her story—she dropped her phone near the woods while vaping. And we stick to ours—we don't know shit."

"That's a nice politically correct answer, Cliff. But you

know just as well as I do that's bullshit." Norah flipped her hair over the right side of her head, then jerked her arm back down. "Winchester knows what we know. About the Penns. The left wing. JC and Piper and the setup. There's no way he'll believe we have nothing to do with this."

"We don't," Cliff replied, his brows raised higher than Norah's.

"Cliff is right," Casey said. "We're innocent. Unless they start asking questions, there's nothing to worry about."

"Ron sort of questioned me," I mumbled.

Kyle shot straight up in his seat. "What do you mean?"

"A while back I asked him what I should do if I had incriminating information or suspicions about someone at my school. I didn't clarify, but I was referring to Piper. He brought that conversation up today and asked if I knew anything about the fire."

"No way," Kyle whispered. "What did you say?"

"I told him no. But I don't know if he bought that either."

Cliff ran his hand over his hair. "Everyone just keep your mouths shut. Nobody talk about the woods. We weren't in the woods. We weren't near the school that night. We don't know anything."

"And we can't draw attention to ourselves in the meantime," Norah added. "If I'm dragged into a scandal, my mom will kill me."

"Well then, don't let her find out about the entire hockey

team you—"

"Winston!" I interjected. "Not the time."

"Are we done here?" Ari abruptly stood to her feet; her thighs bumped against the table, causing everyone to jump a little.

Kyle reached for his hoodie and followed suit. "I'll walk you out," he mumbled under his breath, turning his head away so the table couldn't hear him. But I heard every word, and unfortunately for Kyle, so did Cliff.

"I thought you two were done?"

Kyle paused, then continued scooting out of his seat.

"I'm sure Dean can walk her." Cliff cut his eyes at him. "Right?"

"I can," Dean replied, cutting his eyes at Kyle. I was hoping with all of the cutting going on that someone would take a stab at the tension, but that didn't happen.

"Sit down, Dean." Kyle put his hand out to stop him. "You don't take orders from him."

Cliff took a swig of water, glaring at Kyle over the side of the bottle. "You two got plans?"

"What business is it of yours?" Kyle asked, raising his voice a little. Everyone looked up from the table in surprise. Other than a short "good call" text Cliff had sent Kyle after he decided not to quit the team, the two hadn't spoken since everything exploded between them, and their conversation was almost as uncomfortable to watch as I'm sure it was to have.

"Just making sure you aren't trying to revive a dead relationship."

Kyle smirked. "Yeah? Well maybe had you not been hooking up with Ari behind my back, it wouldn't have died."

"I don't think you want to have that conversation," Cliff replied. "Not with your other girlfriend sitting right here."

I leaned forward. "Cliff—"

"No." Kyle seemed unmoved by his words. "Let him talk."

Cliff lifted his chin and shrugged. "Maybe I was in the way, Ky. After Lana and I broke up, maybe I was a lonely, selfish piece of shit who knew Ari would come running if I opened the door again. And maybe I was wrong for that. No, *I know* I was. But I'm not why your relationship ended."

Kyle widened his stance and grabbed his biceps. It was clear by the smirk on his face that he couldn't wait to hear Cliff's explanation.

"You found out the truth and you had a choice to make. You could have tried salvaging what was left between you and Ari, but you broke up with her."

"Yeah. That's kind of what you have to do when your girlfriend tells you she's been cheating on you with your brother."

"Don't forget the part where she said she was never in love with you," Winston added, concentrating on whatever game he was playing on his phone.

Cliff leaned forward, but not enough to make anyone think he truly cared to be having the conversation. "You can blame me if you want, Ky. You can blame Ari. We'll eat it. But the truth? Whatever weird thing you have going on with Langdon is what stopped you from working things out. I can promise you—I had little to do with it."

"It kind of seems like you had a shit ton to do with it. Don't you think?"

"You want to know what I think? I think you should stop blaming me for the way you treat women."

"Me?" Kyle laughed.

Cliff didn't take too kindly to his laughter. "I don't play with girls' emotions. I tell them how it is, whether they like it or not. Everyone wants to look at me like I'm the dick who screwed over his best friend, but the only one who screwed anyone is you—and you screwed yourself into not knowing who you want."

"You don't know what you're talking about."

"Really?" Cliff nodded. "Then choose one."

"All right, guys, that's enough," I said, hoping to bring an end to their conversation.

"If you still want Ari, then take her." Cliff raised his brows, staring at Kyle with dispassionate eyes. "If you want Casey, then be a man and take her before Sawyer does."

Kyle swiftly walked toward Cliff, and Cliff stood to his

feet. The two were nose-to-nose, and all everyone else could do was watch.

"You have a lot of nerve saying his name," Kyle said. "I'd watch yourself."

"Or what? You gonna hit me?"

"Nah." Kyle grabbed Cliff's hurt shoulder and gave it a little squeeze. "It wouldn't be fair."

"Don't let the sling fool you." Cliff's straight face remained unprovoked, although I knew he must've been in pain. "Don't push me this time. Hit me."

They stared at each other for what seemed like minutes, and when Cliff realized Kyle wasn't going to swing, a supercilious smile appeared on his face. "Don't use me as the reason your relationship failed," he mumbled. "It's pathetic."

Kyle couldn't win the staring contest. He dropped his shoulders and stepped backward toward the exit, then disappeared behind the dining room wall. Everyone knew the conversation would heighten, but no one thought things would go so poorly so quickly. Maybe the status of their friendship was worse than anyone knew, and maybe the damage wasn't going to be quick patchwork. Then again, when your childhood best friend hooks up with your first love, *is it ever*?

After watching him walk away, Cliff rejoined the circle, and Ari walked around the table to meet him. "Why'd you do that?!"

Cliff reached for his bottled water, ignoring her entirely.

"You are such an asshole, Cliff! Why do you care if he walks me to my car? Why do you care what I'm doing?!"

Cliff took a sip, holding eye contact with Ari. After swallowing, he twisted the cap back on, then placed the bottle on the table. "I told you." He fell backward into his seat, then shrugged. "I don't."

Ari glanced at Casey, then at me, then at everyone else at the table. But before anyone could say anything, she jerked her body toward the exit and left.

The dining room seemed to be muted, hushed as if it were unoccupied. I knew Cliff didn't want to admit his feelings for her were stronger than what he said they were on the night of the scrimmage game. His goal was to make it seem as if their summer romance was strictly physical. That he may have liked Ari a little, but not enough to truly act on it. That their secret "rendezvous" happened out of pure loneliness—but I wasn't convinced. I knew Cliff. I knew the way he operated. I knew the way he loved. I saw him love my sister, after all. I watched their interactions for months and I could never forget the way he looked at her. Ironically, *it was strikingly similar to the way he looked at Ari*.

Buckets walked into the dining room. He was thirty minutes late but couldn't have come at a better time.

"Where have you been?" I asked, hurrying him into his

seat.

"With Winchester."

"What? Why?"

He took off his black cotton jacket, wiping his perspiring forehead with a sleeve before folding it on his lap. "Whoever started the fire hacked into the security system. He asked me to trace the hacker."

"And? Did you?"

"Not exactly. I was able to confirm they turned off the cameras—which we already knew."

I studied him; he was hiding something—it was obvious by the way he side-eyed me while speaking.

"Buckets . . . what aren't you telling us?"

"This . . . this person—" He choked on his words, then took a huge gulp of water.

"This person what?" I asked.

Buckets lowered the cup from his mouth. "They turned the cameras back on a few minutes after midnight."

There was a brief pause as everyone tried wrapping their minds around his statement.

"But the fire didn't start until then," Casey mumbled.

"Who would override an entire campus security system, light a building on fire, and then take the time to turn the cameras back on minutes later?" JC asked.

"Someone who would want them back on." Buckets's voice lured us in. "For a reason . . . a reason like catching

Sonny on one . . .”

I swallowed. “What are you saying?”

Buckets looked up and waited for the server to put Winston’s pasta down before continuing. “I’m saying whoever set the fire is the same person who left you the note. They tried luring you there. To have you on camera in the parking lot. *To frame you for arson*.”

As I looked at the tall dark door in front of me, my knees nearly buckled. I curled my knuckles underneath the sleeves on my baggy jean jacket and knocked. Taking a step back, I stared at the door with uncertainty, wondering why I decided to go there. I told myself I’d wait for one of the guys to confront him the following morning, but after Buckets made the connection between the note and the fire, I couldn’t get through the night without clarity. However, the longer I stood there, the less necessary it seemed. I eventually changed my mind, managing to get halfway through the front yard when I heard the lock turn and the front door swing open.

“Sonny?”

I closed my eyes tightly and wished for the earth to swallow me whole, but when that didn’t happen, I turned around and walked back toward the house. “Did you do it?”

Jacob looked behind him, then closed himself outside and met me on the lawn. The white T-shirt he wore hugged his chest, and the scent of musty cedarwood filled my nose. "Do what?"

His words seeped into my eardrums like warm water; I welcomed them, but not long enough for them to truly reach me. "Please don't act like you don't know what I'm talking about, okay?"

Jacob squinted. But I don't . . . know what . . . you're talking about."

I grabbed my elbows and stared into his soft brown eyes. Without warning, everything came flooding back to me. Everything he said—everything he didn't. But what truly drowned me was Jacob's departure and the way he chose to do it. "You know what . . . I don't know why I'm here." I turned around and bailed. "It's not like I can believe a word you say anyway."

"Sonny—"

My feet kept moving.

"Did you really drive all the way here just to leave?"

They stopped. I whipped around, not knowing I was going to change the subject. "What was this? Was this whole thing between us a setup? I write my paper about Farrah Klein while your dad pumps me for information?"

"God, Sonny, you think I set you up?" He stepped a little closer. "Look, yes, I knew about the case. But I wasn't supposed to know, and I couldn't tell you about it. When I met you . . . I just . . . I wanted to get to know you without falling for you. I couldn't fall for you. I couldn't like you, Sonny. I knew what was coming for your dad, and I knew you'd hate me for it. So I tried convincing everyone I liked Norah. I thought that would keep you at arm's length while still allowing us to hang out."

"Yeah? And when you kissed me, was that you 'keeping me at arm's length'?"

"It was a stupid plan," he shot back. "It didn't work. It was never going to work. I shouldn't have opened the door knowing what I knew about your dad. I can see how it looks. I can see why you felt set up, but I swear to you, I would never do something like that." He ran his tanned hand through his hair. "Before I even had time to fix everything, your dad was going to be arrested, my dad told me to pack up, and that was that."

"You told me you and your parents moved here, Jacob. Your mother decorated the entire house. You joined the basketball team. For God's sake, you're on a first-name basis with the servers at the club's café. You never told me your stay here was temporary." I stared at the home behind his head. "How were you even able to move out and move back so quickly?"

Jacob's eyes plummeted. He didn't speak for a good thirty seconds, and I began to wonder if I made a mistake by asking that question. "This isn't my *parents*' house." He lifted his eyes and stared into mine. "It's my mom's."

"I don't understand," I replied, my voice taking a softer shift.

"They're separated. My mom moved to Westcott years ago." I could tell he was struggling to get the words out, and for a nanosecond, I felt a little bad for him. "She travels so much for work, plus I already had my life back home, so I stayed with my dad in Long Beach. She said we could stay at her place while my dad worked on the case, and we didn't know how long it'd take, which is why I joined the team."

"And you're staying at your mom's again?" I asked. "How does that work out when they're separated?"

"I guess she'd actually have to be around for it not to."

My mind raced back to the conversation we had at the café weeks prior. About his parents. His home life. I couldn't have known his parents weren't living together. He never shared that information with me, and when I poked around, it was clear he didn't want to talk about anything personal. I certainly wouldn't have known judging by his cookie-cutter house, his reliable smile, or the way he always seemed to be okay.

I guess Jacob was correct. . . . Maybe perception isn't reality.

"Look, Sonny, I should have told you. Everything. I wanted you to get to know me, I wanted to be more open, I just didn't know how to knowing I wasn't being honest with you about so many things. I try to be an honest guy, I really do, but there are things in my life that are complicated." He took a moment to collect his thoughts. "I understand why you've been ignoring me, and I'll understand if you continue to. I know I disappointed you, Sonny, but just know that I *really am* sorry."

Many seconds of silence passed. Confusion engulfed me; I was drowning in it. All I could do was stand there and let it swallow me. I wanted to hate him—blame him so my father's decision hurt less—but my voice of reason within whispered it wasn't his fault. *And maybe it wasn't.*

"I wanted to tell you that in person the second we got back to town. But we didn't pull into the driveway until like nine on Sunday night. I barely had time to unpack before school on Monday. And with the craziness of the fire and cops and all—I don't know—I've just been waiting for the right time to do it."

"You sure you didn't drive to Westcott on Saturday night for anything?"

Jacob gave me a curious stare. "I'm pretty sure I was hanging out with some friends on Saturday night."

"In Long Beach?"

"Why are you asking me this?"

"I just need to know you weren't in Westcott," I replied.

Jacob walked sideways toward his Jeep, still confused. He opened the door and rummaged through the console, then pulled out a slip of paper and walked back toward me.

"Bowling," he said, placing the receipt in my hand. "In Long Beach."

"So you didn't leave me the note?" I mumbled, staring at the sagebrush bush behind him.

"The note? About the photos of Piper?" Jacob placed his hands on his lower back; his muscles peeked out from underneath his sleeves. "Just thought it looked strange. I wasn't sure if it meant anything."

I temporarily set aside my confusion and broke eye contact with the greenery. "Well, it did. Piper framed JC."

Jacob's eyebrows furrowed. "Wait, what?"

"Winchester used her to plant the answer key into his wrestling bag—in exchange for an itemized list from Princeton's admissions."

"*Principal Winchester*?"

"You remember that manila folder you saw them exchange in the parking lot? Well, Kyle and I saw Piper shortly after he gave it to her. We watched her stuff it into a bag from the sunroom, right before speeding off on her golf cart." I folded myself into my jacket. "Then we broke into her house and found it on the night of the dance."

"That's where you snuck off to?"

I nodded. "There was a Princeton catalog inside. Piper told us about the itemized list later on."

"Wait." He pinched the bridge of his nose. "I'm so confused. How do you know all of this?"

"Guy Penn left a riddle on JC's doorstep a week before school started—except we didn't know it was Guy until three weeks ago. We thought an old teacher left it. We thought he was trying to lead JC to answers, or proof, or evidence. I'm not exactly sure what we thought, but a group of us ran around town trying to solve it—and it only led us to the school's safe."

Jacob collapsed a little. "Sonny, you didn't—"

"It was empty," I replied. "And we had it wrong. But we all met up in parking lot C later that night, and Cliff figured it out. Winchester had JC kicked off the wrestling team so Guy Penn could take his spot, in exchange for land owned by Guy's grandpa. Land the left wing is on. We devised a plan to turn Winchester in, but the following Monday, my dad was arrested instead."

Jacob's guilty conscience forced him to look away.

"That's when Winchester confronted us. The cameras we didn't know were installed on the light posts picked up our conversation in parking lot C. He heard us talk about the break-in . . . the safe . . . everything."

"What did he say?"

"After threatening each of us, he told us to drop it. So we did—until I picked up your pictures. I called everyone to a meeting the other day and showed them to the table. I thought the photos and Princeton profile would be enough to turn him in, but Piper wasn't willing to help."

"Man," he whispered. "Maybe my dad can—"

"NO!" I lunged forward. "Nobody knows about it! Not even our parents. If Principal Winchester knows we're talking about it, he could ruin us. Have us kicked out of Westcott for everything we did."

"What about what *he* did?"

"There's no proof," I replied. "With Piper unwilling to talk, we have nothing on him other than the photos you snapped. And what exactly do they prove?" My question went unanswered. "Besides, JC transferred to Jefferson to wrestle and essentially told us to let it go."

"But you guys are still here under Winchester's thumb. That's not fair."

"None of this is fair."

He paused. "If Winchester knows you guys found out about the left wing, do you think he suspects you for the fire?"

A gust of wind blew by us; autumn leaves tricked down from the trees. I traced them with my eyes as they touched down on Jacob's front lawn. I didn't know what to say, so for a moment, I said nothing. I stood in front of him, staring down at the grass in a daze. His presence sent a calm through my body that I hadn't felt in weeks, and although every rational part of me said not to trust him, for some reason I felt I could.

"I'm not sure," I told him. "But JC and I found a note on

my welcome mat Saturday night. We sort of thought it was from you . . ."

Jacob peered at me. "What did the note say?"

" 'Meet me in parking lot C at midnight. We need to talk.' JC convinced me I should hear you out. The others found out we were going and came with us. We all went into the woods next to the parking lot and waited for you to show up, but you never did. A few minutes later, we saw the fire." I lowered my voice. "We were in the woods that night. We were there."

His eyes dropped.

"We took off running when we saw it, and Ari didn't know it at the time, but she dropped her phone near the woods."

"Did she get it back?"

"From your dad, yes. He told her he found it this morning. Ari explained she must have dropped it while vaping yesterday afternoon, but she's not sure if he believed her."

Jacob tossed his hands behind his head. "Shit."

"I know," I replied, looking side to side. "He already asked me if I know anything about the fire."

"And?"

"I said no, but I'm not positive he bought that." I took a deep breath and let it out. "Principal Winchester asked Buckets to trace the hacker, and he couldn't. But he did confirm they turned the cameras back on a few minutes after midnight—right after they started the fire and ran."

"Why would they do that?"

"Because they wanted me to be caught on camera in parking lot C," I told him. "Whoever left me that note lured me there on purpose. It was a setup. And if you're saying it wasn't you—"

"You think I would do something like that?" His voice let me know he was offended. "You think I'd light a building on fire and try to frame you for it?"

"I don't know!" Another cool breeze blew in between us, causing my eyes to water. "When you say it like that it sounds pretty bad."

"Because it is! *You know* I would never do that to you."

"Do I?"

He squinted at me, the softest wrinkles appearing on his forehead. "What reason would I have to—"

"Maybe you were mad that I was ignoring you?"

"You do realize how insane you sound, right? Jesus *Christ*, Sonny, I might've been upset that you weren't responding to my texts, but that doesn't make me an arsonist." He sighed as I dropped my shoulders and backed down. "Just give me a few days to look into this."

"Absolutely not, Jacob, no."

"Please! I want to help you." He gently grabbed my upper arm. "I won't involve my dad. I just want to ask around."

"You don't have to get involved, Jacob."

"I've been involved ever since someone was standing outside of my living room window. This could be the same person who took photos of us."

"I hadn't thought of that," I whispered, my eyes running wild across his white shirt.

"Maybe you need me." His fingers slid down my arm as he let go. "Just let me help."

"But—"

"God, you're stubborn," he said, the tiniest smile in his eyes. "Please?"

I caved. "You can't tell anyone you're involved. Dean's supposed to talk to you tomorrow morning, but there's no way he would have given you this information. Everyone will kill me if they know I told you we were in the woods."

"You have my word."

I reached for my keys. "I should go," I said, slowly walking backward toward my car. I got halfway through the front yard, then turned around and picked up my pace. As soon as my foot hit the curb, he stopped me.

"Sonny!"

My fingers resting on the door handle, I looked back.

"You know you can trust me . . . right?"

The air shifted, once again blowing against my eyeballs and causing them to water. My hair whipped against my face and stuck to my lip balm, and without saying a word, I entered my warm car and drove off.

Wind comes in many forms. Some peaceful. Some scary. If you aren't still, you'll hear the wrong things. If you aren't observant, you'll sense the wrong vibrations. And if you aren't careful, you may miss the warning . . . *and you may regret it.*

6 MISSED CONNECTIONS

I often wonder how many times I've passed by a stranger, not knowing we used to play in the sandbox together in kindergarten. Or strolled by old sitters who fed me bottles and tucked me in while my parents were away. Shopped next to teachers who nestled me into their classrooms week after week, and got me safely back on the bus en route to home. Or drove past the bus drivers who drove me religiously and carefully to ensure I made it there. It's funny when you think about it. How we can walk right by some of the very people who are the reason we're alive? It's sort of sad to think that if our paths crossed again, we'd never know it.

But some missed connections remain the saddest of them all—and unlike old babysitters, you won't be able to forget them.

"We can x out Jacob," I mumbled as I caught up with Kyle on the way into school the next morning. "It wasn't him."

"What?" He stopped in his tracks, searching for answers in my eyes. "I thought you said—"

"He didn't come back to Westcott until Sunday night. He was in Long Beach on Saturday."

"How do you know this?"

"I just know."

"Is that what he told Dean?" he asked. "Did he already confront him?"

I didn't reply, but I knew based on the way Kyle looked at me that I'd have to explain myself.

"Sonny?"

"That's what he told me," I said, looking side to side. "We talked."

"What do you mean you talked?" He stared into my eyes so intensely, he nearly suctioned an admission from my voice box.

"Look, what was I supposed to do? I wanted to know if it was him!"

"Damn it." Kyle took a few steps back, clasped his hands over his head, and stared at the school before returning to the conversation. "What the hell were you thinking?! You were supposed to let Dean confront him!"

"Would you please keep your voice down?" I whispered. "What's the difference?"

"You aren't Dean! You're emotional!"

"I—"

"What did you tell him? Did you tell him we were in the woods that night?"

I stared around the parking lot as I tucked my hands into my back pockets.

"Sonny! We all agreed we wouldn't talk to anyone!"

"It's just Jacob!"

"Exactly! We can't trust him!"

"He's not going to say anything."

"How do you know?"

"Because I saw it in his eyes."

Kyle let out a quick laugh. "You saw it in his eyes," he repeated. "I think your vision is skewed."

"I'm going to let that comment go."

"Look, this isn't a joke!" He pulled his hands down his head. "If anyone knows we were there that night, if anyone finds out, we're—"

"Jacob won't say anything! He's just as spooked as we are."

"How can you even say that? Just yesterday you couldn't trust the guy, now you believe everything he says?"

"He showed me a receipt that put him in Long Beach late Saturday night." I grabbed his wrists. "He wasn't here, Kyle. He didn't leave the note. But someone else did."

Out of the corner of my eye, I spotted Ron Harrison

walking toward the throng of vehicles, meeting Cliff at his Mercedes as soon as he stepped out. He pretended to help him out of his car, but I knew he wasn't there to assist the handicapped. We watched as they engaged in what seemed to be a quiz-like conversation, and when I saw Cliff look down at his sling, I knew who was quizzing who.

"I hope he's not saying anything," Kyle mumbled.

"It's Cliff," I replied, slowly shaking my head. "He's definitely not."

"He better quit playing around and get his arm looked at."

"I thought he did . . ."

"Why? Because he's wearing a sling to school?" Detest filled his eyes. "He takes that thing off the second he steps on the field. Both Coach and his dad think it's sore—that he's just babying it a little—but I can tell something's up."

"Cliff said it was fine."

"Yeah? Well, the Cliff I saw running drills the other day wasn't *fine*." Kyle paused, staring ahead at his former best friend. "It's only a matter of time before Coach realizes something's wrong. He'll kill him for keeping it from him."

"So why is he?"

"Because this is Westcott." Kyle looked my way. "You're only as good as your throwing arm."

"HEADS UP!"

I jerked my head to the right and saw a football coming full speed toward Kyle's chest. He caught it, but barely. We both looked out into the parking lot as Sawyer closed in on us. Casey was dragging her feet behind him, keeping her distance.

"Ahh, come on, Winchester! You have to stay ready!" He dedicated his attention to me, his eyes dropping to my feet and climbing their way back up. "And how are you doing this morning?"

"She's good," Kyle replied, shoving the football against Sawyer's chest.

He grinned. "Can't wait until we share the field next season."

"You'll be a good backup quarterback."

Sawyer turned around to find Cliff standing behind him. He gave him a good stare before exhaling slightly in his face. "Come on." He looked behind him at Casey. "I'll walk you to class."

Casey stared at us, then at Sawyer, then back at us. She grabbed her book bag straps and reluctantly followed Sawyer toward the double doors.

We watched them walk away—Kyle especially.

"You good?" Cliff asked him.

Kyle looked him up and down. He lifted his shoulders and stood up tall, then cut his eyes at me. "I've got to get to first." After Kyle walked far enough ahead, Cliff and I followed.

"What did Mr. Harrison say to you?" I asked.

"What do you think?" he replied, walking quicker than I

could. "He asked me about my sling."

"And?"

"And I told him it's fine." He sniffed, which is how you knew he was lying. "Has Dean talked to Jacob yet?"

"Not that I know of," I answered. "But it wasn't him."

Cliff came to a halt and stared at me. "Who told you that?"

I looked at him with shameful eyes, and although no other words were exchanged, he picked up what I was putting down.

"What's going on?" Dean held his keys in the air, locking his car as he walked to meet us. "Anyone seen Harrison?"

Cliff remained silent, and my eyes ping-ponged between them. I knew I had to speak, but the lump in my throat was making it difficult.

"Dean . . ." I dug my fingernails into my palms. "It wasn't Jacob."

"What wasn't?"

"He didn't leave me the note," I replied. "He didn't come back until Sunday. He has proof that he was in Long Beach on Saturday night."

Cliff took a few steps back and stared at the pavement, kicking his sneaker against the cement while he waited for the awkward conversation to be over.

"How do you know?" Dean asked.

"Because . . . I . . ." My eyes traced the faded gray stripes on his T-shirt as if I'd find my answer across his chest. I was stalling, but Dean knew me well enough to know that, so I didn't have much time.

"Sonny? How do you know?"

I lifted my head; our eyes met. All I could see was the hurt guy from the gym and the shaky promise I made while standing in the middle of the court.

"Jesus, Sonny. How do you know?"

"Because I talked to him." Cliff stepped forward. "Wasn't him."

"You talked to Jacob?"

He shrugged. "That's what I said."

I found myself leaning in closer and closer, nervously waiting to hear if he accepted the story; when his eyes left Cliff's and met mine, I knew that he had.

"Then who did this to you?"

"I don't know," I replied, pulling my body back before I toppled over. "I'm still trying to figure that out."

"Okay." Dean reached over and kissed my cheek. "Look, don't worry about it. I'll catch up with you in second block."

I smiled at him with my lips, but not my eyes, and after he walked away, I immediately looked up at Cliff. He stared at me for a dreadfully long five seconds, then spoke. "Get your shit together." With raised brows, he rocked backward toward the school.

As I watched him walk away, I wasn't sure which was

worse—keeping a secret from Dean . . . or knowing Cliff Reynolds was keeping one for me.

"All right, class, everyone should have read the last portion of *Romeo and Juliet* by now." Wearing a tight black pencil skirt and a black blouse, Mrs. Penn leaned against the front of her desk. With crossed arms, she looked through her emerald-green frames at her third-period English class.

Other than the multiple interruptions from cops who were pulling kids from class for questioning, it was a relatively normal hour and a half. I watched the door, wondering if I'd be next.

"Thus, begins our big debate," she continued. "Now, it's important to remember why a healthy debate is beneficial in the first place." Mrs. Penn stood to her feet, swaying a ruler back and forth through the air as she walked up and down the rows of desks. "The debates you have in my class will allow you to express your beliefs in a structured, controlled environment. They will help you develop valuable critical thinking skills. It's important to feed your curiosity while simultaneously retaining a certain level of skepticism. Be quick on your feet, articulate your thoughts, and most importantly, polish and perfect your presentation. Gentlemen, for this debate you'll be standing in Juliet's corner. Ladies, you'll be defending Romeo. We'll discuss five different topics, and both teams will need to pick a representative to speak on behalf of their teammates. I'll give you three minutes to pick your captain."

All at once we stood to our feet, walked to the front of the classroom, and separated into two groups. The girls stood off to the left, the guys to the right. It was no surprise that Kyle and I were picked.

Mrs. Penn skated to the back of the room and sat at a desk. Staring pointedly at us from a distance, she continued. "You've picked your representatives. Ms. Carter, Mr. Winchester—please shake hands."

I wanted to roll my eyes at her, but fearing she may see me, I stared at Kyle and extended my arm toward him instead. "Good luck."

"Likewise." He shook my hand.

Mrs. Penn cleared her throat and put on her lecture voice. "Discussion number one: The timeless love story of *Romeo and Juliet* was not about two kids who committed suicide for love's sake. Romeo was a villain who only killed himself because he murdered Tybalt and Paris, had been banished, and realized his life was beyond repair. Do you agree? Five minutes on the clock, and go."

Kyle nodded for me to go first.

"Absolutely not," I replied, glancing beside me at Casey. "To imply Romeo wasn't head over heels for Juliet is not only a complete contradiction to his display of passion throughout the entire play, but it also contradicts the very thing that was most important to him: falling in love."

Kyle coughed. "Romeo was a Montague, a rich kid who almost always got what he wanted—which was what he couldn't have. He didn't really want Juliet. Just like he didn't really want his first *love*, Rosaline. He just wanted to sleep with her and was pissed that she wouldn't. We're supposed to believe the second he laid eyes on Juliet, he suddenly knew what love was?"

"Maybe Romeo was impulsive and immature." I stared at the corner ceiling, scrambling for words to say. "Maybe his adolescence was to blame for his stunted definition of love. But tell me, what made his definition wrong?"

"What made it right?" Kyle asked. "The guy knew their families were feuding enemies. He knew from the start he couldn't be with her peacefully. Why lure an impressionable girl into your arms, make her fall in love with you, and drag her through a war, all so you can fulfill your selfish desires? Had he never gotten involved with her, Juliet would have married Paris like she was supposed to."

"That's not what she wanted. Her true love was Romeo, hence their desire to be together."

"Which was moronic," Kyle replied. "That was never going to work. Romeo knew his life was over. He'd made unforgivable mistakes. That's why he drank the poison. Not because he was heartbroken that Juliet was *dead*."

I laughed a little to throw him off. "Are we to believe the

reason he drank the poison is simply because he'd been banished from Verona? Made a few poor choices?" Then shook my head. "Romeo was not a villain who ended his life due to mistakes. Only love could have driven him to kill himself. Only grief."

"So which it? Love or grief?"

"It was both. He believed Juliet was gone. Overcome with grief, he ends his life. How could anyone interpret that to be anything other than a young man's expression of what he believed love was? It was the ultimate display of affection."

"Killing yourself?"

"Choosing death with her as opposed to life without her," I replied.

Kyle stared at me for so long I thought I'd won the debate. I waited for him to gather his thoughts, but it didn't take me long to realize *Romeo and Juliet* was the last thing on his mind.

Mrs. Penn scratched her chin. "Mr. Winchester? A rebuttal?"

He stared down at his new shoes—shoes that cost almost five-hundred dollars. "I, uh . . ." He swallowed and lifted his head, looking straight at Casey. "I think the problem lies in the initial statement."

"Okay." Mrs. Penn leaned back in her seat. "Go on."

"It's—" Kyle swallowed again. "It's not a timeless love story. It's not a story about passion or the double suicide of two star-crossed lovers. *Romeo and Juliet* has nothing to do with love at all." He clenched his jaw, staring fiercely into Casey's eyes. "*Romeo and Juliet* is about loss. Juliet was a slave to the expectations of her parents, and to the ones she put on herself. She was never allowed to find what brought her joy because she lived to make others happy. If you think about it, Juliet was born lost, and she stayed lost. Until Romeo." Kyle dropped his chin. "I believe she felt hope from what she thought he could bring her—freedom. Freedom to be herself. Permission to feel something she'd never felt before. The only problem with that was—" He looked up and locked eyes with Casey once again. "Romeo was lost too. Just as lost. Sure, maybe he came from money. Maybe he had more than the average person had. But that didn't buy him an identity, and it sure as hell didn't mean he knew how to save her. They were just two young kids who let passion drive them to believe that come hell or high water, they were meant to be together—and they'd do whatever it took to make that happen." He started shaking his head. "But that's not love. Love is sacrifice. Sometimes that means sacrificing what you really want for the betterment of the other person. Sometimes that means losing them."

Kyle's argument tugged at my heartstrings. For the first time in a long time, I was speechless. But I knew I had to say something—even if while trying not to cry. "Maybe you're right," I replied, brushing my pointer fingers across my bottom lashes. “Maybe *Romeo and Juliet* is about loss. Because they died as two kids who never got to find out what could have happened between them. . . . I can’t think of a bigger loss than that.”

The debate had ebbed to nothingness, but the silence that followed my rebuttal was meaningful. It meant it struck a chord with everyone in the room.

“Very interesting, Ms. Carter.” Mrs. Penn peered at us over the top of her cat-eye glasses. “Kyle? Anything?”

He tapped me on my upper arm. “No. I think Sonny took that one.”

Small talk erupted as we prepared for our text topic, and as soon as I turned to face Casey, she turned the other way.

“Bathroom?” Casey asked, her finger in the air.

“Quickly, Ms. Langdon.”

She dropped her finger and half smiled at our peers while she pushed her way toward the classroom door. Kyle’s attempt at explaining why he ended things with her was disguised as a rebuttal, but Casey saw through it—and couldn’t handle the emotions that were resurfacing. He had ripped the band-aid off—poked at the wound—and it was obvious by the way she bolted *that she wasn’t ready to bleed again*.

“Happy Thanksgiving!” I extended my last-minute store-bought pumpkin pie toward Kyle with a forced smile.

“Yum,” he said, staring down at the price tag.

I relaxed my face and stepped onto the Brazilian walnut hardwood floor.

“Hi, Ms. Carter.” Kyle reached his arm around my mother’s upper back and embraced her for a hug. “How are you?”

It had become a tradition of ours to cat Thanksgiving lunch with Kyle and Ms. Winchester. My father rarely cooked, and unless I wanted frozen lasagna, neither did my mom. Ms. Winchester never remarried, but she did walk away with a large empty home, and the only thing that filled her heart more than spending time with Kyle was spending time with me.

“Sonny! Darcy! Come in!” she yelled from the kitchen. “I made a special cranberry sauce for you, Sonny!”

I reached inside a nearby coat closet for one of Kyle’s hoodies and tossed it over my head. “How does it feel knowing your mom loves me more than you?”

“Great if it allows me to go watch football in peace.” He walked into the living room and plonked down on a leather chair-and-a-half.

My mom and I walked toward the kitchen, letting the aroma of yams, stuffing, and green-bean casserole lead the way. The counters were covered with cookbooks and windup timers; the sink was stacked to the top with dishes. Christmas music was playing softly from Ms. Winchester’s phone, and the screen was covered in food. You'd think she would've catered Thanksgiving in with all the money she had, but that just wasn't who she was. She was homey. Motherly. It was almost unbelievable that she was ever married to Principal Winchester.

After taste testing nearly everything in sight, I walked into the living room, pushed Kyle's feet over, and sat down at the end of his chair.

"Who are you texting?" he asked, flipping through channels.

"Dean."

He pressed his lips together and nodded, making it obvious he was judging me; I noticed.

"What?"

"Nothing," he replied.

"It's never nothing."

He flipped some more, pushing my head from in front of the cable box with his foot. "You do know if Dean finds out you went to Jacob's house, or that you've involved him in this—"

"I didn't plan to. I was driving home and my emotions got the best of me." I fidgeted with the hoodie's strings. "I'm scared, Kyle. Who would try framing me for arson? And why? Do you know what could have happened to me had I gone into the parking lot that night? I could be in jail right now."

"But you didn't go." Kyle pulled himself up, removed the throw blanket from his lap, and wrapped his arms around his knees.

"But what if they find out we were in the woods?"

"Look, no one knows that. Not even the person who tried luring you there. And even if my dad finds out we were in the woods that night, at the end of the day, none of us lit the fire."

"But I'm the reason why it happened!"

"Hey." He gently pushed me on the arm. "You're my best friend. I won't let anything happen to you. You know that, right?"

I nodded, dragging the aglets across my fingernails as if I were painting them.

"We'll find out who did this, and once we do, we'll figure out how to prove it was them."

Before I could respond, the doorbell rang. I rolled off the end of the chair and stood to my feet, then trotted toward the foyer. "My guests are here."

Kyle shot up from his comfortable chair with a surprised look on his face. "Guests?"

"I hope you don't mind," I replied. "Your mom said I could invite a couple of people!"

Dragging my fork against the porcelain china plate, my eyes made a circle around the dining room table. When they landed on Kyle, he gave me a very specific death-like stare. The room was lifeless, quiet, and way too uncomfortable to handle.

Ms. Winchester cleared her throat. "So! Norah! Your parents don't host Thanksgiving?"

Norah swung her finger in the air. "No, actually, my mom has to work." She dipped a piece of turkey into my special cranberry sauce and tossed it into her mouth. "And my father chose a life of crime over his family and abandoned us years ago."

My fork tracing came to a grinding halt. I once again stared at Kyle, this time in apology. He shook his head at me as he chomped down on a roll.

Ms. Winchester smiled in confusion as she studied Norah. "That's . . . well . . . JC!" She cleared her throat again. "What's new with you? How's Jefferson? I heard you transferred."

"Yes, ma'am," he replied, taking a swig of sparkling grape juice. "I like it so far."

"What made you want to leave Westcott?"

"Sonny!" Kyle shot up from his seat. "Can you help me with the pies?" He tilted his head to the left. "In the kitchen."

"Sure . . . ," I replied, dabbing my mouth with my napkin. With hesitation, I followed Kyle into the next room. He walked until we were far enough away from the others before he turned around to face me.

"What in the actual hell, Sonny! Why would you invite Norah Soros to Thanksgiving?"

"And JC," I replied, hoping that'd make it better.

"You could've just invited *him*."

"No." My eyebrows furrowed. "Three's unlucky."

"Sonny!"

"What?!"

He grabbed a pie from the corner of the counter. "Why are they here? What are you up to?"

"Nothing."

"It's never nothing," he replied, holding up air quotes.

"I'll explain everything after we eat."

"No." He looked at me like I was out of my mind. "No, no, no. Now. You'll explain now."

"I—I came up with a plan," I said, reaching for a pie. Kyle went to scold me, but I beat him to it. "Look, I know Norah is the last person you want to spend Thanksgiving with, and today is the worst day to do this, but I swear it will all make sense. Just get through lunch. Please?"

"Sonny—"

"It's just a couple of hours," I argued, putting on my trusty needy eyes.

He struggled with the idea for a moment, but when he sighed, I knew I had won. "Thank you." I took the foil off the pumpkin pie. "Now let's serve these beautiful things."

"You ruined my Thanksgiving, you know that?" Kyle

tried dipping his finger into the top; I smacked it away.

"Yeah, well, there's always next year." I pushed the hair out of my face, stood up straight, and began walking back toward the dining room. After eating way too many carbs, exchanging hugs, and starting my mom off on her third glass of wine, the four of us put on our coats and walked outside.

"Now I know why you're such a wimp," Norah told Kyle as we bolted for his Range Rover. "Your mom literally wipes your ass."

"Don't blame me because your mom chooses to work on Thanksgiving."

"No, dude," said JC. "She brought a blowtorch out to toast your crème brûlée. And you let her."

"It was to caramelize the sugar, you assholes." Kyle locked his car doors with his key. "Someone tell me what the hell is going on."

We all stopped in the middle of the driveway.

"We're going to Piper's house," I told him.

"Piper's house? Why?"

"JC thinks she could've left the note."

"JC also thinks it's cool to wear leather pants," Kyle replied. "You really want to listen to him?"

"Hey, dude?" JC lifted his hands. "I'm standing right here."

"There's no way Piper did this," Kyle continued. "Come on, Sonny, you know her."

"I thought I did, but look at what she did to JC."

"She admitted that was a mistake."

"A mistake she carried through," I argued. "To be honest, I can't believe we didn't think of her before."

He sighed. "So that's what we've come up with? You guys want to follow *Piper* around town again?"

"Think about it, Winchester." Norah crossed her arms. "She was so uncomfortable with the thought of turning your dad in that she had to leave the bakery. Later that night, the fire was started. Maybe she got scared that Sonny would talk so she wanted to get rid of her."

"Piper's not crazy enough to burn down the left wing."

"I don't want to believe that she is," JC said. "But look at the facts. She's done this before—to her boyfriend. What makes you think she wouldn't try to set Sonny up if it meant saving her ass?"

"So what, JC? We're going to go confront your girlfriend on Thanksgiving?"

"She's not my girlfriend." JC raised his brows; his eyes went blank. "And if she did this—there won't be any covering for her. I can promise you that."

"So what's the plan?" Kyle asked, uninterested.

Norah looked over at the house, then back at him. "She spends Thanksgiving with her dad. We're going to her mom's to check the print history on her computer. That's where she was on the night of the fire."

"Two of us will distract her while the other two go inside," I added.

"Sonny, we can't keep breaking into people's homes!"

"It's not breaking in if someone opens the door!"

Kyle sighed and stared at the clouds, battling with the idea for nearly a minute. "Fine. But JC and I go through the computer." He dropped his head and honed in on me, then Norah. "Not you two."

The car ride there was quiet. JC was leaned against his window with his hood up, fast asleep. Norah sketched in a notepad, music blaring through her headphones. Kyle stared through the windshield, looking around at all the vacant stores we were passing. "Nobody's out today. Everything's so empty."

I looked at the buildings disappearing in my window as quickly as they appeared. It distracted me for a minute, but my mind kept prompting me to ask Kyle the *burning question*. I tried to fight the urge. I even tried to physically bite my tongue. But poking around was a skill of mine, and I couldn't let another day go by without getting to the bottom of it.

"Kyle?"

"What's up?" he asked as he pulled up to a stoplight.

"Is there . . . is there anything going on between you and Ari?"

He lifted his fingers off the steering wheel, his thumbs still in place. "Why do you keep asking me that?"

"I don't know. You offered to walk her to her car the other night."

"I was being a gentleman." The light turned green and he accelerated. "I've told you a hundred times—we broke up."

"That's not what I asked."

Kyle clenched his jaw and tightened his grip around the wheel. "Look, just let me worry about myself."

"Ky—"

"I'm serious, Sonny. Stay out of it." Silence engulfed us, and all I could do was stare at him. Bare trees were whipping by on the other side of his head like a subway train, and before long, the entire driver-side window was just a sheet of sticks. He was speeding up. I could feel the pull underneath me as the floorboard seemed to disappear. It was as if we'd taken flight—as if we were miles away from my question. I knew he'd have to face it eventually, but based on his reaction, I figured he wasn't exactly ready. I turned to the side and waited for him to change the subject.

He eventually did. "Is Casey okay?"

"Oh, you mean *Juliet*?" I stole a piece of gum from his cupholder. "Why do you want to know?"

"Don't be an ass," he replied. "It looked like she'd been crying when she came back to English. Wasn't sure if she said anything to you."

"Like what?"

"I don't know," he replied, losing patience. "Aren't you supposed to be keeping me posted on her?"

"I technically never agreed to that."

"Sonny!"

"She's fine," I said, bringing my knees to my chest. "She just has a lot on her mind right now. . . . She's under a lot of stress."

"I hope my speech didn't make her upset. I was just trying to find a way to—I don't know—explain my logic to her?"

"It's not just you."

"What do you mean?"

I rested my chin on my knee. "Casey wants her and her brothers to be placed into foster care."

He looked over at me, jerking the car a little. "What?"

"Mr. Ellington has offered his assistance. Apparently, he has connections to a private placement agency. He's going to help them start the process."

Kyle's eyes danced across the street in front of him. "Why?"

"My thoughts exactly . . . but I didn't say it." I lifted my head and turned my body all the way left. "Sawyer brought up the showcase."

Before Kyle could respond, his GPS yelled at us, causing JC to shoot up out of sleep.

Norah removed her headphones, and just like that, our

conversation was over. For then, at least.

"Park behind that bush on the curb," JC said as we pulled down the street. We were sandwiched between two conveyer belts—both stacked with sizeable two-story brick homes. Every house seemed to be cut from the same cloth—so similar to the next—it was difficult to tell them apart. The trees were almost done shedding so I expected to see neglected dead leaf piles covering the yards, but there were none in sight. Every lawn was kept. Every car was washed. Every kid running down the sidewalk was happy—or so they looked.

"I've never been here before," Kyle mumbled as he put the car in park.

"That's not a bad thing," Norah said, rolling her headphones into a ball. "Run this plan by me again, Sonny."

"You and I are going to ring the doorbell. We'll tell Ms. Clemmons we were in the neighborhood and wanted to say hello. After she invites us inside, we'll unlock the door behind us and ask for refreshments. Kyle and JC will sneak in while we're in the kitchen."

"Refreshments?" Norah yanked her shirt down and tightened her bra straps. "Do you kiss your mother with that mouth?"

"What the hell are you doing?" JC asked.

"Piper's mom hates me." She reapplied her lipstick. "But her boyfriend doesn't." When she noticed the eyes on her, she dropped her hand and sighed. "You want in or not?"

Kyle unlocked his doors. "Out. Go. Text us when you've unlocked it."

I stepped outside; Norah followed. Her stiletto hitting the pavement sounded foreign. I was in unchartered waters, and I didn't want to be. The upset feeling in my stomach amounted to full-blown knots as we walked up the driveway, and I was suddenly thankful we had Norah's low-cut shirt to fall back on.

But disturbing noises from inside the house caused us to slow our pace. Doors slamming. Yelling. Loud thuds—so loud JC and Kyle heard it too. They stepped out of the SUV and jogged up the driveway. JC ran by us toward the front door, but just as quickly as his Chuck's hit the welcome mat, he was ushered off.

"What are you guys doing here?" Piper asked, stepping outside with a trash bag in her hand.

"Oops," Norah mumbled as the three of us caught up to JC. "Maybe her dad gets Christmas."

"Are you okay?" JC poked his head around Piper, attempting to sneak a look inside.

She closed the door and dropped the bag by her leather moccasin. "I'm fine," she said, wrapping herself into her argyle sweater.

"What's going on? What was all of that?"

Piper looked behind her, then turned back around and

stared at each of us. "Just a fight."

"Your mom?" JC asked, but it sounded like he already knew the answer.

Piper had an estranged relationship with her mother. She was extremely tough on her—even tougher than Principal Clemmons—and I suppose not even Thanksgiving could ease the tension between them.

"Why are you here?" she asked again, this time expecting an answer from me.

"I'm—" I glanced at Kyle, then at Norah. "We're—"

"Oh, for God's sake." Norah pulled her V-neck up and stepped forward. "Did you burn down the left wing?"

"Come again?"

"Drop the act, Piper. Did you do it or not?"

"*Of course* I didn't! Are you insane?" She tightened her mouth but couldn't keep it closed. "The cops already questioned me. I was cleared. I don't know anything about the fire."

"Why should we believe you?" I asked.

From inside the house, her mom yelled her name. Piper closed her eyes and exhaled. "My grandparents will be here any minute," she said. "You guys should leave."

"Answer her question," Kyle demanded, quickly jumping ship. "Why should we believe a word you say?"

"I have an alibi," she snapped back. "I was in the hospital. Okay?"

JC scrunched his forehead. "Wait, what?"

"It was nothing." She reached down and picked up the trash bag. "I just had a small panic attack. I'm fine. Everything's fine." She closed her eyes again and took a deep breath. "Everything will be fine."

I knew she wanted to believe that—maybe she *had* to try to believe it—but nothing about her life seemed fine. Her outfit looked like something you'd dress your American Girl doll in. A khaki skirt. A hemmed crewneck sweater with a collared shirt poking out. Even her headband was beige. Everything about Piper's life was routine. Plain. Dare I say boring? JC was the only exciting thing to happen to her. It was sad to think she didn't have that anymore—even if it was her fault.

"Do you know anything about a note?" Norah asked.

"Norah!" Kyle yelled.

"A note?" Piper grabbed her pearls. "What note?" When we didn't answer her, she answered us. "I don't know anything about a note."

Her mom shouted for her again, and again, she closed her eyes and took a deep breath.

"You really should go," she said.

JC stepped forward. "Piper—"

"Go . . . JC." She opened her eyes. "Please."

"I'll go," he replied, lifting his hands. "Just tell me you're okay." He paused, taking a moment to take her in. "I need to know you're okay."

Piper held their gaze for as long as she could before answering. It was almost painful to watch them look at each other, and I could sense they were in pain too. "You don't need anything from me, remember?" She abandoned the trash bag on the doorstep and stepped back inside, slamming the door on more than just our faces.

Later that night, around nine o'clock, I sat outside in my car as I stared at the house in front of me. My tires warmed the curb for fifteen minutes before I realized I had to make a move, but I wasn't exactly sure why I was there. I finally turned my car off and instantaneously felt my face and legs get cold again. The heat was gone, and the sad song playing in the background was too. I leaned my head against the headrest and took deep breaths. Suddenly, my phone rang.

"Hello?" I answered.

"Okay, you're either sleeping, crying, or crying yourself to sleep. Which one?" Lana asked.

I lifted my head, mindlessly staring out the windshield. "I wish, almost, and most definitely later."

"Give me one second. I'm going in for round three on my Ben and Jerry's as we speak—I am grabbing a spoon—and then I'll be all ears." She opened a drawer and threw silverware around. "Got my spoon . . . and . . . go."

"You know I hate countdowns."

“Is that why you always used to leave the room right before the ball dropped in Times Square during the New Year’s Eve broadcast?” She made slurping sounds while eating her Ben and Jerry’s, which I knew had to be brownie-batter.

“Ringing in the New Year on a ‘three, two, one’? How can you say that’s not enveloped with anxiety?”

“Well, when you put it that way . . .” Lana’s TV turned on in the background. “So? What’s wrong?”

I sighed. “Nothing. Everything.”

“Let’s start with everything,” she replied. “Let me guess. Boy problems?”

I glanced at the house. “I’m just not sure if I’m making the right decision giving Dean a second chance.”

“How is he, by the way?”

“Fine . . . I guess. . . . I don’t know.” I rested my chin in my palm and wrapped my fingers around my cheek. “I spent so many weeks of my summer vacation writing about my breakup with Dean. I wrote about it so much I almost convinced myself it was a novel and not real life.” My eyes became watery. “But it was. He really did date Norah. It wasn’t fiction—he left me. He left me, and I just took him back.”

“You can’t blame yourself for not being the type of girl to punish your ex. Me? I’d make him squirm and chase me for months. You? You forgive, Sonny. And that’s not your

Achilles heel. That's your strength. So what if you forgave Dean? So what if that makes you look pathetic? Weak? Desperate?"

"Hey, you could just take me out back. It'd be quicker."

"All I'm saying is—you don't have to explain your relationship to anyone. If you want to be with Dean, be with him unapologetically."

"I guess that's the problem. I'm not sure that I do." A bug crawled on the outside of my window; I traced it with my fingertip. "How did you know you wanted to be with Cliff?"

"Oh boy." Lana swallowed and turned down her television. "This is one of those convos."

"I'm serious," I replied. "How did you know?"

"I guess it was just something I felt. Cliff was different. Sure, I caught shit for dating a sophomore. But when I was with him . . . I guess it didn't matter. I loved him." She shoveled another spoonful into her mouth. "Look, sis. All I can tell you is this: Guys will come and guys will go. But family is forever."

"What are you talking about?"

"Oh." Lana paused. "It's just now hitting me that I mixed Jamaican rum into this ice cream last Friday night."

"Not going to ask how you got that." I exhaled. "If you loved him so much, why'd you break up with him?"

"I didn't break up with Cliff, Sonny. Cliff broke up with me."

The conviction in her voice caused me to perk up. I'd heard her say that a thousand times before, but something about that time was different.

"He told me he couldn't be with me anymore," she added. "I assumed it was the Mr. Hill thing, or my decision to go to New York, but on second thought, yeah, I'm not sure that's what it was."

My eyes made circles around the steering wheel, and I couldn't help but think of Ari.

"You know what? Maybe that's the key."

"What?" I asked.

"We're never really sure about anything. So just do what you want at the moment, and if it's wrong, you'll figure it out."

Her sentence sunk in, and we sat in silence while I gathered up the nerve to say what I said next.

"Lana . . ."

"Yeah?" she mumbled through her mouthful of spiked dessert.

But I never did gather it. I *wanted* to tell Lana I knew she leaked her video—it was the only thing I could think about every time we talked—but it didn't seem like that would be some huge revelation. In my heart, in my bones, she knew that I'd figured it out. And I wanted to hate her for it. I wanted to hate her for the stained legacy she'd left behind. But part of me understood how escaping to New York sounded adventurous, and in Westcott, when something adventurous came along, those who wanted off the hamster wheel grabbed for it. Lana wanted off. She did what she had to do. What kind of sister would I have been if I held that against her?

I wiped my wet cheek just as the bug flew away. "See you at Christmas."

"See you at Christmas."

Pulling the phone from my face, I pressed the end button, then stared at the house for another minute or two before starting my car and speeding off down the street.

Maybe the saddest missed connections aren't the ones that are absentmindedly overlooked. Maybe they're the connections we won't be able to forget missing out on—like the ones we could have made, but chose not to.

7 CLOSED DOORS

My father used to tell me if a door doesn't open for you, kick it down. I suppose that tells you more about my dad's behavioral patterns than anything else. Sometimes his advice wasn't worth taking seriously, but that specific saying always seemed to ring true. Because there's nothing worse than a stubborn door standing in your way of what's behind it. Unless, of course, what's behind it is something you never wanted to see.

"So that's it? Piper slammed the door in your face?" Winston walked beside me through the hallway the Monday following Thanksgiving weekend. "Sounds like a complete waste of time."

"It was," I replied as we approached my locker, a coffee in one hand, a stack of books in the other. "I still have no idea who left me the note."

He adjusted his red-and-green Tis the Season to Be Naughty scarf, welcoming Christmas just a tad too early for most people's liking. "What if she's lying?"

"She has an alibi," I said, organizing my books and setting the topic aside. "How was your Thanksgiving?"

"Full of political conversations, booze, and regret."

"Cozy."

"There's nothing cozy about politics," he replied, staring down the hall. "Norah looks like she put on a few. Should I call her out?"

I took a sip of my hazelnut coffee. "I believe that's called fat shaming."

"So what? She once told me I look like Julia Child."

"Some would argue that's a compliment."

"Sonny!" Kyle rushed up behind me and grabbed my arm. "Harrison just questioned me."

"About the fire?"

"About Ari."

"Okay, just calm down." I gripped his arm, battling to hold onto my paper cup. "What did you tell him?"

"I told him that we're friends," he replied. "That we used to date but we broke up, and that we aren't close anymore."

Winston blew a bubble and let it pop over his mouth. "Define *we aren't close*."

Sweat emerged on Kyle's forehead as he stared into my

eyes. “He asked me about Cliff’s arm . . . and how well I know you.”

“*Me*?”

“I told him we aren’t that close either because I didn’t know what he was fishing for.” Kyle shifted his weight from one foot to the other so many times I began to think the floor was hot. “We have to find out who did this. If he starts suspecting us . . .”

“He won’t,” I told him, realizing how quickly our roles had reversed from our conversation in his living room. “Look, he’s probably just doing his due diligence to cross Ari out. Questioning people close to her.”

Suddenly, Sawyer crashed into Kyle from behind, causing him to fall into me. My coffee turned in its cup and spewed all over my clothes.

“Are you okay?” Kyle grabbed my wet arms.

I pinched my shirt and peeled it off my chest, staring down in shock with a wide-open mouth.

“Oh, shit, man. I didn’t see you there.” Sawyer continued walking down the hallway with his Bella View clan.

Kyle didn’t accept his reaction. “You didn’t see me?”

Sawyer’s feet slowed. He stopped, then turned around to face Kyle. “Nah, man. I didn’t.”

“How the hell did you not see me?!”

Everyone in the hallway huddled around us and stared; the room got so quiet you could hear the coffee dripping down from my cup onto the floor.

"I just didn't," Sawyer said, stepping closer.

Kyle glanced at me, then turned back around and did the same. "Apologize."

"For what?"

"Apologize to Sonny for spilling her coffee."

"You know I would—but I don't really take orders from lying pieces of shit like you."

"It's fine, Kyle." I pulled him back by the arm. "I have an extra shirt in my car."

Kyle pulled away, unyielding in his request. "Say you're sorry."

Sawyer's lip curled and a grin appeared; his cool green eyes sent a chill up my spine. "All right. I'm sorry." He reached forward and grabbed Kyle's shoulder, then sauntered closer. "I'm *super* sorry for kissing Casey last night."

Maybe it was his condescending smile. Maybe it was his nauseating voice. Or maybe it was the thought of him touching Casey. Whatever the reason might've been, before Sawyer could blink, Kyle reached back and punched him straight across the face.

"Bro!" Dean ran down the hall and tried breaking them up, but Max Crimson grabbed Dean by his shoulders and stole his balance from underneath him.

I jumped in the middle of the chaos, pulling at Max's shirt

with what I thought was a strong grip. Suddenly, I felt two hands grab my stomach. Cliff ripped me off, then took Max by his collar and punched him in the nose. Dark red blood trickled down Max's face; Cliff's knuckles were covered in it.

London Vanderbilt, with her long ash-blonde ponytail, pulled at Cliff's hood. Ari surged forward, pushing London so aggressively she lost her footing. She jumped from one foot to the next, stumbling backward into the crowd until she finally managed to ground herself and fight back. Alice Kennedy tried breaking them up, but not faster than Norah, who almost shoved the royal blue out of her. She grabbed a handful of Alice's red curls; Alice swatted at Norah, landing a few good slaps on her face—and one could argue she deserved them.

Buckets jostled his way toward a front-row seat.

"Oh my God!" I glanced at him. "Do something!"

"What do you want me to do?" he asked, hiding behind his lens. "I can't fight!"

Just then, Winston grabbed his scarf and tossed it around Norah's neck, choking her backward toward a classroom door.

"Winston! That's Norah!" I ran to stop him but was instantly knocked over; the cold floor caught my fall. At the other end of the hall, Kyle fell on his back, and just as Sawyer went to throw another punch, Cliff grabbed his arm and dragged him away from Kyle, his sling nowhere in sight. He threw Sawyer up against the lockers; the sound of his back hitting the metal sent a jolt through the hallway.

"HEY! HEY!" Ron Harrison, Principal Winchester, and Assistant Principal Clemmons came barreling down the hall. They forced their way through the crowd and took their shot at breaking up the scuffle. "That's enough!" Ron shouted.

Cliff got a few more punches in before Principal Winchester jerked him off of Sawyer. He pushed Cliff back and held his hand up between the two of them. "ALL OF YOU, IN MY OFFICE, NOW!"

The fighting stopped; everything had stopped. The breathless guys grabbed their jaws, and the girls used their fingers to comb out their disheveled hair. Many seconds of silence passed while we all glared at one another.

"LET'S GO!" Principal Winchester yelled. "NOW!"

Cliff flicked his hand toward the ground and sent a spray-paint-like mist of blood onto the white tile, then walked toward the front office. The rest of us followed him down the hall through a narrow tunnel of repulsed teens. Nobody fought at Westcott, *especially not us*.

The bell rang as we piled into Principal Winchester's office. The Bella View kids sat in a row of chairs to the right, and we sat off to the left. The divide between the two clusters was great. Ron Harrison came in and stood in the corner, his legs wide and fists balled, and we all sat in silence while awaiting our fate. I glanced to the left at Kyle's puffy eye, then at Cliff's swollen hand in front of me. To the right, Sawyer's busted lip swelled like an overcooked sausage. Ari's scratched face was hard to miss, though I tried not looking at it; and aside from Norah's rope burn from Winston's scarf attack, she managed to come out unharmed. Dean too. The office door finally swung open, and our principals stepped inside. Principal Winchester tossed an ice pack at Kyle's gut before walking behind his desk.

Kyle's body tensed up from the hard hit.

"Who are we missing?" He sat down in his chair. "Ah, that's right. Max." He folded his hands before slamming them on his desk. "Unfortunately, Max won't be joining us this morning because he's being rushed to the ER with a *broken nose*." He glared at Cliff, whose remorseless eyes descended toward his lap. "To say I am disappointed just may be the understatement of the year. Fighting is in direct violation of the SCC. You know this. You should all be ashamed of yourselves." He focused his attention on Kyle. "And you? Throwing the first punch? I didn't raise you to behave like trash."

"You're right, Dad." Kyle's arms remained crossed high on his chest, never reaching for the ice. "You didn't raise me at all."

Principal Winchester's dark eyes zoned in on his. "You aren't to leave my house this weekend. This week? School, football drills, home. I'll be calling your mother to ensure she enforces that."

Kyle gave him a smug look, nodding in his direction as if doing him a favor. "Okay, Dad."

"Keep up your disrespectful tone and you'll be off the team next."

Cliff dropped his head, turning it slightly so that Kyle could see his face; his narrowed eyes warned Kyle to close his mouth.

"You have anything else to say, son?" Principal Winchester asked him. "No? Then get your ass up and pack your bag."

Kyle clenched his jaw and stared into his dad's eyes; his own glistened. I reached my hand toward him and placed it on his leg, but as soon as it hit, Kyle shot up from his chair and exited the room.

"The rest of you gather your things," said Principal Clemmons. "You're all being sent home for the rest of the week."

"The rest of the week?!" Sawyer removed the wet rag from his lips. "But, sir! Kyle punched me first! I was just defending myself!"

"Is that what you call that?" Norah mumbled.

"That's enough!" Principal Winchester stood to his feet. "You should all be thankful I'm not writing you up. You're welcome for the grace—now get your things and get home.

Your parents are expecting you."

No one was quite sure why he extended mercy, but we all assumed it had something to do with the Bella View kids.

"Great," Winston whispered as we headed toward the door. "My dad will be really proud of me for kicking Norah's ass."

"I would hardly call that an ass-kicking." Norah grabbed her throat and pushed her way to the front of the line. "My mom is going to kill me."

"Same," Ari said, aggressively swiping at the blood seeping from her cuts.

We all walked into the hallway; Mr. Harrison followed closely behind. As we turned the corner, I saw Kyle holding himself up against the lockers halfway down the hall. His head was down, and his breathing was heavy. Cliff closed in on him, and I took small strides in their direction so I could hear their conversation. When Kyle saw Cliff's white shoes, he unenthusiastically pushed himself off the lockers, standing upright on his feet.

"You good?" Cliff asked.

Kyle's heavy eyes fought to stay open. "I don't need you to fight my fights."

"I didn't."

Kyle paused, taking a moment to get a good look at Cliff. It almost seemed like he was reacquainting himself with him. "Your dad's gonna kill you when he gets that hospital bill."

"Yeah." Cliff's chin hit his chest; he allowed for a tiny smile to crack, then stared at Kyle.

Ever since grade school, any scuffle the two of them got into was quickly squashed with a fist bump or a little football talk. They never let anything, or anyone, get in between their friendship—and they were used to forgiving each other for their mistakes.

But forgiveness can be a tricky thing. Sometimes you find you have room for it, but no space for the person who hurt you. Sometimes they don't make sense anymore . . . and sometimes that hurts . . . and you just have to let it.

"Look, my, uh, my birthday party is this weekend," Cliff said, staring down at his raw knuckles. "You should come through."

Kyle stood there in silence, not knowing how to respond to the offer on the table.

"If you can," he added, stepping back down the hall. "Put some ice on that eye."

After a long afternoon of self-loathing, working on my paper, and multiple hours of binge-watching reruns, my doorbell rang. I tightened my messy bun and brushed my eyebrows with my fingers on the way down the stairs. As soon as I opened the door, my heart skipped a beat.

"Are you in as much trouble as I am?" Dean asked, a foil-covered plate in his right hand.

"My mom said we'll talk when she gets home, so I'll let you know." I stared at the plate. "What's that?"

He lifted the foil. "Pie. I hear it's good for a week."

I pulled the door open some more and ushered him inside.

Dean walked into my foyer, placed the pie down on the entryway table, and took off his hoodie. I closed the front door and pretended not to watch, but the gash on his stomach was hard to ignore.

"What happened?" I asked, leaning down and yanking his shirt up.

"It probably just, uh—" Dean slowly pulled his shirt back down, his hand pushing mine off on the way. "It probably happened during the fight."

I reached over, grabbed the plate, and held it between us—which desperately needed to happen. "I'll grab two forks."

"Great." He followed me into the kitchen. "What have you done all afternoon?"

"Just worked on my paper . . . or tried to at least." I opened the silverware drawer, and Dean sat down on a barstool. "I haven't been able to think straight since I got the note."

"And you're sure Piper isn't behind all of this?"

I handed him a fork and laid the pie between us on the counter. "I'm sure."

"Not to be mean, but I strongly dislike that girl."

"The feeling is mutual," I replied. "She strongly dislikes

us too." I glanced up at Dean while I shoveled a bite into my mouth. "But she's been cleared by police."

He walked to the fridge, then poured himself a glass of milk and gulped it down. "I just don't understand who would want to frame you."

I looked out the kitchen window; rain came out of nowhere and trickled down the glass. "I hope we find out sooner than later. Mr. Harrison questioned Kyle this morning, and not about the fire, about Ari . . . Cliff . . . me."

Dean rinsed his cup out in the sink, twirling the glass around until he heard my name. He paused for a second, but in an attempt not to worry me by showing concern, he continued washing. "Really? Why?"

"Maybe he didn't believe Ari. Maybe he thinks she was involved and is questioning everyone close to her." I turned and tossed my fork in the sink. "If he finds out we were there, we're dead."

Dean placed the glass on a nearby dish towel and leaned against the counter. "But no one knows we were there. Not even the person who really did this. We were in the woods. No one saw us."

"Yeah." I leaned against the counter with him. "I hope you're right."

The kitchen was dark, calm, with only the sound of raindrops filling the room. I looked over at Dean and saw that he was already looking at me. "What?"

"Nothing. . . . I was just going to tell you how beautiful you are but I don't want to be cliché." He glanced at the window. "With the rain and all."

I followed suit, slowly nodding while biting my lip and smiling. "Doing anything in the rain does typically scream cliché."

"Like dancing in the rain."

I tightened my bun again. "Or kissing in the rain."

Dean put his hands on the counter behind him; his muscles emerged. "What about kissing near a window with rain on it? Is that considered cliché?"

My playful demeanor diminished and a nervous one appeared. "Yeah . . . I think so."

"That's too bad." Dean dropped his head, then pushed himself off the counter. He walked in front of me, grabbed my waist, and then hoisted me up on the green-tile countertop. "Because I hate clichés." His hands left my waist and slid down my legs. He stared into my eyes, then reached up and removed my ponytail. My hair fell around my neck and covered the sides of my face. I wanted to tuck it behind my ears, but something about it looking messy felt right. His hands made their way back to my legs, and he stood there staring, almost in admiration. "You're beautiful."

I dropped my chin, but he lifted it, forcing me to keep eye contact and accept the compliment. Without warning, Dean leaned in and kissed me. At that moment, my good judgment went down the drain beside us and all I could feel was a burning sensation across my skin. My mind was saying everything about the timing was off, but it somehow felt like the universe had aligned for us. It had been too long since we touched . . . we both knew it. Pulling away, he searched my eyes for permission before continuing. He moved my head to the right, but just as his lips met my neck, I jumped. "Oh my God!"

He pulled back. "What's wrong?"

"The window!" I slid down off the counter, taking a phone charger with me. "I just saw someone at the window!"

Dean turned around and hurried to the entryway. He jerked the front door open with one strong pull as I stood behind him. "*Buckets*? What the hell, man? What are you doing out here in the rain?"

He gave Dean a confused look. "Uh, didn't you hear me ring?"

"No, man. I didn't."

"Okay? Is Sonny here?"

I stepped beside Dean. "I didn't hear it either."

Buckets's hypercritical eyes moved back and forth between us, and just as he went to ask questions, I pushed my hair back into place and beat him to it. "What do you need?"

Dean's disappointment came out through a loud exhale as Buckets stepped inside uninvited.

"I think I overlooked something," he said as he walked into the living room and sat down on the couch. Buckets looked a little twitchy, and he seemed to be on a mission to explain.

"And what's that?" Dean sat down on the coffee table in front of us.

"This person—whoever lit the fire—they had to have driven there. But not to the school. No one would be stupid enough to do that—other than all of us." Buckets pulled out a paper from his damp messenger bag and placed it beside Dean's leg.

I made eye contact with Dean; he looked me up and down, his stare conveying his desire to finish what he started moments prior.

"They must've parked somewhere else and walked," Buckets continued. He opened the paper; a sketch of a map appeared before our eyes. "Here are all of the surrounding shops in close proximity to the school."

"Why are you showing this to us?" Dean asked. "I'm sure the cops have already thought of that."

"You want to wait around to find that out?" Buckets retorted. "I'm trying to help."

"Go on," I told him.

He sighed, then pulled out a red marker. "Only nine shops are within walking distance of the school—making it a relatively quick trip for the arsonist." Buckets put eight dots on the map. "Only thing I don't know is how they got back to their car without being spotted by someone. A Saturday night in Westcott? This person would've had to know that by parking at any of these eight shops, they'd risk being seen walking down the street. But there's one place you can get to by crossing over a couple empty back roads and treading through one or two wooded lots." His marker made a long line across the paper. "Laurel's Bakery."

"Not a chance." Dean shook his head. "Laurel's has security cameras out front. Everyone knows that."

Buckets pointed his finger at him. "But there's someone who may not. Someone who just moved here." He reached for his laptop and pulled up the security footage from the bakery's camera on the night of the fire. We didn't know how he got his hands on it—we didn't ask—but within seconds of watching the recording, I recognized the car parked along the curb out front, as well as the person walking down the sidewalk. I watched as he jumped inside and slowly pulled away.

Dean looked closer. "Is that—?"

Buckets nodded. "*Guy Penn*."

"Since when do we go to Cliff Reynolds's parties?" Winston asked as we followed the music up his driveway.

The Friday night air was chilly, and the sky was flecked with deep orange clouds as the sun descended. My burgundy blouse blew in the wind, and I tucked my hands into my high-waisted dark jeans to keep them warm. "Since Cliff invited me."

"He invited you?" Winston tossed his plaid scarf around his neck. "I don't like who you're becoming. Can't we just go back to your place and watch romance movies like good losers?"

"Had you thrown in chocolate chip cookies I may have obliged." I looked side to side as we approached the flat-roofed mansion. The two Maseratis parked out front floated on a sea of bright white cement. The driveway was so clean, you almost felt guilty for walking on it, and the striped green grass beside it was a distinct shade of rich. The colossal modern structure loomed proudly at the top of the steep hill, tucked behind a horseshoe driveway with perfectly trimmed shrubbery outlining it. The open windows allowed anyone to see straight through the home. I searched for a happy paint shade or comforting décor that hugs you, but it wasn't there. There wasn't even a plank of wood, or a wicker basket, or those cozy throw blankets you can always depend on. His house, as it appeared, was more like a museum.

"Have you told Cliff we think Guy's behind the note and the fire?" Winston asked.

"I think Norah filled him in." I should have been more talkative, but my eyes were twirling around the yard, making it impossible to focus on our conversation. "Supposedly the guys are going to approach him on Monday morning."

"Is 'approach' the new word for 'slam up against a locker'?"

I ignored him and continued to study my surroundings, and that's when Winston's skepticism came out to play.

"Wait a minute. I know what this is about."

"What do you mean?" I waved at my peers as I walked through the threshold of Cliff's home. Once inside, I spotted dozens of tipsy teenagers scattered throughout the bottom level, and a few who were making their way up the stairs. The house lights were dimmed, the music was blaring, the vibe was Violet, and the parental supervision was none. I was overwhelmed by the smell of various designer colognes, all meshing together into a stale expensive scent.

"You aren't here for Cliff," Winston yelled over the music, his voice barely audible from behind. "This is about Jacob! You're hoping to run into him!"

I continued weaving through the crowd of brocks. "I don't know what you're talking about. I'm not here for Jacob."

"Right. And I'm not here for the charcuterie board and chocolate-covered nuts." He grabbed me by my arm, and as I whipped around to face him, I gave him an annoyed look.

"I'm not here for Jacob," I repeated, exaggerating each word. "That's ridiculous. I'm just here to have a good night."

I wanted him to believe me. I willed my words to be true

as they seeped from my lips and into the atmosphere. But all week long I had thought about the next time I'd see him, our encounter in his driveway, and why Dean's kiss didn't wash it all away.

"Kid!" Cliff yelled as he strolled toward us.

Winston rolled his head in Cliff's direction, then looked at me with a scowl. "I'll be in the kitchen being ridiculous if you need me." With a raised brow, he walked backward into the crowd, managing to bump into almost every person in his path.

"Your commitment to our eye contact is impressive!" I shouted.

Cliff stepped in between us. He wore a fitted long-sleeved beige shirt, his most expensive watch, and dark jeans in place of khakis. "You showed up."

Our eyes met. His were a little glazed over, but I hadn't seen him so calm, cool, and collected in months.

Squeezing my lips together, I nodded.

"With Winston." Cliff stared in the direction of the kitchen, then back down at me. After five seconds of an awkward staring contest, a small smile appeared on his face. "Glad you're here."

I placed my hands on my lower back. "You are?"

"Sure. Why not?"

I wanted to believe we were making progress, but I knew the liquid in his cup was to blame for his attitude. "Where's your sling?"

"Ah." He took a swig. "I don't need it."

"Cliff . . . if you hurt your shoulder . . ."

"I told you it's fine."

"Well, Kyle said it's not."

He scoffed. "And how the hell would Kyle know that?"

"Something about drills, I think?" I lifted my shoulders. "I don't know. . . ."

"Tell Kyle to worry about himself. His stamina on the field yesterday afternoon was laughable." He took another sip. "My shoulder's fine."

"If Coach finds out—"

"Jesus, Sonny. What do you know about football? It's a fucking tweak. Nothing to alert the boosters about." His attitude was getting angrier by the second. "Just drop it."

I didn't believe him, but in an effort not to further ruin his mood, I moved on. "Happy birthday, by the way. I'd get you a gift, but what does one get for *Cliff Reynolds*?"

He paused, perhaps attempting to shake off our heated conversation. "I don't have your sister. You could get me her."

I looked into his blue eyes, wondering how he managed to convince himself *Lana* left *him*. Maybe it was his way of denying how strong his feelings were for Ari—and that he more than likely broke up with Lana because of them.

"Where are your parents?"

He glanced at a family photo. "Skiing in Vermont."

"On your birthday?"

"They promised they'd make it to my eighteenth." Cliff lifted his cup in a cheers gesture. "Hey, maybe Kyle will show up to that one too."

Becoming uncomfortable, I changed the subject. "I heard Norah filled you in about Guy."

Cliff nodded at a pack of overzealous pom-pom shakers, then looked at me. "Yeah. I'll handle it."

"I hope sooner than later. Ron Harrison questioned Kyle."

Subtle panic appeared in Cliff's eyes. "About the fire?"

"About Ari . . . me . . . you."

"What about you and Ari?"

"I don't know. Maybe he's just questioning her friends." I flicked his hurt shoulder. "Which is likely why he questioned you."

"You think he suspects we—"

Suddenly, one of Cliff's friends wrapped his arm around him, causing his drink to spew from the cup. "Come on, buddy! We need you in the kitchen for this round!"

Cliff stared down at the small circle of liquid on the marble tile below us.

"I'll . . . get that. . . ." I stared at his drunk friend, then at Cliff.

His friend offered me the most belittling smile. "Hey, aren't you Lana's sister?" He tried to share a laugh with

Cliff. "How is she?"

"Don't be stupid." Cliff pushed him. "Go."

I grabbed a napkin from a nearby table, and as I bent down to clean it, Cliff was being pulled toward the kitchen. "Sonny!"

I looked up, my right hand wet from the potent liquid.

"I'll handle it," he managed to say before drifting off into a mob of his football friends.

I stood to my feet, hurled the napkin into a trash can, and looked around the room at my fellow purples. *What am I doing here*? I thought as I made my way through the sliding glass door and into the backyard. The pool was lit up, but it was way too chilly to swim. Instead, the fire was roaring in the stone fireplace, and Adirondack chairs were scattered all over the cobblestone patio. Market lights hung above our heads, and music played from a nearby speaker. It was more my scene, so I decided to stay for a while. I grabbed a water bottle, sat down in a chair, and watched a game of beer pong on the other side of the pool for nearly twenty minutes.

Eventually, someone joined me.

"Rocky Balboa!"

I turned my head to the right as Jacob dropped into the neighboring chair. His burgundy sweater caught my eye; I couldn't help but notice we matched.

"How are your hands?" he asked.

"Very funny." I peeled my eyes off his chest and stared

into the yard. "Does Cliff know you're here?"

"He invited me. But, uh"—Jacob swiveled in his chair and looked back into the house—"I don't think Cliff knows much of anything right about now."

I nodded. "You're probably right."

"What are you doing out here by yourself?"

"Well, I was with Winston."

"Winston?" Jacob tossed his thumb over his shoulder. "I saw him ten minutes ago. He's watching *Elf* in the guest bedroom with a huge plate of cheese."

"Sounds about right," I replied, staring ahead at the beer-pong players.

"Cliff's house is pretty nice, huh?"

"Yeah. But so is yours."

Jacob settled into his seat, curving his back and shifting into a comfortable position. "My mother did a good job with the place."

I slid my hands underneath my legs. "I'm guessing you two aren't close?"

"I've always been closer to my dad," he answered. "After my mom moved out, she would come back to Long Beach almost every weekend to spend time with me. I even spent a few weekends with her here in Westcott. But those visits eventually slowed down, and within six months, she was hardly ever in California. Her interior decorating business requires so much out of her but—I don't know—something tells me she's okay with that. I know she said I could stay in Long Beach so I didn't have to transfer schools or lose my friends, but it's hard not to think she just dumped me on my dad and bailed. I almost wish they'd just sign the divorce papers and get it over with." He paused, staring down at his knee in a daze. "You know, when you were telling me about your relationship with your dad, I wanted to tell you how much I understood the feeling. I should have."

"It's okay," I replied, hesitant to let my guard down. "It's a personal thing."

"Yeah?" He swallowed. "Well, there's nobody else I'd rather be personal with."

I melted in my seat, removing my hands from underneath my thighs and tucking my hair behind my ears. "Do you miss home?"

"I do." He cleared his throat and paused. "Specifically, the waterfront. I used to wake up early every Sunday and jog for miles up and down the pathway. Sometimes I'd run for so long I forgot where I was." He cracked a small smile. "But I always made time to sit on a bench and wait for the sun to rise, just thinking about life and how beautiful it is. It was the best."

"You, um, you kind of sound like someone who's never been to Long Beach before."

"Nah." He lifted his head. "Just someone who knows never to take things for granted."

I bit my bottom lip. "Well, Westcott certainly can't compete with that."

"Ahh, I don't know." His beautiful brown eyes sparkled underneath the lights. "You're here. . . . That definitely counts for something."

"Right. I'm a real tourist attraction."

"You know, it's funny." He shook his head in disbelief. "Everyone thinks you're amazing but you."

My eyes trickled down his body as I turned my face. I wasn't sure why I usually looked away at the first sound of a compliment, or why I could never accept one. Especially not from Jacob—his always seemed to hit differently.

"Will you guys be leaving again once this investigation is over?"

"I'm not sure," he said. "Do you think we should stay?"

Our eyes met; his begged for the answer he wanted while I hoped mine were telling him what I wasn't saying. What I couldn't say.

After a brief moment of silence, Jacob cleared his throat again, then changed the subject. "Everyone, uh, everyone was talking about the fight all week. It was the topic of every conversation during lunch." He paused. "Well, that and the fire."

"Speaking of which . . ." I glanced behind me at the house. "Your dad questioned Kyle."

"Really? About what?"

"He asked him about Cliff's arm, how well he knows Ari, how well he knows me."

"Shit." He wiped his mouth, his eyes treading across the bricks beneath us. "I asked around about the note. I didn't give details, but nobody knew the slightest thing about it."

"I think we figured out who will."

"Who?"

"Guy Penn," I replied. "Buckets pulled the security footage from Laurel's Bakery. Guy was on it—walking down the sidewalk and into his car around the time of the fire. The guys plan to confront him on Monday morning to tell him what we found."

Jacob didn't seem too relieved or convinced. "Look, maybe you should tell my dad what happened with Piper. About all of this. Get Guy kicked out and get JC back. He can help get rid of Winchester if he knows what he did."

"No." My voice heightened. "You promised me you wouldn't involve him!"

"I know . . . but . . ."

I reached over and grabbed Jacob's wrist. "You promised me."

Jacob's eyes left mine and traveled down to my hand, but I unwrapped my fingers and pulled away. "If Guy won't admit it, then we'll figure out how to prove it was him. But we can't get your dad involved when he already thinks we know something. Just let us handle it."

"Okay," he replied. "I won't tell him." He turned his head and stared out into the yard with me. "But do you want to tell me what you were doing parked outside my house the other night?"

My face burning, I turned to look at him.

"I sort of saw you through my bedroom window."

"I don't . . . I . . ."

"You could've come in."

I also could've told him the truth—had I known what that was. But I didn't know why I drove to Jacob's that night. Blame it on the sad songs that were playing through my speakers, or my exhausted mind, or my mixed emotions regarding his return; whatever the reason might've been, I found myself being pulled down his street without a clear understanding of why. And I pulled away, without knowing what would have happened had I gone inside.

"I was going to ask your dad a question about my paper."

"Really?" Jacob wasn't buying it in the slightest. "At nine on Thanksgiving night?"

"I realized it was Thanksgiving so I took off."

"Took you a while to realize that."

"It's a public street." I tried digging myself out. "I can technically park there for whatever reason I want."

"Oh. Okay." He nodded a little. "Yeah, except that it's not public . . . at all. . . . It's actually pretty private. At least that's what I took from the huge wrought-iron gate out front."

I shrugged. "Never noticed it."

"Oh . . . that's crazy because . . . you sort of have to punch in a code to get through it."

"Well, it must've already been open." I pushed my hands against my jeans and raised my shoulders.

Jacob grinned. "Okay, Sonny Carter. Whatever you say."

I refused to look at him. My cheeks were blushing big time, and I wanted to wait for the red to pass before I said another word. But Jacob continued staring at me, and I couldn't fight the urge to look back.

"What?" I asked him, giving in to a glance. "What are you staring at?"

Jacob took a sip of his drink, then looked ahead. "Nothing," he replied with a playful smile.

His smile—it was dangerous. The egotistical way he curled his lip was barely perceptible but just visible enough to make you believe he knew something you didn't. His lips were soft—I remembered that from our kiss—and he barely had to move them. He did all of his smiling with his eyes. It was charming—and I'm pretty sure he knew it.

"But I do have one more question," he continued.

My deep breath lacked the smoothness Jacob exhibited. "What's that?"

"You and Dean?" His formerly charismatic eyes were now blank. I could tell he already knew the answer based on the way they faintly pleaded for it not to be true.

"Yeah," I replied, our sadness seeming to correlate. "We're trying to work things out."

There was a long pause as Jacob let reality sink in. "I guess I sort of figured that when he slammed the basketball into my gut my first practice back."

I relaxed my face, suspiring a little. "To be fair, Dean wasn't always so . . . aggressive?" Staring up at the stars, I allowed my mind to take a trip down memory lane. "When his mom died, he turned into a different person. I think he used to feel invincible. Captain of a nationally ranked basketball team. Money coming out of their ears. His eyes on Penn. Mrs. Ballinger's passing made him realize he was human. That he could lose things . . . and people. He's never lost anything in his life so it really messed with his head. He's a little tougher now—a little different—but he's a good guy. And any anger he throws your way is only because he's scared of losing me."

"I get it." Jacob nodded; his voice subdued. "Losing you sucks."

I looked away, digging my chin into my chest until my spine hurt.

"Maybe we can be friends," he suggested. "Like we talked about before I left?"

Dean's request flashed across my mind; I stalled, hoping he'd pick up what I was putting down so I didn't have to say it, but he waited me out. "It's just that Dean would prefer I don't speak to you."

Jacob's cheeks turned so red they had to have been hot to the touch, but he managed to nod as if he understood. "Okay."

I didn't know what to say, so I said nothing, and by then he was pretty used to that.

"I should . . . probably go." He stood up and tugged down on his sweater. "We have a game tomorrow morning."

"Yeah, I should go find Winston." My voice was loud and overcompensating. I stood and ran my fingers over my blouse, then stared down at the grass. My eyes became so wet that I could only see a cloudy sheet of green. It felt like minutes had passed before I said what I said next. "Hey, thank you for the brooch."

Jacob stood there waiting, maybe hoping I'd say something else. Anything else. Anything but an empty filler statement. But nothing came. "Yeah." He swallowed his feelings. "Yeah, of course."

I turned around to watch him walk away, and I couldn't understand why, from the moment he left, I wished he wouldn't have.

After dropping a cheese-stuffed Winston off at home, I pulled into Dean's driveway. He had asked me to swing by. I initially told him I had to get home to work on my paper, but after I broke my promise to him, my guilty conscience wouldn't allow me to. I stepped onto the porch and rang the bell.

"Well, if it isn't Sonny Reynolds."

I rolled my eyes and stepped into the foyer. "That has the worst ring to it."

"How was the party?"

Jacob instantly came to mind. "I don't know. It wasn't really my scene."

"I could've told you that," he replied, pulling me in for a hug. As he pulled away, he gently lifted my chin and looked into my eyes. "You okay?"

"Why wouldn't I be?"

"You just patted me on my back," he said, laughing a little, squinting a little. I knew nothing was funny; he wanted answers.

"I'm just tired."

"Tired, huh?" Unblinking, he continued staring at me so intensely I thought he'd be able to see my conversation with Jacob play out across my pupils, but he dropped his hand and smiled. "Let's go lay down."

I followed him up the stairs and into his room. Once inside, Dean reached for the lamp and turned on the light. Within seconds, I noticed a horribly wrapped gift with my name on it sitting on top of his comforter. "What is that?"

He jumped back on his bed, pushing himself up against

his headboard. “It’s just an early Christmas gift.”

“Dean, we promised we weren’t doing gifts this year. Not after everything that happened.”

Once his dad’s reputation was retrieved from the gutter, Mr. Ballinger was able to leave the call center and find work with an old colleague of his. Their financial situation was slowly improving, but they were far from their old life, and I didn’t want Dean wasting money on me—regardless of how badly I wanted to know what was underneath that reindeer paper.

“It’s small,” he replied. “And don’t worry about me. We have plenty of money.”

“You’re sure? You can take it back if you—”

“Just open it.”

I sat down at the end of the bed, reaching for the present with joy in my eyes. After pulling back the wrapping paper, I caught my first glimpse. “Oh my gosh! I remember this day,” I said, staring at the photo of us in nostalgic bliss.

“It was the first time you came over after we started dating.”

“And we baked stuff and watched movies all day,” I added.

“You broke a glass in our kitchen and stepped on a piece. Remember?”

“Don’t remind me. I still have the scar from when you refused to ask your dad to take me to the hospital.”

"It was a little scratch."

"I was gushing blood!"

"Ahh, the blood." Dean covered himself with his blankets. "I spent all night cleaning that off our hardwoods."

My laugh was weak but sincere. "Your mom was so mad. If she could have grounded me, I'm pretty sure she would have."

"She was a germaphobe, that's for sure." Dean smiled, then sniffed and cleared his throat. "Do you like it?"

"I love it," I replied, taking another glance. "We look like babies."

"You'll always be my baby," he mumbled, barely awake. I looked into his blue eyes and saw his pain and gentleness all at once. Without a word, he communicated his feelings with one stare. The previous year had done a number on him, but he was finally ready to get back what he lost—starting with me. "Lay with me," he whispered, pulling up the corner of his comforter.

I turned off the lamp, then slowly crawled into his arms. Dean pulled the covers over me; he pulled me against his chest. I breathed in the scent of his clothes, his sheets, his skin.

He grabbed my chin and pulled my lips toward his. One kiss down, and I could feel more coming. He slid his hand underneath my arm, grabbing my back and pulling me closer. Two kisses down. By the third one, his hands were moving faster.

I pulled away.

"I'm sorry," he whispered.

"No." I sat up and swung my legs off the bed. "It's fine. It's um—"

He propped himself up on his elbow. "What's wrong?"

I exhaled, scrunching my nose. "Can we just . . . take things a little slower?" When he didn't respond, I started to ramble. "It's just that . . . I . . . I love you, and I love being with you, but—"

"Hey." He sat up and joined me on the edge. "You don't have to explain yourself. Of course we can slow down." He kissed my forehead, letting his mouth rest there for a moment. "Whatever you want."

"Thank you." I ran my fingers over my lips, feeling a little embarrassed, feeling a little bad. But mostly I felt shame because the real reason I wanted to pump the brakes had very little to do with Dean and not wanting to kiss him. We both laid back down and went to sleep. I could have stayed there all night—and maybe I would have *if only my thoughts hadn't woken me*.

An hour or so later, after I was sure he'd fallen asleep, I snuck out of his bed and tiptoed down the steps. Once outside, I quickly walked to my car and backed out of the driveway. The quietness inside had a presence to it and made me feel like someone else was in the car. I was more confused than ever, and I couldn't understand how I became *that* girl. The girl who, even after inexcusable betrayal, found it difficult to walk away from her ex-boyfriend. The girl who didn't even know if she wanted to.

I rolled up to a stop sign—the irony wasn't lost on me. Maybe I should have stopped—stopped myself from giving Dean another chance. But the truth is we don't always know what we're supposed to do. We don't always have big red signs staring us in the face, telling us not to move forward with certain things, to slow down, to pause. Sometimes we just have to guess. Sometimes we get it right; sometimes we don't.

And I guess that's the rub with life: *it doesn't give you answers until you've already figured it out yourself.*

I pushed down on the gas and drove back to the hillside. Stoplight after stoplight, I raced to my next stop. I stepped outside of my car and into the crisp night, still wearing my burgundy blouse—plus a few tear stains. Barely standing, I managed to knock on the door.

"Coming!"

I bit my nail, thinking about the night I had, thinking about the hole I'd dug myself into, and as soon as the door flew open, the waterworks began.

"Oh, God," Kyle said.

I walked into his arms and ugly cried.

"Okay . . . okay . . ." He dragged me into the house with

him. “Dean?”

My sobs continued, but louder.

Kyle slung his arm around me and walked me into the living room. He put the remote in my hand, tossed a throw blanket on top of me, and walked into the kitchen to grab snacks. “I was just about to watch a movie. You pick one,” he yelled. “Cookies? My mom made like two sheets full! Chocolate chip!”

I wiped the mascara from underneath my eyes, Dean’s scent lingering on my trembling fingers.

“I’ll take that as a yes!”

I curled up into a ball while scrolling through Netflix. The last thing I remembered hearing was the sound of plates clanking and cabinets closing before my eyes finally gave in to sleep. When they crept open early the next morning, it was the first time in a long time I remembered feeling well-rested. I yawned, reached my arms out beside me in a stretch, and noticed Kyle was sleeping on his chair-and-a-half, a bag of chips by his side. I smiled, shaking my head at the thought of him choosing to sleep sitting up instead of going to his bed.

“Ky!” I whispered, rubbing my head.

He jumped, locked eyes with me, then rolled over and covered his face.

“Wake up,” I whispered again, walking over to his chair and forcing my way onto it. At the foot of the chair sat the laptop. I gave the screen a tap and up popped foster-care articles—nearly fifteen different tabs' worth. My eyes squinted as I scrolled through the pages, wondering why the massive search.

"I see you're back to being your annoying self," Kyle mumbled through the throw blanket.

"Um." I closed the laptop in a hurry, pinching my finger in the process. "What happened last night?" I asked, shaking it off.

He rolled over, removed the blanket, and sat up. "You fell asleep," he said, rubbing his eyes. "I didn't want to wake you."

"Oh no! My mom—"

"I texted her," he said. "You're fine."

I let out a sigh of relief. "Thank you."

"I've got to get up and get to my dad's." He yawned and gave me a small push to the arm. "What happened to *you* last night?"

Before I could reply, the doorbell rang. I jerked my head toward the entryway so quickly my neck cracked. "Who's here this early?"

We exchanged a mutual look of confusion before Kyle jumped up and walked toward the door, pulling yesterday's shirt down over his bare chest. He made a sharp right turn into the office and peeked between the blinds. "Shit," he whispered, his voice still raspy. "It's Mr. Harrison."

"Ron?" I walked in behind him. "Are you sure?"

Kyle dropped his finger. He turned back around and his eyes paced across the hardwoods. "What the hell is he doing here?"

"Don't open the door!"

"I have to." He ironed his wrinkled T-shirt with his hands. "Stay in here."

"Ky! Hold on a second!"

He waved me off as he walked out of the office. Against my wishes, he opened the door and sunlight lit up the foyer.

"Kyle!" Ron exclaimed. "Sorry to bother you so early. I was passing through the neighborhood. Thought I'd pop in to check on you."

"Uh . . . why?" Kyle stepped onto the porch.

"Sort of making my rounds," Ron replied. "Wanted to make sure you were doing all right after the fight."

"Oh, right. The fight. Yes, sir, I'm fine."

I peered through the blinds, sucking them closer to my lips with each breath I took.

"Good." Ron propped his loafer on the porch step. "Well, listen—thanks for talking to me the other day. I'm sure you can see things are pretty hectic around the school right now . . . trying to figure out who's responsible for the fire and all. Narrowing down suspects is a necessity at a time like this."

"Was I . . . was I a suspect?"

"Oh, no. No. No. No." Ron's hands remained hidden inside his pockets. "You and your friends are good kids, but that doesn't mean you'll be exempt from questioning."

"Got it." Kyle ran his fingers across his abs—which is what he did when he was nervous. "I'll answer any questions you have."

"Thank you, Mr. Winchester. You know, I do have one if you've got a second."

"Sure."

"Ari Ziegler . . . your friend. . . . Would you happen to know if she's ever been a smoker?"

"I know that she vaped."

"Vaped?"

"Vapes," he corrected himself. "She vapes."

"I see. Where does she typically do that?"

"Uhh, I don't know, usually in her car before school. Sometimes in the parking lot if no one's watching. Sometimes she'll trail off."

"Trail off?"

"Yeah, I don't know. You'd really have to ask her."

"Sure, sure." Ron nodded. "Reason I ask is I found her cell phone not far from the left wing following the fire. She claimed she was vaping when she came into my office to retrieve it."

"I see."

"But you know, there's something I still can't figure out."

"What's that?"

"Well, Ari told me she dropped it after school on Monday. Said she walked off to a side street so she wouldn't get caught, and that it must've fallen out of her pocket right then and there."

"Sounds like Ari," Kyle replied, laughing a little.

Ron smiled. "You know what's even funnier, Mr. Winchester?"

"Tell me."

"I found her phone on Monday morning."

Suddenly, Kyle wasn't laughing anymore. His smile slowly faded, his eyes slowly narrowed, and his urge to protect Ari kicked in. "She probably mixed up her words. She must have meant to say she dropped it on Monday morning, that's all."

"She would've had to drop it pretty early. I got to school an hour and a half before the bell rang." Ron's eyes were squinted so tight they were nearly shut. "Does Ari typically vape on side streets at six thirty in the morning?"

"I don't really know what Ari does anymore," Kyle replied, his voice threatening to crack. "Like I told you—we broke up."

Ron held intense eye contact with him, then broke character and grinned. "I won't keep you, Mr. Winchester." He pulled out his buzzing phone. "I should get going myself. Headed to the hospital to visit a friend. He was assaulted last night just outside of town."

"Jesus. I'm sorry."

"Yep." Ron glanced down at his cell phone, then looked back up. "Wrong place, wrong time. . . . That'll get ya." He smiled, then pushed himself off the porch step with his loafer. "Have a good one." Halfway down the driveway, he stopped. "This your car?!" he shouted, staring at mine.

I closed my eyes tightly, my eyelashes brushing against the white plastic.

"My mom's!"

Ron gave his keys a shake in his pocket. "Sonny drives one just like it!" He slowly turned around to say goodbye, but really he was just looking right through him. "See you Monday, Mr. Winchester."

Kyle closed the door and I ran out of the office to meet him. For a moment, neither of us said a word, and not because there was nothing to say, but because the panic in our eyes spoke for us. The door took the sunlight with it when it shut, the blinds were still closed, and only our bare feet were visible on the dark hardwoods. I could hear the ice cubes dropping in the freezer, the noises a house makes only in the quiet, the birds chirping on close-by branches. But more than anything, I could hear the sound of normalcy speeding off down the street, and I had a feeling it didn't intend to return anytime soon.

"Kyle . . . when are you planning on talking to Guy

again?"

Perhaps the only thing worse than a closed door is opening one you never should have opened.

8 SECOND CHANCES

Does everyone truly deserve a second chance? I've always liked to think people show us who they are, and whether we choose to believe them or not is up to us. That begs the question: Who's at fault when they hurt us again? Will it be you—for extending grace to someone who has already shown you their true colors? Will it be them—for accepting the olive branch despite knowing your relationship may end the same way it did the first time? Or will it be both—for ignoring your gut instincts not to give another chance . . . or refuse one.

I'd spent all weekend knowing what Monday stood to bring, but nothing could have prepared me for it. The sky seemed to be right on top of us that morning, with a scarce layer of charred-gray fog blowing through it. I walked a little slower—maybe because I feared what Guy would say. Maybe it was the way my peers looked me up and down in disgust for engaging in a fistfight, although one could argue I didn't. Perhaps it was just another sluggish Monday morning. Or maybe it was something else. An intuition. A gut feeling something bad was going to happen. And you know what they say: *you should always listen to your gut*.

"Why do you look like you stayed out all night making bad decisions?" Winston appeared beside me as I walked through the parking lot, his sapphire-blue shirt rolled up to his elbows.

"And I thought everyone was staring because they missed me."

"You know, my dad woke me up with a bullhorn and threatened to kill me if I got into any more trouble, yet I somehow look more alive than you."

My red eyes met his. "I've had a rough weekend, okay? And the first draft of my paper is due tomorrow. I stared at my computer screen for fifteen hours straight yesterday. Between that, and knowing someone's trying to ruin my life, I'm a little stressed."

"Looks like it," he replied. "Kyle told me Mr. Harrison stopped by to visit him on Saturday morning."

"If by 'visit' you mean 'interrogate.' "

"He filled you in?"

"No, but I was there."

Winston chewed on a Twizzler. "Why were you at Kyle's that early?"

"I spent the night."

"You spent the night? At Kyle's? Why?"

"I just . . . did."

"Okay . . . what aren't you telling me?" he asked. "You're not telling me something and it's showing more than Norah's weight gain."

"Would you knock that off? Norah's skinnier than your left thigh."

"How dare you. I'll have you know my left thigh is comparable to my right one if I stand on my toes and pop a knee." He tugged down on his shirt. "Now start at the—"

"End? I wound up at Kyle's, crying over Dean. The beginning? I went to Jacob's house to confront him about the note."

"What? When?"

"After we left the club that night. I was the one who talked to Jacob and found out it wasn't him. Not Cliff."

"But I heard Cliff—"

"He covered for me. I didn't want to tell Dean I went to Jacob's house and involved him in this. Especially not after I promised Dean I wouldn't speak to him. So Cliff stepped in and lied for me."

"Cliff?" Winston choked on the red rope in his mouth, coughing for dramatics. "Cliff Reynolds?"

"Cliff Reynolds." I held my hand in front of me and let the fog slip through my fingers. "Then he told me to get my shit together."

"As opposed to his shit that's all over the place?"

I dropped my hand.

"If you didn't want Dean to know you went to Jacob's house, make sure he doesn't find out the two of you were sitting fireside at Cliff's birthday party."

"Weren't you eating cheese in the guest bedroom? How would you know what I was doing?"

"The guest bedroom has a window," Winston replied. "And I could see your feelings for Jacob through it."

Maybe I should have fought back against his statement. I wanted to. I didn't want to admit my feelings for Jacob, especially not to Winston—my judgmental best friend. But I couldn't fight it any longer. I needed help sorting it out—even if Winston was the only help I could find.

"I don't know what to do," I said as we opened the double doors and entered the hallway. "I like Jacob, but I love Dean. And every time I begin to question our relationship, he pulls me back in. I'm more comfortable with him than I am anyone."

"I don't know, you seemed pretty comfortable in those photos of you and Jacob on his couch."

"How observant, Winston. Thanks." I clenched my book bag straps. "I can't unlove him. I just can't. If that makes me stupid—"

"That doesn't make you stupid." Winston took a sharp right turn down the hallway where our lockers were. "That makes you *you*."

"Liking two guys at once is not me," I replied. "It's Ari."

"You're far from Ari."

"Am I? Because there's Dean, and then there's Jacob. That's not one guy. That's two guys."

"No one can say you can't count." Winston shoved another Twizzler into his mouth. "Look, just tell Dean the truth. Tell him you're confused. Tell him you might have feelings for Jacob after all, and that you need time to figure it out."

"That will crush him."

"Not more than learning you're only with him because you're scared to let him go."

"Sonny!" a voice yelled from behind.

I turned around, searching for a pair of eyes to lock in with mine. Within seconds, I found myself face-to-face with the guy who was causing me so much confusion. At least one of them, anyway.

Jacob approached me, a sense of urgency across his face. "Can I talk to you?"

Winston raised a brow, then walked ahead toward his locker, leaving Jacob and me behind.

"What's up?" I asked, my eyes scanning the halls in

search of Dean, hoping he was running late.

"Look, I thought about our conversation at Cliff's party. I respect you, Sonny, and if you don't want to talk to me because of what I did, or because you're happy with Dean, or for whatever reason—then I'll back off. But I need to hear that from you."

I tucked my hair behind my ear as Kyle passed by us. He glanced at Jacob, then nodded at me. As he walked by, Ari and Norah passed him. I made eye contact with each of them before turning my attention back on Jacob. "What do you want me to say?"

"Tell me what *you* want. Not what Dean wants."

"Jacob—"

"Look, I told you before I left that we could be friends because I thought it was the right thing to do. But it didn't feel right. It still doesn't. And avoiding you every day, having to pretend that I'm okay with not talking to you, watching you and Dean together—I'm sorry, Sonny, but that doesn't feel right either."

"I—"

"You came to my house for a reason," he interrupted. "You could have let Dean handle it, but you came to hear me out. You parked outside on my curb for nearly an hour, and I don't know what you would have said had you come inside, but I'm pretty sure you weren't going to tell me you don't want to talk anymore." He placed his hands on my waist; the heat from his fingers nearly melted me. "So please . . . just tell me what you want."

"I can't, Jacob."

"No, bullshit—you can. Don't think about him. Don't think about what he wants from you. What do you want?"

Just then, my eyes were drawn to Cliff. He was standing at his locker, staring inside at a growing heap of problems. I knew he'd been filled in on Kyle and Mr. Harrison's conversation—everyone had. Ron knew Ari had lied, and it was clear he thought her friends knew why. It was no longer just about Ari's phone. It was no longer a matter of *if* we'd all be suspects; it was a matter of when. I stared around the hallway at the people who were in the woods with me on the night of the fire, and suddenly, they were the only people I could see. Every one of them stood out like boldface letters on a paper full of words. We were all in a waiting game, and only one person could end it.

Guy Penn walked down the hall toward his locker, and before I could reply to Jacob, Cliff came barreling through the crowd toward him. He grabbed Guy by his collar and slammed him against the metal wall, his forearm pressing against Guy's neck. "You think this shit is funny?!" Cliff asked, his face centimeters from Guy's.

We all gathered around and watched from a safe distance. It was all most of us were willing to do after our week off. Kyle approached my other side, and the others surrounded us.

"I don't know what you're talking about," Guy mumbled. "But you and I both know I can maneuver my way out of your grip and pin you to the floor. If you don't want to be embarrassed, I recommend you release me."

Guy's reply only made Cliff push harder. "Yeah, bullshit—we saw you."

"Saw me what?"

Jacob walked over and separated the two of them. "Don't get expelled," he said, pushing Cliff back toward Kyle. He held out his hand to stop Cliff from coming forward again.

Guy aggressively brushed off his shirt, his face flushed red. "Not one for Mondays, Mr. Reynolds?"

"If you come near me, or any of my friends again—"

"We'll both kill you." Kyle stepped forward. His eyes were empty and unforgiving; they looked black as night. "Do you understand that, Guy? We will kill you."

Remember that dark shift I was telling you about? *This was it*. This was the moment everything changed. To normal kids, riddles and unflattering photos can be chalked up to adolescent games or unimportant gossip that doesn't deserve any attention. But to Westcott students, everything mattered. Every single word you spoke, text you sent, grade you earned, mistake you made—it all counted. Because people watched us. Influential people. People who chose us—or didn't. There were no *games* at Westcott High. There was no humor in rumors. And when our futures were on the line, there was no mercy. Kyle meant what he said—and we knew it.

Guy bent down to pick up his books. “Look, I don’t know what you’re talking about. If this is about the riddle—”

“This isn’t about the FUCKING riddle,” Cliff grunted. “It’s about the note.”

“What note?” Guy laughed. “You’re insane.”

Cliff broke through Jacob’s arm and stepped in front of Guy’s face. “You need to come clean.”

“About what?!”

“Everything okay down there?” Principal Winchester asked from the opposite end of the hall.

His voice caused everyone to scurry.

Jacob tossed his arm around Cliff and pulled him away from Guy. “Yes, sir! All good!”

My eyes shifted between Principal Winchester and the guys. He nodded but stood there watching. “Good to see you back, Mr. Reynolds,” he shouted, still patiently standing at the head of the hallway.

Cliff finally broke eye contact with Guy and looked his way. “Yes, sir,” he yelled. “Glad to be back.”

Principal Winchester eventually walked on, and once he was out of sight, Cliff gave Guy one last threatening look before heading toward first.

“Let’s go,” Kyle said, pulling me down the hall away

from Guy. Away from Jacob. We made it to Kyle's locker, and so did the others.

"Let's kill Guy now," Norah suggested. "Why wait for him to admit it?"

"Let's just turn in the footage from Laurel's," Ari said, spinning her rings around her fingers. "We have him on surveillance camera—"

"Doing what? Walking to his car, blocks away from the school?" For the first time all year, Dean seemed specifically nervous about the matter. "We have to get him to come forward."

"By what? Beating it out of him? Thanos just proved that won't work," Buckets said.

"You think this is a joke?" Kyle gave Buckets a quick shove to the chest. "Do you have any idea what this could mean for us? Harrison thinks we're involved somehow. If our names are even mentioned in another Westcott scandal, no ILS will touch us."

Buckets brushed off his chest. "We're aware."

"Kyle, calm down," Ari whispered sternly. "You're going to draw attention to us if you keep fighting people!"

"More attention than the orange phone you dropped near the woods like an idiot?" Dean grabbed his hair. "My reputation—"

"Everyone's reputation." Kyle tossed his hood over his head and pulled the strings. "We can't talk about this here.

Let's meet tonight to figure out a plan. My house."

"What about the club?" Winston asked.

"No more meeting in public. My house. Eight o'clock. Someone tell Cliff."

"He's invited?" Buckets questioned.

"This isn't about us." Kyle lifted his shoulders to readjust his backpack. "Someone tell him."

We all watched as Kyle walked toward first period, passing by Casey on his way.

She reached over to stop him. "Hey, Kyle . . . I wanted to give you—"

"Not now, Casey." He walked on, dismissing her entirely.

She stood there in the middle of the hall, staring down at the folded-up paper in her hand. Her long-sleeved baggy gray T-shirt looked like something she snagged from her dad's closet, but that couldn't have been the case. It covered the back of her hands, but I saw the way she clung onto the note with her fingers—so tightly her knuckles must have been begging for release. We watched as she turned around, tossed the paper into a trash can off to the left, and walked briskly toward her first class.

Everyone dispersed in opposite directions until only Dean and I were left.

"This is all my fault," I whispered, falling against the lockers in defeat. "I shouldn't have gone to the school that night. I've dragged you all into this mess."

"Hey." Dean pulled me in for a hug, and this time I welcomed it. "It's not your fault. We're all in this."

Before I could pull away, I saw Ron Harrison walking toward me out of the corner of my eye. His pockets jingled, and his dress shoes reflected off the sunlight coming in through the open doors.

"Sonny!" Ron tapped my shoulder as he passed by. "See me in my office in ten."

"Um . . ." I glanced at Dean, then back at him. "Am I in trouble?"

Ron turned around and used his eyes to smile—kind of. "Ten minutes, Ms. Carter!"

"What do you think that's all about?" Dean asked as I played out different scenarios in my mind.

"I don't think I want to know."

Ten minutes later, I walked into the front office. To my surprise, I wasn't alone.

Cliff looked up at me from a chair. His hair was a little messier than normal, his face a little paler. I wanted to think his flushed demeanor was a result of his scuffle with Guy, but something told me Cliff was beginning to crack.

"What are you doing here?" I asked him, descending into my seat.

Using his fingers as a brush, he combed his hair until every strand was back into place. Cracking or not, Cliff knew we would all unravel if he did, so he put on a brave face. "Harrison called me down here."

"Me too," I replied, watching the secretaries watch us.

Suddenly, the office door swung open, and Ari walked inside. Kyle came in right behind her. The four of us made uncomfortable eye contact as they joined us.

"Mr. Harrison called for you too?" I asked.

Kyle sat on the edge of his seat and prepped me. "Don't say anything about the woods."

"Or Ari's phone," Cliff added, staring ahead at the front desk. "We don't know shit, got it?"

"And what about me? What am I supposed to say?" Ari's leg bounced up and down, shaking the row of chairs.

"You say nothing," Cliff replied. "You've already told him your truth."

"Yeah, except it wasn't the truth." Her monotone voice took flight. "He told me he found my phone on Tuesday to try to catch me in a lie—and he did. He knows I'm lying. He knows—"

"He doesn't know shit," Cliff quickly interjected. "He's baiting us. He thinks we know something, and we don't. Everyone keep your mouths shut."

I wasn't sure if we were taking orders from Cliff, or just too nervous to speak, but everyone stopped talking. Kyle slouched down and closed his eyes. I sat up straight in my chair, watching the clock, waiting impatiently for our meeting. Minutes passed when out of the corner of my eye, I saw Cliff's right hand slowly move toward Ari's left thigh. He placed it on her knee and pushed down, putting a stop to her violent shaking. One would think he was just trying to ensure she didn't make herself look guilty, especially since the two of them hadn't resolved anything since she stormed out of the club, but I knew it meant more.

"Mr. Harrison will see you now," Ms. Pamela said from behind the front desk.

We stood to our feet and marched toward his office. As we approached the door, Cliff turned around to face us. "Don't say anything stupid." He made sure to make eye contact with each of us before opening the door—me especially. One by one, we walked inside and sat down in the four chairs in front of his desk. Previously, there had been two, but that time four of them were lined up.

He was prepared for us.

"Sonny! Kyle! Cliff! Ms. Ziegler!" Ron looked up from the bottom desk drawer he'd been digging through and stared at us. "Thank you for coming!" He pulled out four folders. "And how is everyone feeling after their little vacation?"

Cliff nodded. "Good. But glad to be back."

"Very glad," Kyle added.

I peeked at Ari. Her face looked like milk, one shade away from blending in with the wall behind her cheek.

"Glad to hear that," Ron replied, shuffling through the folders. "I'm sure you're all wondering why you're here."

When we didn't reply, Ron stared at us over the top of his thin metal glasses.

"Uh." I cleared my throat. "Yeah. I guess we are."

He looked back down at the folders. "I was hoping you four could help me with something if you have a second." He removed a piece of paper from each and spread them across his desk. "These are your grades from the beginning of the school year."

We all took a look.

"Do these stats look correct to you?"

"Yes, sir," Cliff answered while the rest of us nodded.

Ron pointed at the middle of each paper with the tip of his ink pen. "But if you look right here, a little over a month ago, all four of your grades collectively took a hit." He stared at each of us. "Any idea why?"

I swallowed as the parking lot C conversation with Principal Winchester came up in my throat. "Well . . . my dad was arrested. I was sort of going through a bad time."

"Understandable." Ron tapped my paper with his ink pen. "Mr. Winchester?"

"I don't know. Girl problems I think."

He turned his attention to Cliff. "Mr. Reynolds?"

Cliff shrugged. "Do I have to explain my grades to you?"

Ron paused, clearly taken aback by his attitude. "An

explanation would be appreciated."

"It was the end of the season. I was probably just slacking a little."

"Slacking?"

"Yes, sir." Cliff raised his brow, challenging him to disagree. "Slacking."

Ron removed his glasses. After looking at Cliff for ten long seconds, he moved on to Ari. "Ms. Ziegler. Why the decline?"

"Just . . . had a lot going on."

"Anything you'd like to share with me?"

"She's good," Cliff replied for her.

Ron smirked. "Well, it's certainly understandable that you kids were each going through some things. That *would* explain the sudden change in grades. But you know, if you look here"—he pointed to the bottom of each paper—"your grades tanked again. The Monday after the fire, all four of you received Cs on your precalculus quiz. And in the weeks since, you have all failed to turn in miscellaneous assignments." He glanced at Cliff. "Mr. Reynolds, you even managed to flunk your history test. You have straight As in that class."

Cliff leaned back in his chair. "Yeah, well, our school was set on fire. . . . I'm sure we aren't the only four who haven't turned in some homework."

"Funny you mention that." Ron pulled out another small

stack of folders. He put his glasses back on and peered at each one. "There have been a few others. Mr. Banks, Ms. Langdon, Mr. Poland, Mr. Ballinger, and last but not least, Ms. Sor—"

"I'm sorry, are you allowed to be discussing their grades with us?" Kyle interjected.

"No, he's not," Cliff replied, sure of himself. "And why aren't they in here being questioned?"

Ron's eyes surveyed Cliff's; he studied him with piercing scrutiny. "I only have four chairs."

Just then, the heat kicked on; the loud noise caused me to jump in my seat. It was almost eerie the unit knew how cold the room had gotten—in more than one way.

"It appears your grades take a slight hit when you're going through something intense. Something heavy." He made eye contact with me. "And I can certainly sympathize with something like an arrest shaking your world a little." Then with the others. "But what I can't wrap my head around is why, in the weeks following the fire, the nine of you specifically have been impacted to the point of letting your grades slip. As you know, you're all required to maintain a certain GPA, and these types of grades are alarming. Maybe something's going on? Maybe you'd like to get some things off your chests?" He honed in on Ari. "Maybe you know something about the fire?"

Ari went to speak, but Cliff put his hand up. "You know

what? Maybe I should call my dad."

"For?"

"You clearly think we did something, and it's a little unethical to question us without our parents present. Don't you think, Mr. Harrison?"

A wry smile appeared on Ron's face. "Well, it doesn't really matter what I think, Mr. Reynolds. I'm not a cop."

Cliff entered into their death-stare competition to win, shrugging right before he spoke. "Then I'm not a suspect." He pushed himself off the chair and walked out of the office.

Later that night, at eight o'clock on the dot, I stepped outside of my car and buttoned my coat; my wavy hair kept my ears warm. It was time for our meeting. The closer I got to the door, the more I questioned my being there. The more I questioned everything I stood for. But he saw me through the window. He saw me, and I saw him, and there was no turning back. He stood up from his comfortable chair, then slowly walked toward the front door to meet me. His hand on the opposite side of the chipped teal-blue coffee-cup logo, he pushed open the glass door and ushered me inside.

Second chances. Sometimes you give them to people who are deserving of grace. Sometimes you give them in vain. Other times, you give them to Guy Penn, in the middle of Geraldine's, when you're supposed to be somewhere else.

9 GOODBYES

Some people say there's nothing good about goodbyes. I'd have to agree. We've never been taught how to end something. Goodbyes, and how we do them, are completely up to us. What we say—and what we don't. There is no rule book. There's nothing to follow. There are no standards to go by. It isn't like that—only good things are like that.

"Welcome back," Guy said, holding open the door to the coffee shop.

I gave him a cautious look, then walked in. Only a few other coffee drinkers sat inside, working on papers, reading books. I didn't recognize the barista behind the counter—it wasn't Ashley. In fact, I saw no one I recognized. It almost looked like the perfect scene for a setup, and I considered for a moment I was in one. But I took my chances and collapsed into a black-and-white houndstooth chair.

"Would you fancy a latte?" Guy asked.

"I'm not here for coffee. I'm here to talk."

"Honest." Guy nodded and dropped down into the chair across from mine. "I like that about you." He lifted his cup to me in a cheers gesture. "And hey, thankfully I can still talk after your friend nearly crushed my windpipe."

I closed my eyes so tight I was sure I'd left permanent wrinkles. "Look, what do you want? Do you want money? Cliff can—"

"Whoa, whoa, hang on a second. You called *me* here."

"Why are you doing this? If this is some sick game, or riddle, or some twisted version of fun for you—"

"What exactly do you think I did?"

"The note. The fire."

"What note?"

"The note you left on my doorstep that told me to meet you in parking lot C so we could 'talk.' JC and I found it."

"Ah. So JC found it and assumed it was from me?"

"No. JC thought the note was from Jacob. We all did until we found out the timeline didn't fit." I waited for a customer to pass by and then leaned forward. "We know you burned down the left wing. It makes sense. You were furious that Principal Winchester fired my dad, and if you couldn't have him, he couldn't have his precious new building."

"You're right. That does make a whole lot of sense."

"You tried setting me up," I continued. "You wanted to

get me in the parking lot so I'd be on camera when you turned them back on."

Guy slowly lifted his coffee cup to his lips. He took a long sip, keeping eye contact with me. As he lowered his cup, he smiled with his eyes. "Well, sorry to burst your bubble, Sonny, but I've already been questioned by police. I've been cleared."

"Is that so?"

With raised brows, he cocked his head to the left and waited for me to continue.

"And what if they saw surveillance footage of your car parked outside of Laurel's Bakery on the night of the fire? What if they saw you hopping into your car shortly after the fire was started?"

"I was parked at the bakery because I stayed until closing, then walked to Geraldine's to catch up on homework. It was a nice night so I thought I'd take a stroll instead of driving." He rolled his pointer finger in the air. "Go ahead. Rewind the tapes. You'll see me pull up at Laurel's around eight, walk out at ten, take a left toward Geraldine's, and of course, as you've already seen, walk back around one. Multiple people confirmed I was at Geraldine's when the fire started." He reached for his cell phone. "This photo I posted on my page that night certainly doesn't hurt my case."

I stared down at the picture of textbooks and lemon bread, thinking of how fitting it was he liked *lemon*.

"You really think I'd douse my grandfather's land in gasoline?"

Leaning forward in my chair, I set my humiliation aside and pressed on. "Don't act like it's far-fetched. We all know what you did to get into Westcott."

"Sorry, madam, that's between my grandfather and Principal Winchester. I had nothing to do with that."

"But you sure are proud of it, aren't you? Leaving JC a riddle. Shoving it in his face."

"I like to play games . . . have a little fun . . . big deal."

I leaned forward some more. "You watch me. You've been watching me since the day we met. Everywhere I look . . . there you are. On the football field, in the auditorium, in the halls. Maybe you didn't do it, but maybe you know who did. Maybe you knew it was coming."

Guy tapped his fingers against his cup. "I told you, Sonny, just wanted to be friends."

Scooting to the edge of my seat, I continued bargaining. "Then as a *friend* . . . please do me this one favor and tell me who did it."

"Why do you care so much?"

I struggled with what to say next. I knew I couldn't tell him we were in the woods that night, but I needed to assure him there was a *very* good reason I cared. "Look, I can't say. But I can tell you that Mr. Harrison may think we're involved somehow. That's why Cliff—"

"You can say it." He motioned for me to continue. "Crushed my windpipe."

"Look, you must know something that can help me."

He took another swig; I could hear him swallow. "I come from a *really* shitty family, Sonny. But you know that. You hate my mom, don't you? At least that's the rumor. Don't get me wrong—I hate her too. The woman's a nut. Always has been." He cracked his neck; each pop caused me to blink. "One time when I didn't clean my room, I came home and all my clothes were in trash bags on the curb. A little weird? More like psychotic. The woman's always been tough on me. I put up with it as long as I could but eventually decided adopting the title of *weird child* was a lot easier than trying to prove myself to her. The same goes for my dad. My only saving grace was my grandparents. They paid for all my wrestling camps. They believed in me. No one's ever believed in me, Sonny. Do you know what that does to a kid's head?" He glowered at me. "No, I don't suppose you do. My grandpa is a strict guy. No bullshit. All work, no play. He's successful and I've always wanted to be like him. One day I asked him how he got to the top. He asked why I wanted to get there. 'Only lonely people live there,' he said. But I wanted to be the best wrestler anyone's ever seen. Looking back, I think I just wanted to be seen." Guy took a straw paper and began folding it into little squares. "He told me I'd have to be willing to take out my opponent. No matter the risk. No matter the way." He flicked the paper off to the left and stared at me. "If my seventy-five-year-old grandpa took out JC . . . Sonny Carter can surely find a way to take out this amateur."

I gritted my teeth in place of reaching for his neck. "Do you know who that amateur is?"

"Even if I did"—his dark eyes were unmoved—"you know I can't tell you."

Knees to knees, I continued pleading with him, inches away from falling off the chair. "Please, Guy, just point me in the right direction."

My words hit his tongue like honey; he cracked a crooked smile. "Do you know what it's like to see things, Sonny? To know things? To harbor secrets? Do you know how heavy it is to carry someone else's? I'm not talking about the who-likes-who, who-cheated-on-who bullshit. No. *Real* secrets. Ones that come with long nights of trying to fall asleep so you can forget you know them, despite knowing the second you open your eyes you'll have to wear them like yesterday's T-shirt. I've seen many things, Sonny. I've seen you. I know you. You eat salad on Tuesdays, but pizza on Fridays since you know you'll be running the mile in gym class. You wear oversized sweaters because you can't stand to dress like your fellow Violets, whose fingertips ooze more advantage than your Cobalt friends will ever have in their lifetime. You hate that you're rich. You hate that you're not ugly or nerdy enough to be the underdog you feel you are in your heart. Your Chuck Taylors are always dirty—you could wash them—but it authenticates your underdog persona. You hate your ex-boyfriend because he banged the hottest girl in school, but you're not strong enough to walk away. You skip out on weights in P.E. so you can write in your journal about guys like Jacob who will continue to screw you over, yet you somehow manage to convince yourself it's poetic. You take shit from guys like Cliff Reynolds, whose haircuts cost more than what it'd take to feed a small village in Kuwait, and you keep your hair medium length so you won't ever look like your sister, Lana. You'd hate that—she's a slut. Sonny Carter is *no slut*. She's just a girl who came crawling in here on hands and knees, begging me to tell her secrets she doesn't really want to know. Because once she knows them . . . she'll have to face the fact that someone out there in this world doesn't like her. *And everyone likes Sonny Carter*."

Like a popped tire, I deflated. What little space I had between my lips disappeared as I closed them and ground my teeth together to keep myself angry—but even that was a challenge.

"I didn't do it." Guy took another sip from his cup, never closing his eyes, not even to blink. "But ask yourself—do you really want to know who did?"

Later that night, I pulled into my driveway with a tear-stained shirt and ten missed calls. I'd missed Kyle's meeting, and I was in no mood to explain why. All the way home, I replayed Guy's words in my mind like a broken record. I was shocked to learn he wasn't behind the note, and even more scared to find out who was.

I put my car in park, unlocked the side door of my house, and walked inside. Gliding lazily into the kitchen, I opened the fridge. Mom had left me a plate of spaghetti. I could tell by the size of the meatballs that it was from the club—likely more than a few days old. I happily passed.

After staring at the front of the fridge without reason for nearly five minutes, I walked back toward the front door and up the stairs. Three steps in, I noticed a slight drop in temperature. The farther I climbed, the colder it got. I dragged my fingers across the wallpaper; it almost felt wet.

I reached the top of the stairwell; the hallway was filled with brittle silence and the carpet underneath my feet felt more like an ice pond. With narrowed eyes, I walked over to the thermostat. The heat was on, but the goosebumps covering my arms begged to differ. I crossed them, hoping the overlap would provide warmth of some kind.

My eyes shifted down the hall toward my mother's room. *Maybe she left her fan on*, I thought. I crept down the hallway and peeked my head inside. Her cheap perfume, the kind she wore out with her girlfriends, met me at the door.

The moonlight shined through her sheer white curtains, allowing just enough light for me to see a lipstick-stained glass of Merlot on her nightstand, and that her fan was off. I looked side to side, then closed her door and walked back down the hall toward my room.

When I reached the bathroom, I stepped inside and flipped on the light. The tiles underneath my feet sent a chill through my body. I leaned over the sink, turned on the hot water, and splashed some on my face. *You're going crazy*, I thought as I stared at myself in the mirror, blotting my cheeks with a hand towel before walking to my room. I pushed open the door with a false sense of confidence.

That's when I saw it.

Jacob's black Jeep hurried down my street. He pulled onto the curb and hopped out of his car with a baseball bat in his hand.

I met him on the front lawn. "I'm so sorry! I didn't know who else to call." I could have called ten other people, or the police, but for some reason the only person I thought to dial was Jacob.

"Don't be sorry," he said. "Are you sure no one's inside?"

"I'm sure. I checked the house."

"Next time you should really call the cops." Jacob walked around me and made his way toward my side door. His cologne was barely hanging onto his clothes from the long day, but I could still smell it, and it brought me a little relief.

"It wasn't a random break-in," I said, jogging behind him up the steps.

Jacob reached the top of the stairs. He looked side to side, then took a left turn in the direction of the only room with a lamp on. "How do you know?" he asked, stepping inside. He walked over to my previously open window and made sure it was locked.

"Because they took my paper," I replied, standing in the doorframe, out of breath.

Jacob turned around; his eyes were just as wide as mine.

"It's gone." I walked over to my laptop and ran my pinky finger over the side. "My flash drive is gone."

"Sonny—"

"My notes. My rough draft." I rummaged through the stacks of papers on my desk. "It's all gone."

"Who would do this?" he asked.

"The same person who'd stand outside your living room window and take photos of me. The same person who tried framing me for arson." I rubbed my forehead. "This isn't a game anymore, Jacob. They broke into my house. *My house*!"

"Calm down," he said, placing his hand on my shoulder with a firm grip.

"That's not an option," I argued. "We have a Chosen Ten meeting tomorrow morning. Our pieces are due."

"Well, maybe that's your answer. Whoever took this must know your draft is due tomorrow. Maybe it's someone on the Chosen Ten who views you as competition. Maybe it's a Bella View kid."

"Sawyer? London?" I tossed out their names, trying to determine whether or not they'd do something like that. "I don't know."

"Do you have any other enemies?"

For a split second, I stopped listening. I no longer seemed to care that Jacob was standing in the middle of my bedroom. The past few months had finally caught up to me and the composure I could always depend on fled. For once, I was enraged. My fury sprang to life as I swiped my hands across my desk like windshield wipers, sending jars of pens and papers flying. I didn't stop chucking items until the entire desk was wiped clean.

Jacob quietly snuck up behind me. "Let's rewrite it."

I whipped around.

"I can help you," he said, walking past me toward the wreckage, unaffected by my breakdown.

"You don't—"

"I want to," he cut me off, bending down to pick up my mess. "Besides, other than my dad, no one knows the Farrah Klein story better than me. I know more than I want to."

"But we'll never finish it in one night," I replied, my pessimism making an appearance.

"So we'll pull an all-nighter."

I kneeled to help, grabbing handfuls of colorful ink pens. "I don't know, Jacob."

He placed a stack of papers on my desk. "I'm not leaving you here alone. So we can just sit here until your mom comes home, or we can work on your draft. It's completely your choice."

And with no other choice but to be removed from the Chosen Ten, I picked up my laptop, took a deep breath, and caved. "I guess an all-nighter doesn't seem like the worst idea."

Multiple cans of Red Bull later, I shot up from the floor with a finished first draft in my hands. What was left of my hair looked like I'd walked through a windstorm, and I could've passed as a raccoon with the amount of smudged mascara underneath my eyes. I knew I looked like a crazy person who'd just convinced herself she found Atlantis. "We did it!" I yelled.

"Shhh!" Smiling, Jacob scooted backward until his spine hit the side of my bed. His brain had been picked beyond the recommended amount for one's mental health; his voice was raspy from talking so much. "Don't be so loud."

Like a proud mother, I beamed down upon my paper and sat beside him on the ground. Dropping my head against the side of my mattress, I stared at the ceiling. The ceiling-fan blades squeaked each time they came full circle and I hadn't noticed the noise until that moment. "Tiptoeing the line of mental exasperation," I mumbled.

"Huh?"

"Nothing," I replied. "Just . . . thank you."

"No problem. It was fun."

"Liar."

His chin hit his chest and he smiled again.

"No really," I continued. "I can't say thank you enough. The Westcott Awards mean everything to me, and without your help tonight, I would have been kicked off."

"Any excuse to hang out with you," he replied. "Even if that means talking about Farrah Klein."

My cheeks began to burn.

"Hey, look, I'm, uh . . . I'm sorry about the other day in the hall. I shouldn't have been so pushy. I don't really know what I was thinking."

"I guess I'm not exactly innocent. One day I'm telling you we can't talk, the next day I'm asking you to come over to chase away intruders."

"Not gonna lie—that was pretty confusing. The come-over part, not really the robbery, which is sort of saying something."

"Right." I curled my lips. "Look, I'm sorry for leaving you hanging. I wish I could explain how I feel."

"You can try."

I wondered if it was time to open up, and when I saw that Jacob couldn't even look at me, I realized it probably was. "I think I'm just—" I bit my lip. "I think I'm scared of you?"

"Scared?" He turned his head; his eyes narrowed. "What have I done to—"

"It's not you. I've just . . . I've never loved anyone but Dean. Okay, sure, I considered Kyle for like a split second in fifth grade."

"Does he know that?"

"No, and don't ever tell him. His head is big enough and I've kept that secret hidden ever since I punched him." I looked at the corner of the ceiling and sighed. "But Dean was the first guy I fell in love with, and who fell in love with me. He's all I know."

"I mean look, Sonny, it's definitely understandable to be intimidated by new things. I'm new. I get it. You don't know me that well, and what you do know so far hasn't necessarily painted me in the best light. But staying with someone because they're safe—"

"What's so wrong about playing it safe?"

He shrugged. "I guess you forfeit opportunities to take risks. Risks you want to take but don't because you're choosing someone else above yourself." He rolled his head to the left, his eyes weighing him down. "But I can't force you to choose you, Sonny. You have to do that."

The consequence of responding was great. I knew if I did,

I could easily say too much. Every word I spoke from that point on mattered, unlike before. We sat in silence for minutes, neither of us knowing how to transition from that conversation. Thankfully, I didn't have to.

"I just wish I could have met you under normal circumstances."

I gulped, desperately trying to put his prior statement behind us. "I, um . . . I don't know. . . . Maybe that would have changed everything. In chaos theory—"

Before I could finish my sentence, Jacob recited the entire definition verbatim.

"The butterfly effect," I said, turning to face him with wide eyes. "How'd you—"

"My ex really liked that concept . . . or maybe just the insect." He ran his fingers up and down on his jeans. I could tell his mind left the room. "We should probably . . ."

"Um . . . yeah." I stood to my feet; Jacob followed.

"It's four in the morning. Do you mind if I crash here? I can take the couch."

"Take my bed," I replied, turning off the lamp on my nightstand. The moonlight was taking its time peeking through the cracks between the blinds, so everything was completely black. "I'll go curl up next to my mom."

We were planted underneath my ceiling fan, our bodies merely silhouettes. I couldn't see him, and he couldn't see me, but we both sensed the tension between us. It was so powerful, neither of us moved.

"Goodnight," I whispered.

Jacob's frame moved forward; he gently pulled me toward him. I didn't even have time to think about it or to say no, or yes—he didn't give me a choice. I sunk into his arms and he held me there. My face lay against him until the moment he pulled us apart, and once he did, he stepped back and stared at me. With his right hand, he reached up and tucked my hair behind my ear, his fingers slowly falling down my neck as he let go. "Goodnight."

I walked into the hallway and closed the door behind me. My heart began to beat fast, but it could have been chalked up to all the Red Bull I'd devoured. I slid into the bathroom, opened up a pack of makeup wipes, and rubbed my face. The mirror in front of me showed a cheap reflection of who I was. Upon first glance, you would've thought I'd just come home from a nightclub or a party riddled with mistakes. That with each stroke of the makeup wipe, I was removing a little more shame from the evening. But that wasn't the case. I was just a girl who'd stayed up all night writing a paper. And when the makeup was gone, I stared at that girl. Part of me was proud of her resilience. Part of me wanted to ram my fist into the mirror, shattering it so I could no longer see. Because no amount of makeup remover could rid her of the truth: one half of her heart was sleeping in her bed, and the other half had been calling her all night from his.

The following morning, the sound of cars driving down my street woke me ten minutes before my alarm could. I didn't want to wake my mom the night before, so I slept on the couch, which became a terrible idea once I felt how sore my back was. I slowly tiptoed up the stairs, crept into the bathroom, and hopped in the shower. I turned on the faucet, then jumped to the end of the tub so the cold water couldn't reach me. When it was finally warm, I pulled the lever and stood underneath the showerhead, letting the water hit my face. Every minute I spent there became a chance to figure out who had broken into my room.

It was dangerous that I didn't call the police, a notion I only understood once I had slept on it. A break-in far surpassed picture leaks and rumors. I felt violated, and even though I was able to bury my fears to write my paper, they came back the next morning, consuming me like the steam filling the bathroom. My mind scrambled for answers, but as I turned off the water, I was only cleaner.

I slipped into my robe, then walked into my room. Jacob was nowhere in sight. The bed was made, the pillows were fluffed, and the Red Bull cans were sitting in the trash can. I ran my fingers over my quilt as if I had all the time in the world, but my eyes were eventually pulled to a note lying on my pillow—with the rainbow brooch sitting on top. I grabbed it, unfolded the paper, and his words took me under:

I couldn't let the last note you received be from anyone but me.

I think I love you, Sonny Carter.

Jacob

"Ky! Wait up!" I shouted as I chased him down in the empty parking lot. "We have to talk!"

He continued walking into school. I was sure he didn't hear me, so I tried again.

"Kyle!" I picked up my pace and caught up to him in the hallway. "Hello?"

He stopped in his tracks, looked at the ceiling, and then turned around to entertain me. "What do you want, Sonny?"

"Whoa . . . what's wrong?"

"Seriously? Are you that out of touch with reality?"

I squinted and tossed my hands up in front of me. "Okay, hold on. What are you talking about?"

"Where were you last night?" He popped his lips. "You know what? Don't even answer that. I already know." He turned around and continued walking toward the auditorium.

My meeting with Guy flashed across my mind. "That's what I want to talk to you about, Kyle! I—"

"God, you are *so* selfish, Sonny," he said, coming back for round two. "We're in this mess because of you! Had you never gone to meet Jacob that night, none of this would have happened!"

"Wait. Now I'm really confused."

"Maybe if you'd focus on someone other than yourself for once, you wouldn't be!"

My jaw hit the ground. "What are you talking about?! Why are you so mad at me?!"

"Everyone comes to your aid, Sonny. Everyone's always there to help you. When you asked us to help JC—we were there. When you were about to make a huge mistake by walking into parking lot C—we were there. When you come crying to us about your boy problems—we're always there. And the one time we needed you—you blow us off."

"I didn't know the meeting was so important," I replied. "I figured you could fill me in."

"Before or after you were done hanging out with Jacob?"

Suddenly it felt like I'd chugged six more Red Bulls. "How . . . how do you—"

"Dean drove by your house last night when you weren't picking up your phone and saw Jacob's Jeep on the curb."

Oh, God I thought.

"Did you seriously think you'd get away with that? Jesus, Sonny. Dean called me afterward and had a mental breakdown. I couldn't console him."

"Okay, since when are you a Dean advocate?" I fired back. "Weren't you the one who told me Dean was a dumb decision?"

"Does that justify you sleeping with Jacob when you're working things out with him?"

"God!" I squinted. "I didn't sleep with Jacob, Kyle. I slept on the couch. But thanks for your presumptions."

"Sonny—"

"How . . . dare you . . . try to shame me." With narrowed eyes, I grabbed my temples. "You of all people! I'm selfish for skipping one meeting? I'm suddenly a horrible friend? Everything I do is for my friends! I'm invested in all of you more than you're invested in yourselves! I'll have you know someone broke into my house last night and stole my flash drive. I called Jacob, and he came over to check on me. And thank God he did, because he stayed up all night to help me rewrite my paper."

Kyle stood there, his chin high, taking my outburst like a champ.

I reached into my book bag and removed a folded-up piece of paper. Walking toward Kyle with purpose, I shoved it into his hand. "Here."

He looked down at his palm.

"Casey tried giving this to you in the hallway yesterday but you blew her off. I guess I wasn't 'too focused on myself' to notice that." I glared at him, then brushed by his shoulder in the direction of the auditorium. Halfway there, I turned back around. "Oh, and by the way, it wasn't Guy. I met with him last night. He has an alibi." Leaving Kyle behind me, I completed my walk. After entering the gloomy room, I fell back against the wall, inhaling for what felt like the first time in minutes. A few seconds passed when I heard the sound of Sawyer's voice; I quickly shot up and peeked back into the hall.

"Winchester! Buddy!" He jogged toward Kyle. "Got a minute?"

"What do you want?" Kyle asked.

"To talk," he replied. "Look, I'm sorry for the coffee incident. I deserved that punch."

"You know why I punched you. That wasn't why."

"Ahh." Sawyer grabbed his lips. "The Casey thing. Yeah. Hey, look, I'm sorry about that too. But to be fair, I didn't know you two had a thing when—"

"When what? When you decided to pretend to like her?"

"Pretend to like her?" Sawyer smiled. "Is that what you think I'm doing?"

"Considering what your last girlfriend looks like, yeah, I'm pretty sure that's exactly what you're doing."

"Casey's a pretty girl."

"Not your type of pretty," Kyle retorted. "Cut the shit. You wanna talk? Tell me what you're up to."

"I'm mentoring her brothers and we got to know each other." Sawyer shoved his hands into the pockets on his yellow hoodie, widening his stance. "She told me about her situation, and I wanted to help."

"Doesn't sound like you."

"People change, Winchester." Sawyer studied Kyle's eyes. "Speaking of helping others . . . I was hoping you could help me."

"Yeah? And how's that?"

"By coming clean about your pal Cliff Reynolds."

Memories of the showcase punched me in the gut, and it didn't take long for nausea to set in.

"You and I both know his little secret. Sonny knows it too." Sawyer dropped his smile. "Cliff doesn't deserve to be on the team. He doesn't deserve the respect he gets. He doesn't even deserve a good friend like you, Kyle. I heard about what happened between you two. What kind of a dick hooks up with his best friend's girl?" It wasn't a question. "Look, what do you say you and I request a meeting with the student-conduct council to let them know what their star quarterback does in his free time?"

Their conversation came to a standstill.

"We gotta get in there." Sawyer checked his watch. "How about this? I'll give you a few days to think about it. Just know I'd sure hate it if your unwillingness to help me affected my willingness to help Casey."

"What makes you think I want you to help Casey?"

"Don't lie to yourself, dude. You know who my dad is. You may not like it, but he's the only chance she has at getting out of her aunt's house quickly."

"You need proof," Kyle said. "You'd have to prove it. It won't matter what I say."

"It matters when your last name is Winchester." Sawyer grinned, patted Kyle's arm, and then walked off. "See you in a few days."

"I don't need a few days!"

Over the edge of the doorframe, I saw Sawyer come to a halt. He turned back around and waited for a follow-up statement.

"I have my answer," Kyle said, holding intense eye contact with him. He paused for what seemed like an eternity, but when he finally spoke, it was certainly final. "Fuck you."

"I can't believe we were wrong," Winston said as we sat down at our lunch table later that afternoon.

The cafeteria was somber. The sunlight that usually came through the massive glass windows was hiding behind clouds, and it didn't feel like I was roaming freely through the grandiose space; it almost seemed as though I'd been barricaded inside. I wanted to leave, but it felt like I was surrounded by lions who were waiting to attack me if I made the wrong move. I could feel eyes on me, but I wasn't looking around to verify it. I knew everyone had words waiting for me. By then, everyone knew I'd met with Guy, everyone knew someone had broken into my house and stolen my paper, and everyone knew I decided to call Jacob—not Dean—when it happened.

"I can't believe Guy has an alibi," Casey said.

"Yeah, well, had Buckets done proper research . . ." I bobbed my head from left to right in search of Kyle. I hadn't had the chance to speak with him after our fight and we had a lot to talk about. "Guy knows who's doing this to me. I know he does."

Winston shoved a pizza boat into his mouth. "How do we get him to tell us?"

"We don't," I replied. "He's not going to. We have to come up with a plan."

"Sounds oddly familiar." Winston cracked open his soda. "Pretty sure we called a meeting last night to do exactly that."

"I had to meet with Guy, Wins. I couldn't wait."

"Well, *our* meeting was cut short when Dean got scared you'd been murdered and took off toward your house."

"I see you didn't make that trip."

"I knew you weren't dead." Winston licked the pizza grease off his fingers. "Although I bet you wish you were now that Dean knows you were having a sleepover with Jacob."

I gritted my teeth. "By the time we finished the paper, it was four in the morning. He slept in my bed, and I took a throw blanket and a pillow to the couch. Nothing happened."

Casey tossed her apple core into her brown paper bag. "Does Dean know that?"

"Not yet," I replied. "You think he's *mad* mad?"

Our eyes collectively traveled toward Dean. He was sitting with his head down at the end of his lunch table, buried underneath his navy-blue Westcott hoodie.

"If he were any madder," said Winston, "he'd be me last Christmas morning when I got UGG boots."

Just then, we turned our faces toward the middle of the lunchroom. It wasn't a loud noise or a commotion that commanded our attention. Rather, a hush blew over the cafeteria, which was honestly more alarming than the sound of a tray dropping or a fight breaking out. The loud conversations subsided, and we all watched as Kyle and Ari stood face-to-face. Not talking. Not moving. It was like a scene straight out of a movie—one everyone wanted to watch.

Ari stood there like a statue, wearing black jeans and an oversized black sweater, holding her blue lunch tray with ring-covered fingers—some with three or four stacked up to the knuckle. She had a choker around her neck, and her eyes were frozen. It was almost as if she knew what was coming next.

"I can't keep doing this to myself," Kyle said.

"Oh shit," Winston whispered.

"I'm tired of the humiliation. I'm tired of being the guy

who can't let go of his ex-girlfriend. I don't know how you were able to convince yourself that what you did to me was justified. I'll never know." Kyle's eyes were lethargic, but they managed to look her up and down before he continued. "You're not loyal, Ari. You're not honest. And despite fighting with this for months, you're not the right person for me."

Ari stood there, seemingly in shock that Kyle was finally giving her everything she wanted. Or perhaps just in shock that he chose to do so in front of the entire cafeteria.

"So I'll be around you," he continued. "I'll be cordial. But I'm done going back and forth with this shit in my mind. I'm done, Ari. Go be with whoever you want to be with. I just hope whoever it is—they aren't embarrassed to be seen with you." Clenching his jaw, he glanced at Cliff, then looked back at her. "Because despite everything you *aren't*, you are way too good to be somebody's secret."

Everyone watched Kyle walk by Ari on his way to the other side of the cafeteria. He used his body to push the door open, then exited the lunchroom as if the scene had ended. And I suppose it had. *I suppose it finally had.*

Later that afternoon, I sat alone in the club's café, staring down at my cell-phone screen. I kept typing out texts to Dean, but I never felt brave enough to send them; truthfully, I wasn't sure what to say.

“Hey.” JC scooted into the booth.

“Hi.” I glanced up at him, then tucked my cell phone in between my legs. “Thanks for meeting me.”

A waitress approached our table with a notepad. “You two ready to order?”

“I’ll have a Coke.” JC raised his eyebrows at me. “You want anything?”

“A green tea, please.” I lifted my chin at the waitress as she wrote down our drinks. “And a scone. And you know what? A fry too. With honey mustard.”

It was her job not to judge, but she didn’t hide her emotions well. “I’ll be back,” she said with wide eyes.

“Appreciate it.” JC handed her the two menus on the table. When she got far enough away, he turned and looked at me. “Why didn’t you come to Kyle’s last night?”

“It’s a long story,” I replied. “Did Kyle tell you about Ron Harrison’s house call?”

“Yeah, and that he pulled you all into his office.” He tapped his finger against his glass, staring aimlessly at the sweat. “But we didn’t get to talk much. Dean took off and everyone just sort of left.” He paused, and thank God because I needed a moment to swallow my shame. “Did you guys talk to him?”

“Sort of . . . but Cliff put a stop to it once he practically accused us of knowing something about the fire.”

JC fell back in his booth; his head bounced from the

impact. “Shit.”

“Ron believes Ari did it and that we’re all involved somehow. I know he does.”

“But he can’t prove it, right? I mean, we didn’t do it. Did we?”

I studied him, losing myself for a moment. I couldn’t believe it had come to this—but we both began to wonder if we *were* responsible for the fire. Even though we knew we were innocent, at some point over the course of a few weeks we started to feel guilty. And for a split second, I questioned if I was.

“No.” I shook my head. “This is crazy! The only thing we’re guilty of is being in the wrong place at the wrong time. We just have to figure out who did this, and once we do, we have to prove it.”

“Wait a minute.” JC rolled up his sleeves and leaned forward. “What do you mean ‘whoever did this’? I thought we agreed that it was Guy?”

The waitress placed my green tea, scone, and fries in front of me, and then handed JC his soda. “That’s why I called you here.” I reached forward and took a bite from my scone, then dropped it back down on the plate. “It wasn’t Guy.”

JC stopped mid-sip and peered at me over his cup. He slowly lowered his glass. “What do you mean?”

“I mean . . . it wasn’t him.”

“Really?” His voice went from normal to accusatory as

he snuck some fries. “And how would you know that?”

“Because I . . . I met with him.”

After JC finished chewing, he tried convincing me that hadn’t happened. “No you didn’t. You wouldn’t do that.”

“I had to know!”

By the way he was staring at me, I couldn’t tell if he was going to get up from the table and walk out or sit there to hear more, but I continued talking.

“This is my life on the line. This person—whoever they are—is trying to take me down.”

“Why the hell would you meet with Guy?” he asked angrily.

“I thought I could talk to him—maybe offer him money or something. . . . I don’t know.”

“Christ, Sonny. We were supposed to come up with a plan together. You showed him our cards!”

“It wouldn’t have mattered. Guy’s already been cleared by police. He was at Geraldine’s that night. Parked at Laurel’s, yes, but his alibi checked out.” I leaned forward. “I know he knows more. But he’s not talking.”

“That’s not at all shocking, Sonny. I mean, did you really think he’d help us?”

“Someone broke into my house,” I whispered. “When I got home from our meeting, my bedroom window was open and my flash drive was gone.”

JC paused. “Did you call the cops?”

"No. I wasn't sure I should involve them with the investigation and all. I called Jacob."

"Jacob?"

"He helped me rewrite my paper," I replied, hoping he wouldn't ask further questions. "This isn't a game anymore. This has to stop."

JC grabbed his forehead and rubbed his face. "But if it wasn't Jacob, Piper, or Guy, then who was it?"

Suddenly, Ron Harrison walked into the café. He made small talk with a server, then held a sheet of paper up to her face.

"What is he doing?" I whispered, sinking low and using JC as a shield so he wouldn't spot me.

JC took a look. "I'm not sure. He's clearly showing her something."

"Like what?"

He looked a little longer. "Maybe it's not a *what*. Maybe it's a *who*."

The waitress shook her head and walked off, leaving Ron standing in the middle of the room. He took his seat at the bar and casually read the menu.

"I think he mentioned something about visiting a friend of his," I mumbled. "On the morning he showed up at Kyle's house. He said he'd been assaulted. Maybe he's looking for the person who hurt him."

"Yeah," JC replied. "Maybe."

We peeled our eyes off his designer suit and looked at each other.

"We should go," I said. "I'll talk to the others first thing tomorrow morning, and we'll come up with a plan." JC went to write his club ID number down on the receipt but I stopped him. "I'll grab it."

"I've got it," he replied, reaching for the pen.

"No." I grabbed the paper before he could. "I think my dad owes us one, don't you?"

Later that night, I rolled into Dean's driveway. My headlights lit up his face. He stood at the opposite end, shooting hoops by the garage. I turned off my car and sat there for a minute. Usually, he'd come to greet me, but he continued shooting baskets. That's how I knew it was serious. Once I'd confirmed the severity of the situation, I grabbed my courage from the floorboard, stepped outside, and dragged my feet down the driveway.

"Hi," I said, standing off to the side, a safe distance away.

Dean dribbled the ball, then took another shot.

"Okay." I nodded. "You aren't speaking to me."

He got his rebound and dribbled some more. His face was pale and his cheeks were flushed. It appeared as if he'd been outside for hours. I knew Dean turned to basketball when he needed to clear his mind, but I also knew he hated being cold, so I was a little surprised.

"Dean—"

The sound of the ball hitting the pavement made me blink, and nothing but echoes filled the driveway.

"Will you talk to me, please? I came all this way to explain myself. . . . The least you could do is listen."

"The least I could do," he repeated in a sluggish voice, taking another shot.

"Look, nothing happened last night. Someone broke into my house and stole my flash drive. I called Jacob because everyone was at Kyle's, and I thought he might be the only person I could reach."

"Did you try me?"

"Well, no, but—"

"But what, Sonny?" Dean grabbed the basketball and tucked it underneath his arm. "You know I would have answered. Why didn't you call me?"

"I don't know. . . ."

"I think you do." We stood there, staring right through each other as we listened to the sound of crickets chirping. Dean knew I was being disingenuous. He turned around and dribbled some more, but not quick enough for me to miss his eye roll.

"I know you don't believe me," I said. "But he helped me write my paper, then crashed. I slept on the couch. That's it."

"I believe you, Sonny," Dean replied, shooting a three-pointer with ease. "You might do a lot of things, like humiliate me to every guy on the team by 'crashing' with Jacob, but I know you wouldn't sleep with him."

"Okay, I'm sensing a little sarcasm in your voice, but I can assure you, I didn't—"

"No sarcasm." Without hurry, he grabbed the ball from the pavement. "You really did humiliate me."

I held my elbows, hoping to hold myself together. "I didn't do anything with him."

"No. You fell for him. Which is way worse."

"I never said that."

"Do you think I'm stupid? I know you, Sonny. I know when something's up with you, and ever since he came back, you haven't been acting the same."

"Maybe because someone tried framing me for—"

"This isn't about the fire." Dean tossed the ball off to the side and crossed the driveway. We stood face-to-face. "Tell me right now. Do you want to be with me?"

I dropped my head, but in true Dean fashion, he pushed up on the bottom of my chin and lifted it—forcing me to keep eye contact. "Do you want to be with me? Or am I just wasting my time?"

"I—"

"No, just answer me."

"Dean—"

"Things don't have to be figured out right now, but you have to answer me, Sonny."

The breaths escaping my body were shaky. I knew I didn't have an answer for him—not the one he wanted. "I can't answer that right now."

Dean's cold fingers slowly left my skin. He slid his hands into the pockets on his basketball shorts and stepped away. After nodding a few times, he finally spoke. "Then I think you should go."

Some people say there's nothing good about goodbyes. I'd have to agree. Goodbyes aren't natural. They aren't easy. And in the worst situations, they aren't even your choice.

10 WEDNESDAY

Certain days in everyone's life will stick out more than others. Traumatic experiences can't be erased. Your brain has a funny way of marking them in red ink. Bolding them. Allowing you to remember silly details you'd normally forget. Like the smell in the air, what you were wearing, the color of your nail polish, the color of the walls. Everyone will have that day.

My day was a Wednesday.

"I'm sorry, Sonny." Kyle's deep voice rolled into my eardrum as I walked through the hallway the following morning. "You're not selfish. Most of the time."

"Yeah? Tell Dean that."

"I guess you two talked?"

"That's not important," I replied. "Sawyer—"

"You were listening behind the auditorium door, weren't you?"

I grabbed his arms. "Look, maybe we should think about what he said."

Kyle didn't take too kindly to my idea; he pulled his arms away. "Absolutely not."

"Kyle!" The depth of my voice startled him; you could tell by the way his eyes widened. "You heard what he said about me—that I know—"

"You don't know anything," he interjected.

"Just listen—"

"We aren't turning our backs on Cliff just because Sawyer threatened to cut ties with Casey." He rolled his shoulders back. "If he does, he does. Casey doesn't need him."

I found it slightly comforting that he wanted to protect Cliff, even in their current state, but still, I pressed on. "How can you say that?! Look, I'm not suggesting we turn on Cliff, but maybe you can talk to Sawyer? Ask him to let it go?"

"Wow, Sonny, why didn't I think of that?" He rubbed his forehead in circular motions. "I won't be able to stop him."

"Well at least try to convince him not to pull Casey into this. I don't necessarily understand this whole foster care thing, and it could even be a bad move, but Casey's happy. She's finally hopeful that something in her life is going right. Sawyer may be a horrible person, but *he is* helping her. She needs—"

"She doesn't need him," he repeated, sure of himself. "Just drop it."

"Sonny!" Buckets approached us, Winston following.

I quickly switched conversations, but by no means did I leave that one behind. "I've been meaning to talk to you. We have to come up with a plan, Buckets."

"Losing your magic?" He cracked open an energy drink and downed it. "You're the plan-girl. Shouldn't you have already come up with one?"

"Perspective check," Winston interjected. "No one has been arrested, convicted, or even accused of setting the fire. Just because Jacob's daddy asks us a few questions here and there doesn't make us suspects. Besides, we didn't do it."

"What other leads do they have?" Kyle asked. "They're getting pressure from the community to figure this out and Mr. Harrison knows Ari lied."

"Honestly, I'm starting to believe it was Ari myself," I said.

Kyle raised his brows at me. "That's not okay."

"Neither is your ankle bracelet." Winston placed his hand on Kyle's shoulder and moved him to the side. He stepped closer to Buckets. "What do we do?"

"I—" Buckets's phone buzzed; he checked the message. "I've got to run. Just lay low. We'll think of something."

We all watched him walk away, and with only five or so

minutes before the bell rang, we dispersed in different directions. I knew Kyle had chemistry first period, but he took a right turn down the hall where Casey's locker was. And that could only have meant one thing: I had to follow him. I made that same right turn, quickly burying myself inside a classroom door nook—close enough to where I could eavesdrop on their conversation. Wearing a Cobalt blue sweater, Casey was gathering books at her locker when Kyle inched his way up to her.

"Why didn't you just call me?" he asked, her note in his hand.

Casey looked up and saw the folded piece of paper, then looked back inside her locker. "My phone's been acting weird."

Kyle closed his eyes and exhaled, clearly aware of what that meant. "You could have talked to me at school."

"I tried. You should remember. You had to dig my attempt out of the trash can."

"I'm sorry, Casey. I have a lot going on. I—"

"You aren't the only one with a lot going on. I may not have been in the woods that night, but as far as your dad is concerned, I'm one of you guys." Casey caught herself getting too heated. She paused, then dropped her head. "It's not a big deal. . . . It was just a stupid team pizza night." She zipped her book bag. "I know my brothers really like you, and everyone's dad was going, I just figured—"

"And I would have loved to go."

"Sawyer went," she quickly replied, tossing her bag across her back. "It's not a big deal."

"Casey, listen, I . . . I think we should talk about what I said at the scrimmage game."

Those words caused her to shrink. She looked down at the floor as she pushed her baby hairs behind her ears. "We really don't have to."

"I think we should."

There was a long pause. The hallway was getting quieter, and I swear I heard their heartbeats from my nook.

Kyle reached forward and pulled her hair back out, brushing her jawline with the back of his fingers as he let go. "Can you look at me?" When she made eye contact, he continued. "I'm sorry, Casey. I'm sorry for what I did. For all of it. I never should have dragged you into my bullshit with Ari."

"It's fine," she replied, her cheeks as red as a cherry.

"No, it's not fine. I handled everything like an idiot, and you didn't deserve that."

She rolled her wrists underneath her sleeves and shifted her weight from one worn sneaker to the other. "You sure this apology isn't inspired by your recent revelation that you're done with Ari?"

"My what?"

"Your speech in the cafeteria?"

Squinting his eyes, he shook his head and stepped closer. "Look, no. I'm apologizing because I need to. I want to. I said a lot of things that night—things that hurt you—and I'm sorry for it."

"Well did you mean them?" she asked.

He put one hand behind his head. "I meant it when I said you're too good for me. When I said I'd ruin you."

Casey crossed her arms around her stomach and looked down again, fidgeting with her fingers. It was clear she was uncomfortable with the conversation, and looking away was her only chance at getting through it. "Yeah, well, maybe I should've told you that I'm already a little ruined," she said softly, and without a lick of confidence.

Kyle smiled with his eyes. There was a long pause while he stared at her. "Casey—" He swallowed. "Maybe I was wrong. Maybe I—"

"Hey!" Sawyer slithered around the corner like the snake he was. "You coming?"

She turned around and glanced at him, then looked back at Kyle. "I, um . . . I should go."

"Wait a second." He pinched her sweater, stopping her from walking away. "Why didn't you tell me about the foster care stuff?"

Casey looked surprised. "Who told you?"

"Who do you think?"

She squirmed some more. "I guess I wasn't really telling

anyone . . . and we weren't really talking."

"You could have at least told me how bad things have been." Kyle looked over her shoulder, jaw clenched. "I know Sawyer said he wants to help you but—you have to understand—he's not a good dude, Casey."

"Kyle—"

"Just listen." He stepped closer, his voice desperate and rushed. "There are other people who can help you and your brothers. Other families. Please don't get caught up with Sawyer. Especially not romantically."

"He's just a friend."

"Was he just your friend when you kissed him?!"

She exhaled in his face.

Kyle closed his eyes and did the same. "I'm sorry. That was stupid. I—"

"Everything okay?!" Sawyer shouted, still standing at the other end of the hall.

"I have to go," she said, eager to end the conversation.

"Wait." Kyle pinched her sweater again. "Look, I'm sure he's selling you a bag of bullshit—telling you everything you want to hear—but Sawyer's no good. You just have to trust me."

Her eyes picked a spot on Kyle's shirt and they didn't leave. She was locked in, staring at his chest, lost in thought. "If someone walked into this building right now and offered you a full ride to Cornell, you'd take it wouldn't you?"

"Of course."

"What if I told you I didn't like that person? Would it matter?"

"Casey—"

"Just answer the question."

"No." Kyle shrugged. "But—"

"But what? But that's different?" She pushed her glasses up. "You wanted me to tell you how bad things are, right?" She went to tell him but couldn't manage to. "Listen, I don't want to be sent home. I want to stay here—in Westcott—I want to graduate and get into a good college. This is how I can do that. By taking the help that's been offered to me. Mr. Ellington is a powerful man with resources. I can't turn him down."

"But you don't understand—"

"No." She stepped backward in the direction of Sawyer. "You don't."

Kyle stood there and watched Casey walk away toward another guy. Losing Ari was one thing. Losing Cliff was another. But losing Casey? I knew there was no way he was okay with that. Not to Sawyer. Not with everything he knew about him. The bell rang and I quietly snuck out of my nook, then darted down the hall—almost making it to my first class.

Almost.

"*Would the following students please report to the office?*

Cliff Reynolds, Casey Langdon, Ari Ziegler, Norah Soros, Dean Ballinger, Kyle Winchester, Winston Banks, Billy Poland, and Sonny Carter."

The walls were white. My nail polish—light taupe. The scent in the air was a mixture of cleaning liquids, cologne, and the smell of the school's cafeteria. There's at least one day in everyone's life that will stick out for all the wrong reasons, but if you're lucky, it won't be nearly as traumatic as mine was.

11 CLIFF

I've done a lot of shitty things; I've been taught to not admit them. My childhood was respectable. No brothers, no sisters—just two functioning alcoholic parents and my things. But nice things. Expensive things. My home was filled with Calacatta marble countertops, Persian rugs, and imported artwork from Madrid—sometimes from Paris if my father worked several *late shifts* that month. I guess we all have our ways of apologizing.

My way of making my mother feel better was to draw her pictures. I was no Norah Soros but I was only a fifth grader. I hung one on our stainless-steel fridge once. A red heart. She took it down the next day. I told myself she just didn't like the color red—unless it's in her wine glass.

They did the best they could. Better than most, I guess. Better than Langdon's parents. I guess you've reached a low when you're comparing yourself to Casey Langdon. It was just the three of us. I was their first and only born. Thank God—my sibling would've had a real fucked-up life.

"Your parents should be here any minute," Ron said, checking his watch.

I nodded. I could have told him where they were. My father was with his hot secretary—two glasses of whiskey into the day—and my mother was in her hot-yoga class. But I stood by my motto: I don't know shit. I wasn't supposed to know my father's secrets. I was supposed to think he had integrity, but my mother was a loud crier. Even after the complete disappointment my dad was, I still fought to honor his last name. Because he did teach me some things. How to throw a football. How to ski. How to make money. How to keep it.

"Can I get you a glass of water?"

"I'm good," I told Ron.

He thought I knew something. Probably thought I started the fire. Like I said, I've done some shitty things—but committing arson wasn't one of them.

"Christ, Kurt. How many times are you gonna text me? I'll roll through tomorrow." I honestly don't remember much about that lobby—other than the bright-ass sun coming in through the windows and blinding me. "Yes, I have the cash. Tomorrow." I hung up the phone and sat down on the couch.

My dad was off somewhere—maybe in his office, maybe with the manager—I didn't know. I did know that I didn't want to be there and I was late for football drills.

"Kurt sounds like a real pain in the ass."

I didn't notice her. She was waiting for the elevator with her arms around a box. A moving box. I couldn't really see her. The bright-ass sun was making that difficult. But I could see she was wearing a black tank top and black shorts—the really high ones girls always wear. I lifted my head and raised my eyebrows at her. I made sure to look her up and down. Girls love that.

"Sorry . . . I didn't mean to eavesdrop."

I shrugged. "All good."

"You live here?"

"Nah."

The elevator door opened. "Well, remind me to make a formal complaint that a random guy who doesn't live here is hanging out in my new lobby."

Her voice was flat. Sort of sarcastic. Sort of bitchy. She had tan legs—I caught a glimpse of them when she walked into the elevator. I guess you could say I waited another thirty minutes for my dad to finish up whatever it was he went there to do, but I'm pretty sure I was waiting for her.

"Sorry to keep you waiting." My dad walked into the office and Ron stood up to greet him. "Ron Harrison, is it?" They shook hands. Their shirts were the same brand. Almost the same color. I picked up on details like that. My mother taught me to always be aware of what's going on around me. Irony, right?

"Mr. Reynolds. Nice to meet you."

"Where's, uh . . . where's Bob?" He sat down next to me. I didn't look up. I could sense his disappointment just fine; there was no need to make eye contact to confirm it.

"Principal Winchester is with another student." Ron sat down in his chair; it squeaked as he leaned forward. "I'll be asking the questions."

"And you are?"

"The new student advisor, but I'm also working directly with the Westcott Police Department on the investigation."

"Okay." My dad rolled up his sleeves, a little confused by his title. "Do I need my attorney?"

"Cliff isn't under arrest. I just have a few things I'd like to clear up with him."

They went back and forth for a few minutes. Lawyer talk. Power plays. Bullshit like that.

Ron finally got the OK. "Cliff. How well do you know Ari Ziegler?"

"Random guy who doesn't live here—you're still here."

I had nodded off, but her voice woke me. Or her smell. She smelled like drug-store perfume.

"Are you homeless?"

"Do I look homeless?"

"I don't know what homeless people look like."

"Everyone knows what homeless people look like. They look homeless."

"Wow. Kurt really pissed you off, huh?"

"Do you know Kurt or something?"

"If you couldn't tell by the large moving box you didn't offer to help me with, I'm new here."

"I'm supposed to help you? I don't know you."

"You could, but if you aren't a fan of homeless people, you probably won't be a fan of mine."

"Who said I—"

"We just moved here. I passed the entrance exam at Westcott High."

"So you got in through the lottery?"

"Based on your tone . . . I'm guessing you didn't?"

"My parents pay my tuition. Yours too if you want to get technical."

"Nice."

"What's your name?"

"Ari . . . Ari Ziegler."

"Ari?" I stared at my dad. I stared at Ron. "Why do you want to know?"

Ron cleared his throat. "Well. We have reason to believe

she may have been in the area the night of the fire."

"Hang on a minute." Dad scooted to the end of his seat. "Did Bob co-sign this? You do realize what accusing a Westcott student could mean? You want to announce we let a criminal in through the lottery? As if the Ivy League schools need another reason to question their relationships with us? Come on!"

"We understand your concern, Mr. Reynolds. We're trying to keep this as contained as possible." Dad went to speak, but Ron raised his voice. "*No one* wants another public debacle, which is why we're hoping to eliminate all of our students as suspects. The sooner we can eliminate Ari, the better." He looked at me. "We want the same thing, right? To clear her name?"

It's almost like he knew.

"I can do that," he boasted. "There's never been a better time for you to know me, Cliff."

"I'm Cliff. . . . My dad owns this place."

"Hence the tuition." Ari had brown hair. It was messy. I liked it. She wore all black. Her shoes were black. Her nails were black. But her eyes—they were light brown. They stood out.

"I didn't mean anything by that. It's just . . . none of our parents like the idea of the lottery. It's sort of—"

"Diverse?"

"Sure . . . we'll go with that."

She picked at her nails. "What do you do when you're not hating homeless people?"

Why was Ari funny? Why did I want to laugh?

"I play football."

"Of course you do."

"You want diversity? You're gonna have to bring it."

"Deal." She stood up. "I sing. I'm singing tonight at the karaoke bar on Brevard Street if you want to stop by."

"Brevard Street?" I had no idea where that was.

"It's five minutes from here." She grabbed an ink pen from the coffee table and scribbled on a piece of masking tape that was stuck to her arm. "Look for the jaded musicians hanging around out front. I'll be inside."

I reached for the tape. My fingers touched hers. They had rings on them. Gold ones.

"See you, Cliff." She walked away.

I stared at the address. Her number. The little heart at the end. Why was she so nice? Why was she so bitchy? Why the hell did I care?

"What the hell are you trying to get at here?" I could smell the alcohol on my dad's breath. This wasn't good for Ron. "I respect your position, Mr. Harrison. I want you to find the person who did this. But Cliff can't help you with that."

Ron didn't buy what he was selling. "There'd be no

reason why you'd cover for Ari, Cliff?"

"No."

"Perhaps you two acted together, then?"

"Why the *fuck* would I want to burn down the left wing?"

"Language," Dad said. "Mr. Harrison, I'm afraid we're done here."

"Sawyer Ellington," Ron read aloud, staring down at his folder. "He's a damn good quarterback. Maybe you were worried you'd lose your spot?"

"That's not going to happen."

"Maybe you didn't want to risk it?"

"So I risked my entire future instead?" I smirked. "I thought you were some famous lawyer? This is what you've come up with? Pointing the finger at *me*?"

"Perhaps you can point me elsewhere? Toward Ari?"

"For Christ's sake, the Zieglers are renters of mine," Dad interjected. "I don't think Cliff and Ari run in the same circle."

"Fancy running into you here." Ari found me at the bar. She was wearing black jeans with holes in them and a tight black tank top. She had a black thing around her neck.

"I was in the area."

"You're a bad liar."

"Yeah." I dropped my head and smiled—but not too much. Girls hate that clingy shit. "I was intrigued. Better?"

Ari smiled too. Her hair was pulled back, but it was falling everywhere. Her shoulders were tan. I don't know shit about makeup, but it looked good. *She* looked good.

"Come sit. I have ten minutes."

I followed her to a table in the middle of the room. "Never been here before."

"You're kidding."

"All right . . . all right. . . . I can't exactly hide my—"

"Your privilege?"

"What's so bad about being well-off?"

"I don't know." She lifted her tan shoulders, then relaxed them. "You miss out on places like this."

"Miss out?" I looked around the shithole. I hoped no one saw me there. Not there. Not with her.

"Did you know the owners of this karaoke bar were high school sweethearts? They used to sing together in theatre."

I nodded. She was losing me—but not all the way. "High school sweethearts? Is that still a thing?"

"You know, I don't know. I haven't had much luck in that department. The guys at my old school were all gamers."

"Not your type?"

She scrunched her nose. It was cute. *She* was cute. "Is having a type still a thing?"

"The thing is, Ron—Cliff's a good kid. A good student. He has a lot going for him."

"I agree." Ron took a sip of water.

"And I can tell you that my son doesn't hang out with people who cause problems—people who get in trouble—he stays out of that mess."

"Your son was sent home for punching a student in the nose until he broke it."

"That was self-defense."

"Regardless." Ron diffused the situation—great tactic. "It's important we get through these questions. Now I don't think I've asked anything unfair."

"Is it fair to assume you had a good time?"

I was glad to leave the karaoke bar. It reeked of smoke. We walked down the sidewalk toward the condos. I didn't want her to walk home alone.

"I think that's fair."

"You can tell the truth. It's not your scene."

"It's definitely not." I shook my head. "But I'm glad I came. You have a nice voice."

"Really?"

I raised my brows and nodded while I looked her up and down.

"Thanks." She noticed. "So if this isn't your idea of fun, what is?" She crossed her arms. It was hot outside, but maybe she was cold. If I'd had a jacket, I would have given it to her in a second.

"I don't know. . . . Hanging out with friends, football, watching football . . ."

"That sounds strikingly similar to my nightmares."

"Yeah . . . well . . . everyone has their thing."

We made it to the complex. Mr. Ziegler's car was in the parking lot. He drove an old Volvo station wagon.

"What's your thing, Cliff Reynolds?" She stopped and stood in front of me. Her arms were still crossed. Her eyes were reflecting off the streetlight.

"What do you mean?"

"What's your thing? It can't just be bromances and football. What makes you feel alive?"

"Feel alive?" I was practically dead inside—everyone knew that. But she didn't know me. Not yet. "I don't know. Football?"

She laughed and shook her head. "My new project figure-out-what-makes-Cliff-happy officially initiated."

"Speaking of nightmares." I stared at everything but her.

"Come on! It's just one summer. . . ."

"We hung out a few times the summer before tenth grade. But then she started dating my best friend so we sort of lost touch."

My dad was shocked to hear that. I knew it. Again, I didn't have to look at him to confirm.

"I see." Ron took notes. "Your friend Kyle?"

I shrugged. “I don’t know.”

“You don’t know?”

“What does it matter? This is about Ari, and I told you, Ari and I lost touch.”

“But before that.” Ron jotted more words down. “What did you do that summer?”

I looked behind his head at a photo of Jacob, taking in his question. What did I do that summer? I looked for excuses. I looked for reasons not to like her. She never knew this, but every time we were in public, I searched the crowd for familiar faces, hoping to not be spotted. Ari was wrong for me. She wore black. I wore white. Her jeans had holes. My khakis were pressed. Her car looked like she bought it at an auction. Her family had no real weight to their name. No status. No money. I couldn’t be seen with her around Westcott. What would I say? How would I explain that to my friends?

I wanted to. I was going to. I was going to tell them about her. But then . . . Kyle.

“What happened to you on Saturday? I thought you were gonna swing by for card night?”

Kyle was the best-looking friend I had, but he looked like shit. “My dad didn’t want me leaving the house.”

“Grounded, huh?” I dug through my locker; he leaned against the one beside it. “I still can’t believe your old man is our new principal."

"Yeah. It sucks." He started to tear up. He hated tearing up in front of me. Kyle looked up to me. I had no idea why. "I don't understand why my mom is forcing me to see him. It's like hanging out with a stranger every weekend."

"Hey." I patted him on his upper arm. "He's not that bad." His dad was an asshole, but I pretended he wasn't for Kyle's sake. He hated him. He hated that he was back. I hated it for him. He wasn't the same Ky, and he hadn't been for weeks.

Kyle rubbed his eyes.

I could see he was texting someone. "Who's that?"

"It's no one."

"The cheesy-ass look on your face says otherwise."

He acted like he was going to hit me; I laughed.

"You talking to someone?"

He didn't answer right away. That was my answer.

"Who is she?"

"Just . . . this girl."

"Just hung out around town a couple of times," I told Ron, snapping out of my daze. "Nothing memorable."

Ron's pen came to a halt; he looked up at me. "Did she ever share anything with you?"

Yeah, a lot. "Like what?"

"Details about her home life? Her friends? Her past?"

Yes. "Not really."

My dad was texting someone. Probably our attorney.

"I see." Ron put the lid on his ink pen and placed it on top of his notepad. "Do you have any idea why she would have been near the left wing that night?"

"No . . . I . . ."

"No, dude! I'm not gonna show you!" Kyle held onto his phone.

"I just want to see her."

"You won't approve."

"Why not?"

"She's . . . different."

"You don't exactly go for cheerleaders, Ky. Come on. Show me the damn picture!"

"Okay!" He laughed. It was the first time I'd seen him laugh in weeks. He tilted the phone toward my face. "She's incredible, bro. She's a singer. She's a Cobalt, but—I don't know—she's so . . ."

"Different."

"Yeah." He smiled again. "I showed her around campus on her first day. She was trying to write this song and asked me what I thought about the lyrics. Me of all people, right?" He closed his app and shrugged. "We've been texting ever since."

"Good for you, man." I pulled him in for a hug and stared into the hallway over his shoulder. "See you before practice, yeah? I'll wait for you."

I've hurt a lot of people in my life. I've broken girls' hearts. My last name precedes me; maybe it always will. You didn't deserve a guy like me, Ari. I hid you. I said I would've told my friends about us and showed you off to the world—but I'm full of shit. I wouldn't have done that. You deserved that, Ari. You deserved a guy who would have given that to you. You deserved Kyle. I deserved Lana. She was right for me. She wore colors. Name brands. I moved on; you didn't. Kyle wasn't what you wanted. He kept you warm, and eventually, you teach yourself how to love those people—but you never fell in love with him. And I'm sorry I didn't make it easier for you to. I'm sorry I hurt you, Ari. You're not the same girl I met that summer. She was innocent. She believed in romance. She believed that guys like me would fight away monsters. I messed that all up. I was the monster. I've done a lot of shitty things in my life—I've hurt people and I've hurt myself—but I did manage to get one thing right, Ari: I loved you.

"Cliff?"

I lifted my head. "Like I said . . . I hardly know her."

12 KYLE

I like to think I'm a good guy—and I always try to do the right thing—but I know sometimes I don't. I used to blame that on my bloodline. The last name Winchester had its downfalls, but it also had its perks. It got me to the front of the line. It erased a few of my mistakes. It definitely got me stopped by men at the club who told me how much I resembled my dad.

"Where's Dad?"

Mom smelled like the cinnamon-apple candle from our kitchen. "He called me here. . . . He should be here."

He should've been a lot of things he wasn't. Like a good husband. A good father. A good principal. But he was none of them. And he was never on time. We sat in his office, waiting for him to walk through the door. My mom shouldn't have had to wait for him one more second of her life. She waited for Dad to get his shit together for years. He never did.

"Why are they questioning you?" Mom asked. "Is this about the fire?"

I didn't want to scare her. "I'm sure it's just procedure."

"You didn't do it, did you?"

"Mom?!"

"I know you hate your father."

Maybe everyone thought I did. Maybe I acted like it. I might've even said it. But he was my dad. If anything, I hated that he wasn't a better man. He left when I was younger. I don't remember much about that day; it never seemed to matter. He moved to Arizona, where he was raised. We stayed in California. My mom loved the town of Westcott. She needed to be around things she loved, which is why she was constantly inviting my friends over—especially Sonny.

"Has Sonny been questioned?"

"I don't know."

"This is crazy. You kids don't belong in an interrogation. You're straight-A students. You're going to Ivy League schools. My God, is your father trying to ruin that?"

The office door opened, and my dad walked in with Assistant Principal Clemmons.

Mom stood to her feet. "You have a lot of nerve pulling our son out of class for your witch hunt without my consent."

"I'm the principal, Kate. I don't need your consent to pull

one of my students from class."

"He's your son. Did you forget that?"

"Of course not." Dad wasn't interested in trying to convince her; his tone made that abundantly clear. He sat down behind his desk, and Principal Clemmons stood off to his left.

"Then what is this? You're questioning whether or not our kid dabbled in arson? You're pointing the finger at your child?"

"Have I ever let anything happen to Kyle?" Dad mumbled under his breath, leaning forward so only we could hear him. "He has *my* last name, Kate."

He tried putting my mom at ease, but I wasn't convinced he wouldn't let me crash and burn if he had to.

"I just need to ask Kyle a few questions," said Clemmons.

"It's protocol." Dad tried to calm her, but he couldn't. Only I could do that.

"It's fine, Mom. I'll answer his questions."

She hesitated. "This ends when I say so."

"Should I end the song with a double entendre or just let the music fade?" She had stopped me on my way to first as if she knew me.

"I'm not sure." I didn't know anything about writing lyrics, but I liked her voice. "Both would sound great."

"Decisions, decisions, right?" She had on boots, but other

than that, I don't remember a whole lot about that morning. I was taken aback by her boldness. *That* I remembered.

"Right." I couldn't keep my eyes off hers. They were brown, and they sort of told a story, even at first glance.

"Oh sorry. . . . I never told you my name. I'm Ari." She took a break from writing in her notebook. "It's my first day."

"Kyle. And I figured as much."

We shook hands. Her fingers were covered in rings. I'm pretty sure they were silver, or maybe gold. I didn't normally catch those kinds of details. But I did catch how good she smelled. She must've been wearing expensive perfume.

"I'm guessing you're not new here?"

"No. Been here my whole life."

"You say that like it's a bad thing."

"I love Westcott, but, uh, my dad's the new principal."

"Principal Winchester is your dad?" Her grimacing face said it all. "Say no more. I met him after I won the lottery. He's . . . special."

I pressed my lips together and nodded.

"Wanna walk me to first? Show me around the school?"

I didn't have a chance to respond, but my answer was yes.

"Great." She pulled me down the hall with her. "You're a lifesaver."

"I'll save you the details, but we believe Ari Ziegler may

have been in the area the night of the fire."

"My son and Ari broke up a long time ago. What does this have to do with him?"

Clemmons kindly glared at my mom. It was obvious she was being a pain in his ass. "How long did you two date, Kyle?"

I ran my hands down my legs and shifted in my chair. "On and off for about a year."

"Why'd you break up?"

"We, uh . . . we got in a fight."

"About?"

"It's about time!" I took the finished song from her hands.

"You're not allowed to hate it. That's my only rule."

We walked through the parking lot and into the school. I had so much on my mind that day. Upcoming football game. I had a test. But she trumped all of that. "Why would I hate it?"

"I hate everything I write," she said. "If someone tells me they love my work, I ask them why."

I pretended to read her lyrics, but I couldn't focus. I couldn't stop thinking about how beautiful she was. "This is really good."

"You're just being nice."

"No. No, really, I like it."

"Why? See. Told you." She was funny. I sort of needed

that.

"Who's, uh—" I skimmed some more. "Who's the lucky guy?"

"It's just a song."

"Oh." I felt some relief. "You're really talented."

"And you're a great friend, Kyle Winchester. I'm glad I know you."

"I don't know. It was probably over something dumb. That's what all our fights were—dumb."

Mom coughed. I was probably saying too much.

"Was she an angry girl?"

She chucked a trophy at my cheek once. "No."

"Never? She never once gave you the impression she was dangerous?"

"Dangerous?"

Clemmons pulled out Ari's transcript from her previous school. "Troubled?"

"Troubled how?" I asked, looking down at the folder.

He removed some papers but made sure I couldn't see them while he flipped through. "Was Ari . . . *okay*?"

"Are you okay?"

She was walking quickly down the hallway, away from our locker room. I was headed in there to change for practice. When she passed me, I saw that she was crying.

"Hey, hey, hey." I stopped her. "What's wrong?"

"Nothing." Her red eyes and the black streaks on her face told me otherwise. "I'm fine."

"No, you're not. What's wrong?"

She didn't want to tell me but finally did. "I was sort of just broken up with."

"Oh." I put my gym bag on my other shoulder. "I didn't know you were dating someone."

"I guess I wasn't."

I was late for practice and had to go, but I couldn't leave her there—not until she knew there was nothing wrong with her, and that it wasn't her fault. "His loss, right?"

She sort of laughed, but more tears fell.

"Don't cry."

"I'll try not to."

"Ahh, see, I can't leave until you stop." I checked my watch. "But I'm super late, so—"

She laughed again and wiped her eyes. "Done."

"You sure?"

"I'm sure, Kyle Winchester."

"Good." I tapped her arm. "For what it's worth, this dude must have serious issues."

"I mean . . . she had her issues." My eyes wanted to close, but I didn't want Clemmons to think I was tired or stressed.

"What kind of—"

“Are we done here?” Mom interrupted.

Dad lifted his hand. “Pipe down, Kate.”

“Don’t talk to her like that,” I replied, sitting straight up in my seat.

“Folks . . . let’s just . . . take it easy.” Clemmons put his hand up. “Kyle, if you don’t want to talk about Ari, what *can* you tell me?”

“Can you walk a little faster, Ky? Jesus. You’re ten minutes late.” I don’t remember the look on his face when I walked into the locker room—just that he quickly wiped his eye and tried not showing it to me.

I tossed my gym bag down and looked in his direction. “You good?”

Cliff sniffed. “Why wouldn’t I be?”

I should have known that day, but looking back, I’m not surprised I didn’t. How could I have seen it? You’ve always been better than me at hiding your emotions. You’ve always been better than me at everything, Cliff. A tad bit richer. A little taller. A lot smoother. My dad wasn’t in my life to teach me things, so you taught me things instead. I learned everything I know from you. How to dress. How to play cards. How to talk to girls. You treated me like your brother, Cliff, and I looked up to you. Now . . . I don’t know why. Why’d you choose to do it that way? You could have told me the truth when I walked into the locker room. You didn't give me a gift, Cliff. I spent months—a whole year—trying to convince her that she wasn't broken. And you kept breaking her. You were touching her when I was. You were lying next to my girlfriend hours after she left my bed—for months. It wasn't her fault. You are responsible. You did this, and I don't owe you a reconciliation. I've tried—believe me—I've tried to reconcile things in my head. Every night I think about how this will pan out. How did you think this would pan out, Cliff? I could ruin you. Did you think about that? I know things about you—about Kurt and his boys, about what you do in your free time. I mean . . . I like to think I'm a good guy, and I always try to do the right thing—but you know, sometimes I just don't feel like it.

"Kyle?"

I lifted my chin. "What do you want to know?"

13 NORAH

You don't know pain until you've seen your artwork plastered all over an online auction in Greece. I only hoped the money bought him a nice house. He always wanted one—without my mother and me in it.

"Do you think your mother will be joining us soon?" Mr. Harrison asked me.

"My mom works."

She didn't have to really. My grandpa was filthy rich. He sent her money every month to pay my tuition, and to feed her shopping addiction. I'm pretty sure she worked to take her mind off her divorce and shopped to take her mind off work. It was a vicious cycle, but by all means, swipe away if it means your happiness. The only thing that made me happy was painting. I could easily get lost in it. The world was such a dark place, but when I painted, the colors took the edge off.

It was therapeutic, and one of the only things I was good at. Just ask my dad.

"And your dad is . . . ?" Ron glanced down at the notes in my folder.

"A piece of shit."

He looked up at me over his glasses; I swear he looked identical to Jacob—just a few decades older with a few more wrinkles.

"Sorry. He's not coming."

My mom walked into the office wearing a white silk blouse, a red lip, and a last name she never changed. She was thirty minutes late and already in a rush to leave. "Beck Soros." She extended her hand toward Ron as he stood to his feet.

"Ron Harrison—student advisor. Nice to meet you."

"Right. I remember getting an email about that." She sat down beside me; her overpriced perfume smacked me across the face. "What's this all about?"

He sat back down in his chair; it squeaked. "I have a few questions for your daughter."

"Is she in trouble?"

"No."

Mom tucked her purse on her lap. "Is this about the fire?"

"Fire-engine red or bubble-gum pink?" Ari peeked her head out of my closet; the paint on the wall matched the pink dress in her right hand.

"I'm not going." I hung upside down over the edge of my mattress and made snow angels on my down comforter, minus the snow. "It's Dean Ballinger. He's a Cobalt."

"So am I."

"He's broke."

"So what? So am I."

"He's not my type."

"So what?! He asked you on a date. The least you could do is give him a chance."

"Didn't he break up with Sonny Carter, like, yesterday?"

"Okay, yeah, this may be a rebound situation, but who cares? Just go. Have a good time. When's the last time you remember doing that?"

"Before you got here." I showed her the canvas I'd been working on.

"Nice." She held a green blouse against her chest and peered into my closet mirror. "Get your ass in here and help me find something."

"I told you! I'm not going on a date with Ballinger."

"Please!" She was practically begging. "Just do this for me!"

"My God, Ari. Why do you care?"

"Because—I don't know—I want you to be happy. Dean is a chance at a normal relationship. Just go with it."

I rolled off my bed, walked toward my closet, and leaned

against the doorframe. "You're the worst friend."

"This is about Norah's friend, Ari Ziegler," Mr. Harrison clarified.

"Ari?" I shot up in my seat. "What about her?"

He looked at my mother, then at me. "We have reason to believe she may have been in the area the night of the fire."

"Okay?" Mom checked the time on her diamond-encrusted Rolex. "What does that have to do with my daughter?"

"I'd just like to ask Norah some questions. Maybe she can help shed some light on the case."

"It's a case now?" I crossed my arms and laughed. "You have this all wrong."

"Sort of feels wrong to be on a date with you."

Dean looked across the table at me. He had taken me out to a fairly fancy place. I was surprised. Pleasantly surprised. "Why's that?"

"Let me count the ways." My pointer fingers met. "One, you're Sonny Carter's boyfriend."

"Ex." His voice was cute. I hadn't noticed it until that moment.

"Okay, ex, but recent."

He leaned back in his seat and challenged me with his eyes. "Go on."

"You're a Cobalt."

"Ouch."

"I know—you haven't always been—but that's sort of my third point. Aren't you . . . broke?"

"Depends on what your definition of broke is." He spoke with ease, almost as if nothing mattered. "But what does that have to do with anything?"

"I don't know. I'm not exactly a cheap date."

"Okay." Dean wasn't running. Why wasn't he running?

"Come on, Ballinger. I've known you for years. Why me? Why now? If I'm a rebound, just say so and we can work that out."

"Yeah? And how's that?"

"Look, guys use me to get back at their girlfriends all the time. If—"

"Do you really think that's what's going on here?"

"Do you mind telling me what's going on here?" Mom asked, glancing at both Ron and me. "If Norah isn't the one in question, then you should really be speaking with Ari."

"Well, Ms. Soros, I've been told Norah and Ari are very close."

"Which is why I can tell you she had nothing to do with the fire," I interjected.

"*Did you*?"

"Excuse me?" Mom was angry, the Botox just made it

difficult to tell. “Are you out of your mind?”

“You’re a Chosen Ten, Norah. Maybe you were intimidated by the other competitors? Maybe you thought you’d ruin their chances at attending Westcott by eliminating the left wing, and asked your best friend Ari to help?”

“Let me tell you something, Mr. Harrison, my daughter isn’t scared of anything. She certainly wouldn’t be stupid enough to commit arson. Now I’ve had enough. Norah, let’s go.”

Maybe I should have listened, but I couldn’t break my gaze with Ron. “I didn’t do it, and neither did Ari.”

“Okay.” Ron crossed his arms and leaned back in his chair. “How do you know?”

“How do you know dating a Violet like me won’t be the worst decision you’ve ever made?” I asked as we walked back to his Audi. Dinner was over, but my quest to find out why he wanted to date me wasn’t.

“Impossible. . . . You couldn’t be the worst anything.” Ballinger had game. His sweet replies were on rotation, and he reached for them with ease whenever he needed one.

“I’m sort of hard to deal with.”

“I can deal with that.” He got in the driver’s seat; he smelled so good—like a mixture of fresh laundry and Bergamot cologne.

“But why me?”

"You've already asked me that, and I've told you, I want to get to know you."

"Come on, Ballinger. You can't go from Sonny Carter to me. We're complete opposites."

"Would you stop?"

"Stop what?"

"Stop comparing yourself to other girls. I'm here with you, and I'm not asking you to be anyone else. If I wasn't interested in you, I wouldn't have asked you out tonight."

I looked out the window; it was sparkling clean. Everything about Dean was orderly and clean. It was really attractive. "I guess . . . I'm just . . . not used to being asked."

"Yeah right," he replied. "Plenty of guys like you. You've been asked out a lot."

"On dates," I clarified. "I'm not used to being asked out on dates. Guys may like me but they don't want to date me."

Dean reached over and put his hand on top of my thigh. "I do."

"I just do!" I scratched the indigo paint off my middle finger. "Ari wouldn't do something like that!"

"Calm down, Nor." Mom only abbreviated my name when she was getting impatient. "Now let's go. I need to get back to my office."

"Beck, is it?" Ron looked pissed. "This is a serious matter. Dozens of students have undergone questioning over the last few weeks. Norah isn't an exception. Please have a seat."

I placed my fingertips on his desk and gave him my best bitch-face. "Look, you can think what you want. You can ask your little questions. You can make unprincipled house calls on the weekends, intimidating us with whatever it is you think you know, but at the end of the day—you're wrong. Ari didn't do this."

Ron tapped his pen on top of his paper. "I'll ask one more time, then. Norah . . . *how* do you know Ari wouldn't have started the fire?"

"I wouldn't have come tonight had it not been for Ari."

"Ari convinced you to come out with me?" Dean asked as we approached my front door. "Ari Ziegler?"

"Yeah."

"Whatever it takes, I guess." He grabbed my hand; his were rugged. "I had fun with you."

"Really?" We stood on my porch. "We didn't even do anything."

"Anything like . . .?"

I didn't want to tell him what I'd normally do while hanging out with a guy. I kind of didn't want him to know. But he caught on.

"I'm not that kind of dude."

I hated it when guys said that. "Isn't that what they all

say?"

He paused for a while. "Look, I know what it feels like to be abandoned, Norah. Our situations are a little different, but I had a parent leave too." He lifted my chin and stared into my eyes. I couldn't believe how blue his were—even in the dark. "I'm not your dad. I'm not all these other guys who just want to hook up with you. Give me a chance to prove that."

"Look, I can't prove it. But I know." My eyes tried focusing on Ron's face, but it was becoming rapidly blurry. That usually happened when I got too mad to see.

Mom leaned toward me. "Norah? Do you know something you aren't telling me?"

Yes. "No."

Her face and voice got lower. "Don't you dare cover for Ari. You're months away from the Westcott Awards. This could—" Her cell phone rang; she tried to ignore it, but I knew she couldn't.

"Go ahead, Mom." I glared ahead at Mr. Harrison. "We're done here."

"I'm sorry Norah couldn't be of much help." She stared down at her phone and gave Ron a quick fake smile before answering. "I'll see you tonight," she whispered to me over the side of her screen, then stood up and walked out of the office. The door clicked shut. I sat there with my arms crossed, eyes still blurry.

"Thank you for your time, Norah." Ron grabbed the stack of papers from his desk and straightened them.

"Ari's a good person. She's a good friend."

"Our meeting is done, Ms. Soros. You can go back to class now."

"She's the only reason I've ever felt happiness."

"Ms. Soros," he repeated. "I'll say it again. If you can't answer my question, then I'm afraid our meeting is done."

I looked down; my mind raced back to his question. How did I know Ari wouldn't have started the fire? Other than the obvious—she was in the woods with me—multiple things came to mind. Ari was the reason I made the best decision I've ever made. She was the reason I gave Dean a chance. She gave *me* a chance—something not a lot of people did. Everyone always thought I was stone cold and incapable of being a friend. And maybe those things were true. But dating Dean changed me. I allowed myself to be open. I allowed myself to be loved. What we had wasn't inauthentic. I know everyone thought it was. It was quick, sure, but it was real. I don't know what he told Sonny, or his basketball buddies, or anyone for that matter.

But Dean did love me. And I loved him. I was even going to tell him that. I had it all planned. But then . . .

"What the hell was that?!" I asked, gripping Dean's arm.

"What?"

"You just whispered something into Sonny's ear!"

He looked around the gym at our peers; the disco ball lit up his face. "I was just—" He looked at me. "Just—"

"Just what? Just flirting with your ex-girlfriend?"

"I wasn't flirting. I—"

My eyes narrowed because I could tell something was wrong. He wasn't saying anything but saying everything at the same time. I took a step forward. "What the hell is going on?" I mumbled under my breath. "Tell me."

Dean cut his eyes from left to right, noticing the circle forming around us. "Nothing. Let's not do this right here."

"Do what?" I grabbed his face. "Do what?"

He put his fingers around my wrists and slowly pulled them down. I could see my pink mask in his pupils, but everything else in the room was a blur. "I can't do this anymore, Norah."

"What?"

"I—I can't do this. Us."

"Do *not* do this to me." Locking eyes with him, I pleaded some more. "Please."

"I'm sorry, Norah."

"No." I slapped him across the face. "*I'm* sorry."

"I'm sorry, Mr. Harrison. I can't tell you how I know." I blinked my way out of my trance. "Ari isn't responsible, but—"

"Ms. Soros—"

"But I think I know who is."

We've never gotten along, Sonny. Maybe we're too different. Maybe you're daddy's little princess who always gets what she wants—even if that means someone else's boyfriend. And maybe I'm the school bitch, who adopted the title because in actuality I'm too weak to fight it. I'm not who everyone thinks I am. I have feelings. And Dean crushed them. So did you. You didn't stop to consider me when you took him back. You didn't stop to consider the public humiliation I endured when he dumped me at the dance. The way you stared at me in Piper's room—I know you recognized the look in my eyes. You wore it once when Dean dumped you. But you didn't care. You didn't ask me how I was. You didn't pull me aside to apologize until weeks later in parking lot C when I gave you Jacob's note, after you'd already taken Dean back. I let it go—I wasn't going to make you pay. But Ari's the only reason I've ever felt happiness, and I'm not letting her go down for something you dragged us into.

Ron looked side to side, then leaned forward. "And who would that be?"

14 THE PLAN

We as humans need each other—it's an unavoidable truth. We need baristas to not hit snooze so we can get our morning coffee. We need people to become teachers, so we can learn what they know and become something great ourselves. And what about traffic signal operators? They're important too. After all, don't we need stoplights to avoid dodging and dashing one another on the highways like a game of bumper cars? If everyone gave up, rolled over, and didn't show, no one would get anywhere in life. Because we all need each other to survive—even the people we never expected.

Later that afternoon, I sat quietly on Kyle's bed—waiting with the others for our next meeting. We'd all been questioned, interrogated by Ron, Principal Clemmons, and

Principal Winchester. But none of us knew what the person sitting next to us had said—it was particularly unsettling.

The bedroom door creaked open and Ari appeared. Our meeting began.

"Oh, hey—thanks, Ari. You're an hour late." Winston was crouched down in the corner of the room.

Ari closed the door and fell against the back of it, pausing for a minute. She looked worse than anyone; the color had drained from her face. "They really think it was me, don't they?"

Everyone stared at anything but her. We all knew the answer to that was yes, but no one wanted to say it.

"Great." She nodded, then forcefully smacked a stack of fidget spinners off Kyle's desk; they flew out onto his freshly vacuumed carpet.

Cliff sprung up from the wall. "You need to calm down, Ari! They have no proof."

"They found my phone!"

"And they gave it back," I said. "If Ron thought that was enough evidence—or evidence at all—he would have turned it over to the police."

"Maybe that's next," Casey stated.

"It won't be as long as everyone told them what they wanted to hear." Cliff pinched the bridge of his nose. "That Ari wasn't involved and neither were we."

"And?" JC, who was questioned by an officer that morning, looked around the room. "Is that what everybody told them?"

Everyone remained silent; you could hear a pin drop. Suddenly, that unsettling feeling from earlier felt more like a virus.

Winston stood and brushed off his pants. "Technically, unless they find evidence that places *us* in the area on the night of the fire, they only suspect Ari. I'm good with that."

"Screw you, Winston. You were there too."

"Because of Sonny." Norah was leaning against Kyle's bookshelves with a distant look in her eyes. She had been so quiet up until that point, I almost forgot she was in the room. "We were only there because of Sonny. Why should Ari, or any of us, have to suffer for her dumb decision to go to parking lot C that night? Sonny should come clean."

"Come clean about what?" Dean jumped to my defense. "She didn't do it."

"She's the reason someone did! She clearly pissed someone off!"

"Sonny's not to blame," he replied.

"You would say that."

"What's that supposed to mean?"

Norah pressed three fingers against her forehead and closed her eyes tightly. "It means you're up Sonny's ass!"

When no one agreed, she opened her eyes and looked around the room. "Oh, come on! We're all thinking it!"

Kyle bounced his head against the back of his headboard. "Norah—"

"You guys can all sit here and pretend not to see it, but I can't take this anymore. She played you, Dean! You thought she wanted you back, but everyone knew she liked Jacob. Maybe you could've seen that too had your head not been stuck . . . up . . . her . . . ass." She walked toward him, her words packing a punch. "She liked Jacob then; she likes Jacob now. Yet you still come to her rescue." With a disdainful look, she took one more jab. "It's pathetic."

"I'm not doing this with you," he said, backing away from her face. "Sonny isn't admitting to anything."

"Fine." Norah shrugged. "It can always be handled another way."

"Whoa, whoa, whoa, hold on. What's that supposed to mean?" Kyle jumped off the bed and stepped toward Norah, but not quicker than Dean, who stepped in front of her.

"Easy, all right?" said Dean, holding up a hand.

I glanced at him, thinking my eyes were playing tricks on me while he acted as a human shield for Norah.

Kyle huffed. "Don't do that. Don't act like I'm being aggressive. I'm just making sure she understands me."

"She understands you. Just back up."

"Back up?" Kyle squinted, smiling a little. "I'm nowhere near her. And shouldn't you be the one defending Sonny?"

"I just did."

"It looks like you're defending Norah after she just implied she plans to rat on her."

Dean turned to face her; their blue eyes met. "You didn't, did you?"

"You think I'm going down for some bullshit midnight meeting that had nothing to do with me?" She broke their gaze and went on to address the rest of us. "Wake up, *squad*, I'll throw you all under the bus if it comes down to it. I'm a Violet. I'm a Chosen Ten. I don't belong in the middle of an investigation because Sonny wanted to chase a love letter. My best friend doesn't deserve to be the main suspect because she dropped her phone near the woods, where we never would've been had it not been for Sonny. SHE is the reason someone took a match to our new wing. She may not know who did it, and she may not have done it herself, but she *is* responsible." Norah looked around for validation. "I mean, come on guys. Had it not been for her dragging us along to solve that riddle—none of us would even be on Principal Winchester's shit list. She caused all of this. Her and her dumb plan." Her eyes bored into mine. "Almost as dumb as her sister's."

I couldn't bite my tongue any longer. "I'll take the blame if that makes you happy. But just so we're all clear, this is *not* my fault. You're the one who called everybody to parking lot C to hear Piper out. And it wasn't my idea to go into the woods. In fact, I never asked any of you to come to the school that night. You all just showed up."

"Yeah. We all showed up for you, Sonny. Maybe next time you can show up for us—if you aren't too busy 'writing papers' with Jacob behind Dean's back."

"Please stay out of mine and Dean's relationship."

"Like you stayed out of ours?!"

The way Norah's voice heightened caused me to cower. Her words were disguised as a question, but it wasn't a question at all. I heard the blame in her voice. I heard her misery. She didn't ask me to relate to her woes. She didn't have to; I already did.

Kyle moved in between us, his hands out in front of him. "Everyone calm down. Okay? As long as everybody stuck to the story and didn't say anything to incriminate Ari or anyone else, everything is fine. Questioning is over. Let's just cross our fingers that they believed us and let it go."

"Get out of my face!" Norah shoved Kyle in the chest.

"That's enough, Norah!" Cliff pushed himself off the wall and walked toward her.

"Jesus." Kyle gave Cliff a quick shove to stop him. "I don't need you to come to my aid!"

"What are you talking about?"

"Stop trying to fix my problems. I don't need you to do that."

"Dude—"

"Nah, don't dude me." Kyle pushed Cliff again.

This time, Cliff pushed back.

Ari grabbed her head, then hurtled forward to stand in between them. "Just stop! Just stop it!"

"Stay out of it." Kyle looked at Ari, then at Cliff. "Both of you . . . stay away from me."

"I'm so sick of this." A patronizing smirk appeared on Cliff's face as he stepped toward Kyle some more, but it was clear he found nothing funny. "Or what, Ky?" Ari reached for Cliff's arm, but she couldn't hold him back. "What are you going to do?"

"Be careful. . . . Maybe I've already done it."

My cheeks began to burn as Kyle's words sunk in, and the showcase played out like a horror flick in my mind.

Cliff's smile dropped; he called his bluff. "You wouldn't do that to me."

"Yeah?" Kyle nodded. "And I didn't think you'd hook up with Ari, but you did. Guess we can be wrong about people."

Winston walked to the window and tried opening it.

"What are you doing?" I asked.

"I'll tell you what I'm not doing. I'm not listening to this again."

I pulled him away from the window—but not without a fight.

Kyle and Cliff held their gaze. Another ten seconds went by, each of them unwavering until Kyle finally spoke. "Get the hell out."

Cliff swallowed. We could see it. We could hear it. He backed away in the direction of the door, then turned and exited his room.

Kyle twisted around. "You know what? All of you can get out. I'm done."

"But we have to find the person who did this," Ari said. "We have to come up with a plan. We—"

"We? There is no *we*, Ari." He glanced around the room. "Everybody for themselves."

I stepped forward. "Kyle—"

"GET OUT!"

Winston grabbed his heart with a flat hand, his mouth open. "You don't have to ask me three times. Twice, maybe. Three times?" He walked toward the door, bending down to steal a fidget spinner on his way out.

One by one, everyone cleared the room. With no plan in motion, we left even more lost than when we arrived. The pressure of the case was nipping at our ankles. Everyone was turning on everyone; everything was falling apart. But I knew there was one person who could put aside their emotions to get a job done, and at that point, he was the only person I had.

I stepped onto the football field; something told me I'd find him there. The sky was navy blue with shades of pink swirled about; the sun was leaving. Rather than making myself known, I stayed behind and watched for a moment, taking my seat on the bottom bleacher. It was the first time I'd felt peace in weeks, maybe months. Oddly enough, it was while I watched a mental breakdown take place in front of my eyes.

"GOD!" Cliff slammed the football down onto the green turf amongst a plethora of footballs. "DAMN IT!" He dropped to his knees, then rolled over and sat down in the middle of the field.

After a minute or two, I pushed myself off the cold metal bench and walked his way.

He glanced at me and grabbed a football, stood to his feet, and went on with conditioning—as if I didn't just witness his meltdown. "What are you doing here?"

"Can I not come by to check on you?"

"What for? It's not the first time Kyle spit in my face." He tossed the football down the field, wincing as he let go. "Won't be the last."

My eyes dropped to the ground where his sling sat.

"Besides." He threw another. "Pretty sure he ratted me out. So."

"He was lying," I replied. "There's no way he told anyone about that."

"Well, maybe he should." Cliff reached down and grabbed another ball, tracing my body with his eyes. He turned and chucked it. "Sawyer will soon enough and my football career will be over." He winced again.

"If your shoulder doesn't take you out first."

"It's fine." He reached for another, but I put my hand out to stop him.

"It's not. You can't even cock your arm back without squirming, and no offense, but I can throw longer than that."

Cliff glared at me, then grabbed another ball. He paused for a while, gave it a few taps, then let it fall out of his hand. "I don't know what's wrong with it." Balling his fingers into fists, he struggled to come to grips with what he was saying. "I can't throw. I can't . . . I can't extend my arm without shooting pain. I've been working out with a buddy, on the 'low, trying to regain strength. But I messed it up even more stepping into that fight."

"You have to see the athletic trainers."

"They'll tell Coach."

"You have to tell your coach, Cliff. How long do you think you can keep this up? It's dangerous to play on top of an injury—you know that."

“I’ll take my chances.”

“You’re running out of them,” I replied. “You have to sit out until it heals.”

“Sawyer will love that.” He huffed. “Face it, Sonny. I’m a sitting duck, so just let me ride this out until I’m shot. You know what Sawyer has on me. Kyle knows too.”

“Kyle won’t say anything.”

“How the hell do you know?” Cliff gave me a distasteful look. “Did you come all the way here just to stand up for Kyle?”

“No.” I stared at his face, the absence of the sun creating a shadow. “I came here for your help.”

“Help with what?”

“A plan.”

We need each other. To learn. To grow. To survive. No one can get through life alone. At some point, everyone will need help. And sometimes, that help will come in the most unlikely form, from the most unlikely person. A person like Cliff Reynolds.

15 THE CHRISTMAS GALA: PART ONE

Welcome to the Westcott High Christmas Gala, an event unlike any other. Where cheap party-store streamers and sad plastic mistletoes simply won't do. A tunnel laced with Christmas trees leads you into the gym, white lights so blinding you mustn't look directly at them. A white carpet is rolled out to match the experience—which starts at the curb. Luxury cars roll up in rows; teenagers pour out from the back seats. High heels and loafers meet the concrete; expensive gowns fall and brush the top of the cement. Suits are tailored to perfection, bow ties seamlessly match dresses. Diamond-covered wrists rest on designer clutches. Faux-fur coats warm shoulders. Wavy hair falls across bare backs. Boys' eyes sparkle with excitement for what the night could bring them. Rich, thick magic floats in the air.

I stepped inside; my black heels lined up. I ran my hands over my black dress; it was long-sleeved, sucking the life out of me, and best of all, I'd blend in with the crowd. My eyes took their time looking around the room. The walls were covered with white fabric—the ceiling too. Christmas trees with white lights and white ornaments lined the perimeter of the gymnasium; one particularly large tree sat center, and fake snow surrounded the bottom of it. I could smell the pine from the moment I walked in. White velvet couches were dispersed along the sides, and cocktail tables were randomly placed throughout the room—each one piled with decadent hors d'oeuvres. Exquisite designer gowns were stacked on the dance floor like crayons in a box, each more vibrant than the next. Handsome guys in suits plagued the room; you couldn't miss them—not that you'd have wanted to.

My night began when a server offered me a virgin cranberry cocktail.

"I'm okay." I grabbed my dress and lifted it off the floor, making my way toward the center of the room. Pushing past clusters of strangers, I eventually made it. My eyes scanned the crowd. They were eager to meet her face, and they finally did. I walked her way, weaving through people while simultaneously using them as shields. Her dress was long and navy blue. It had a slit in one leg, and lace at the top. Her hair was wavy, as it usually was, and she was looking around the room. I wondered for who.

"Kid!" Cliff glided toward her. He wore a black fitted suit and a colorful bow tie. His hair was freshly cut and styled. He was striking; it made sense why girls seemed to drop their boyfriends for him. "Sorry I'm late."

I pulled my straight hair over the sides of my face, glaring at them through blonde lines.

"Are we still on?" Sonny asked.

"Yeah." He looked side to side, then stepped a little closer. "You sure this will work?"

"Let's hope so."

Cliff nodded. "Nine."

"Nine."

Nine? My mind raced. *I'll be there*.

He took his eyes off her and then disappeared into the crowd, passing by Winston on his way out of sight.

"Well, if it isn't my best friend." Winston snagged a drink off a server's tray as he wiggled her way. His burgundy blazer bounced off his fitted black slacks, black dress shoes, and black bow tie.

"Well, if it isn't mine." Sonny grabbed his drink and took a sip. "No date?"

"Nope." He took it back. "And you?"

She dropped her chin. "Nope."

"Cheers." He tapped his cup against her forehead; she smacked his arm away. "I thought you and Kyle decided to come together?"

"That was before he kicked me out of his room a few days ago."

"You haven't talked to him?"

"He hasn't really been talking to anyone," she replied.

"And what about him?" Winston asked.

Sonny followed his gaze toward the double doors, and I followed hers. Jacob stood tall, wearing a fitted grayish-blue suit, a light blue shirt, and a bow tie.

"Have you talked to him?"

"Sonny! Winston!" Buckets demanded their attention, walking briskly across the gym floor. "Picture?" He held his camera to his eye as they posed. "Thanks. Yearbook duties."

"You look nice," Sonny said, admiring his cream blazer.

"It's the black tie. The only nice thing I own."

"That camera isn't cheap," Winston replied.

"The tie and the camera. The only two nice things I own." He checked the photo, then lifted his head. "Catch up with you later."

I liked Buckets. Winston too. If only I liked their leader, we all could've been friends—but that was never going to happen.

"He's in a good mood." Sonny watched him melt back into the crowd.

"It's disgusting," Winston replied, reaching for a nearby soufflé. "Where's the damn drama? I came here for *Carrie*, and I want to see *Carrie*."

As he went to take a bite, my eyes were needed at the corner of the room. With a gift in one hand, Kyle was texting someone with his other. He dropped his phone into his pocket and walked toward the side door that led to the hallway.

I glanced at Sonny, then peered at the clock. I had another hour before it struck nine—I had time.

Kyle walked out of the gym, and I waited a good twenty seconds before slipping out the door myself. At the end of the hall, I caught the tail end of his suit turning the corner and I tiptoed in that direction. My calves began burning halfway there, and I considered dropping my heels. But fearing Kyle would hear me, I endured the pain and tiptoed the rest of the way.

I peeked my head over the edge. Kyle stood in the middle of the dark room. He wore a fitted black jacket, which I had to admit looked pretty nice with his rich black hair. But all I kept staring at was the wrapped box snuggling with his arm, and I had to know what was inside.

Suddenly, someone joined him.

"Hi." Casey appeared. Her hair was parted and straight. Her short dress was bright red. Her heels were glossy and black.

"Hi." Kyle's eyes took a trip across her body. "You look very pretty."

She had her arms crossed, and she didn't seem interested in the conversation. But she also didn't strike me as the type of girl who'd tell a hot guy like Kyle to go scratch. She seemed insecure. Nervous. "My, Kyle," I mumbled. "What did you do to her?"

"Thanks."

"I know you're here with Sawyer so I won't keep you long." He removed the box from underneath his arm. "This is for you."

"A gift?" She grabbed the box with caution, staring down at the red-and-white checkered wrapping paper. "I don't—"

"Please," he interrupted. "Just open it."

Casey hesitated, but finally unwrapped the box. She was kind enough to walk the paper over to a nearby trash can but dropped a few pieces along the way. When she returned, she reached inside and removed a slip of paper. "What is this?"

"It's a list of every weather channel on my TV."

She looked up. "What—"

"My mom upgraded to the premium cable package, so we have a ton of channels. Even I was surprised at how many tornado documentaries there are." He slid his hands into his suit pockets. "Thought this would come in handy when you move in."

Casey's mouth opened, but that was about all it did. "When . . . when . . . *what*?"

"I figured there's no need for you and your brothers to go through the hassle of foster care. Not when we have three extra bedrooms." He shrugged. "You were right, Casey. I don't understand what it's like to be you. I probably never will. I have a great mom. A big house. A good life. I think it's time for you to understand what it's like to have those things."

She squeezed her eyes shut as if batting off a brain freeze. "Kyle—"

"My mom wants to help. If it's okay with your aunt, and if we can figure out a way to do this, we'd like for all three of you to move in with us." He shrugged again; the guy was good at that. "When I go off to college, the house will be empty. And if you know anything about my mom, she hates an empty house. Your brothers can stay there for as long as they need. Until they graduate. Until whenever."

"But we . . . we can't. . . ."

"You can," Kyle argued. "And you will. My mom's already out buying little kid comforters and shit." He half smiled. "Probably jumping the gun just a little but I couldn't stop her."

Casey's chest pumped up and down as she stared down at the paper. "But Sawyer was helping me."

"Now he doesn't have to."

She seemed to give thought to his offer, but I could tell it made her skin crawl. "Well, what can I do for you guys?"

She lifted her head. "I can get a part-time job and pay rent. I can—"

"You don't have to do a thing."

Casey's shoulders dropped as if her entire world had just come together. "I mean . . . I don't . . . I don't really know what to say."

"Say you'll move in."

She bit down on her lip.

"I won't take no for an answer, so just say yes."

"K." She nodded, her bottom lip still stuck between her teeth. "Okay. I guess we'll move in."

"Great." He half smiled again. "My mom will make some calls."

"Are you—"

"Yes," he interrupted. "I'm sure."

Casey let out a shaky breath.

"I'll let you get back to the dance." He tapped her upper arm and turned to walk away.

"Wait!"

Kyle's black dress shoes came to a halt; he twisted around.

"Do you think I could hug you?" she asked, pulling on her earlobe.

"Yeah," he whispered, fighting to get the word out, fighting to keep his eyes open. "Of course you can hug me."

They walked toward each other and embraced. His chin over her head, he peered out into the hall. He couldn't see me, but I could see him, and he didn't look like he'd just landed a cute roommate. He looked a bit distraught. It was more than enough to tell me something deeper was going on with him, with them, with that hug. He didn't want to let go.

Casey pulled away, and they stared into each other's eyes. My anxiety went through the roof while I waited for whatever was coming next. She reached up and placed her hand on the back of his head, his black hair peeking through her fingers. She pulled his face toward hers, but in a shocking turn of events, Kyle pulled away.

"Uhh." He looked all the way left.

Casey let go, and her eyes plummeted quicker than the good vibes. "Sorry."

"No." He reached for her. "Don't be sorry. It's not you."

"Oh—okay."

"We can't," he replied.

"All right." She was trying to understand, but the blurry line he'd drawn was hard to read.

"I promised my mom we were just friends . . . and that we wouldn't cross any lines. That was the only way she agreed to this whole thing."

Casey inhaled; it was almost as shaky as her exhale from moments prior. "Yeah. Yeah, of course."

"I hope you understand."

"Of course I do." Her lips struggled to form a smile. "I should probably . . . go call my brothers. . . ."

"Sure." Kyle nodded. "Yeah, good idea."

Casey walked down the hallway, out the back door, and into the parking lot; I could hear her heart break from where I was standing.

"Bye, Casey," I mouthed, watching her walk away.

Kyle reached for the wrapping paper pieces and crumbled them into a ball. He stared down at his closed fists and then shot it into the trash can.

"Hey, you should've been a basketball player," I said, appearing from behind the shadows.

He turned around to face me; he was squinting. "I'm sorry?"

With crossed arms, I walked toward him; my heels clanked against the tile that time. "Sorry, I didn't mean to eavesdrop. I was grabbing a sip from the water fountain and overheard your conversation."

"The water fountain?" He looked over my shoulder. "There's bottled water in the dance. Like tons of it."

"I just needed a breather."

He squinted some more. "Do I know you?"

"I don't go to school here," I replied. "Arm-candy duty called."

"Ah." He nodded. "Who are you here with?"

I couldn't answer his question, so I softly squeezed his arm. Physical contact is electrifying, and a great way to throw someone off. "That was really sweet—what you did for that girl."

He looked over at my hand.

"I know it's none of my business—and I don't really know the whole situation—but she's lucky to have you."

I thought he'd say thank you, but he glared at me instead. That didn't stop me from offering him a soft smile, but it did prompt me to quickly let go. "Have a good evening." I turned around, dropped the act, and then strutted back into the gym—finding the nearest shield and peering over her shoulder.

Thankfully, the two adorable—but naïve—freshman volunteers checking tickets weren't popular enough to know I didn't belong there. I suppose they did their job. I handed them a red slip of paper, and they took it, smiled, and let me into the room. Seemed easy enough. They really should've had better security.

"May I offer you a drink?"

"We meet again," I said to the server. "You know what? When in Rome." I grabbed the cocktail off the tray, took a sip, and lifted my glass to cheers him. He wasn't impressed with my wit like I was. Guy appreciated my wit—so much so he was willing to give me his gala ticket. He really was a good friend, but not because of the ticket. Because he was there for me when I needed him most.

"Can we talk?"

I rolled my head to the right; Kyle and Ari stood in front of each other.

"No," he replied. "We can't."

"Don't make me beg," she said, grabbing him so he wouldn't walk away. "I just want to talk."

"About what?"

"Outside." She motioned toward the doors with her head, her emerald-green jumpsuit forming to her body. She opted out of a dress—bold. Almost as bold as hooking up with your boyfriend's best friend.

He succumbed. I watched her follow him outside, and I paused to think about whether or not I was up for round two with Kyle.

"Why not?" I mumbled, making my way toward the side door. I had to walk around; I couldn't let him see me again for fear he'd think I was following him.

As I walked along the sidewalk toward the entrance of the gym, a plane flew overhead and Guy came to mind. Our introduction wasn't typical. I walked into a coffee shop named Geraldine's one evening. It was summer, just weeks before junior year was set to start. He was sitting in the corner of the café, scribbling in a notepad. I grabbed a few pastries and a coffee while side-eyeing him from the register, and eventually, started a conversation.

"What are you writing?"

Guy looked up at me; his eyes sucked me in. "A riddle."

"Do tell," I said, taking my seat at his table. "I love riddles."

I couldn't believe he trusted me so quickly, but maybe he saw in me what I saw in him—that we'd be fast friends. He went on to tell me about his old school and all of the trouble he got in. He and his parents weren't close. No one understood him; no one cared to try. He told me all about the left-wing exchange and the setup, which made sense once he explained his passion for wrestling and how excited he was to be on Coach Dirk's team. It was a fresh start for him, but he couldn't escape his mischievous ways, and hey, in a town like Westcott, you had to make your own fun.

"I'm going to drop this on his porch. Kid deserves to know what happened—if he can solve the riddle."

A grin slowly appeared on my face. "You're a little crazy."

"A little."

I didn't judge. I'd just been released from Harriet Lange, after all. And if I learned one thing throughout my stay at a psychiatric hospital—it was that timing is everything. They taught me to take time for myself, and that the universe would give it back to me. Meeting Guy was no accident. I needed an "in" into Westcott. *He was my in.*

"Look, I'm sorry for the way I did it. Maybe I should have pulled you aside."

I hid behind a Christmas tree, peeking through the branches.

"No shit, Kyle. I know I don't deserve much of anything from you, but humiliating me in front of the entire lunchroom?" Ari's wavy hair was pulled halfway up into a ponytail.

"And what about the way you've humiliated me?" His voice was loud at first, but then he lowered it. "*Maybe* had it been anyone else, I could have chalked it up to cheating and moved on. But Cliff? He's my brother!"

"I know. I—"

"I'm talking!" And back up it went. "How could you hook up with my best friend? My teammate? We're going to the same college, Ari. We'll play on the same team. I can't run away from him like you can once we graduate. I can't escape what happened. Every time I see him, I'll see you two together. I'll see his betrayal. I can't handle that."

"Look . . ."

He shook his head and sighed. He didn't want to listen, but I wanted to hear her out. I hated cheaters, but she seemed authentic enough.

"Kyle." She grabbed his arm. "I'm sorry. I've said it a million times. At the end of the day—it's not enough. I'm not enough."

"You were."

"You want better than me, Kyle. I've always been bad at relationships, and I've always gone after the wrong guys. You were too good for me."

"I already ended things with you, Ari. I don't need the speech."

"This isn't a speech," she fired back, getting angrier. "I just wanted you to know that . . . that you're nothing like Cliff. You're better. You love better because you aren't afraid to love who you love. Even if that's a Cobalt. Even if that's Casey Langdon." She took a deep breath and let it out. "I wouldn't go back to that day and make a different decision. Dating you was the right one to make. It was bad timing, and I sabotaged our relationship by my actions, but you were exactly what I needed. *Who* I needed. And no one believed in our relationship, but you did. You fought for me. You showed up. You made me believe I was worth showing up for. This last year with you has been crazy, but I'm happy for what we had because you showed me what real love is." She paused. "Go give that to someone who deserves it."

"Uh-oh, Kyle," I whispered behind the branch. Comforters had been purchased. It was far too late to take back his offer. No more Casey—his mother said so.

A tear leaked from Kyle's eye, rolled down his cheek, and hit the white carpet. Ari's eyes were wet; tears were sure to fall if she blinked. They slowly walked toward each other and embraced. It wasn't like the hug he'd shared with Casey minutes prior. This one was drenched in goodbye—the shittiest kind of hug. For minutes they stood in each other's arms, then pulled away and took some time to wipe their eyes in silence.

"You, uh—" He swallowed, wiping his eye once more. "You deserve that too, Ari." He nodded, giving her one last sorrowful stare. "I hope you find it again."

As soon as he turned to walk inside, Ari fell against a brick wall and crumbled. But just as I went to comfort her, Dean passed by, holding a dozen red roses. I was torn—but she wore black in a town where everything was white, so something told me she was the type of person who'd bounce back quickly.

I trailed behind Dean as we strolled into the gym. Between his black suit and my black dress, the red roses were a nice pop. He bobbed his head around as if searching for someone. I had a feeling who.

"Dean! My man!" A basketball buddy grabbed his shoulder, separating the two of us. It sucked because he smelled intoxicating. "Come take some pictures with the team. There's a photo booth."

He was too nice to say no like I would've. "Okay."

"Don't worry," I mumbled as I watched him be pulled off into the crowd. "I'll go find her." I clung closely to my next shield—so close I couldn't believe he didn't ask me to back off. My eyes met the clock. The last time I remembered checking the clock so often was when I was waiting for Guy to show up.

"Sonny Carter," Guy had said to me. "She's Coach's daughter."

"So?" I grabbed a piece of the lemon loaf we split and hurled it into my mouth. Our coffee dates at Geraldine's were becoming a ritual. He enjoyed them, but I needed them.

"So she's probably off-limits. And full disclosure—I creeped her out when I talked to her this morning. She was backing away from me."

"You are a little creepy."

He reached for a chunk. "You aren't wrong."

"Just try again."

"I planned to, but I saw her walking down the hall with this guy ten minutes later. She seemed very content."

"Oh yeah?" I swallowed the lemon bread. "What's his name?"

"I don't know. . . . Jake . . . or Justin." He shrugged, then took a sip of his coffee. "Jacob." He nodded. "His name's Jacob."

"You're going to let a guy named *Jacob* stop you?"

"You're right." Guy nodded, staring blankly at the corner of the room. "If he were a Justin, I'd run. Nobody can compete with a Justin."

I playfully tossed a chunk of bread at his face. "Especially not a *Guy*."

"You look like shit," Norah said, standing by a cocktail table. Her black velvet dress looked painted on, and I'm sure she would've appreciated the comparison.

Kyle was leaned against the wall, and truthfully, I wasn't up for round three so I went to walk away. But then something strange happened.

"Get up," she said like it was a chore. "Dance with me."

"I'm good."

I wanted to tell him that Ari breaking his heart was just karma for when he broke Casey's and that it wasn't the end of the world. Although, if karma comes with luggage, it can eventually make you feel that way.

"Come on, Winchester. You're crying in the corner of the gala. It's embarrassing."

"I'm not crying, Norah, Jesus." He looked at her, totally annoyed. "Weren't you the one falling apart at a dance a couple of months ago?"

"I was. And I'll never let a Cobalt bring me to tears again." There was something sinister about her voice. "Now get your ass off this wall and come dance with me."

I didn't expect him to agree, but maybe he was just as lonely as she was, and maybe they thought an innocent dance could help ease both their pain.

He eventually grabbed her hand, and they walked side by side toward the dance floor. I stayed behind; something told me there was nothing to see there. I stepped around a couch—the very couch Sonny was sitting on. Pulling my hair over my face, I turned sideways and took slow sips from my glass while I watched her every move. Her dress was pretty on her, but it looked better on me. I made sure to hang it back up, over the hinge on her closet door, just the way I found it. I especially handled her flash drive with care. Some may say taking it the night before her paper was due was intentional—but that was just a bonus. The lure was the shape, and how pretty it was. It was calling my name and I knew it had to come home with me. But I'm not some malicious burglar who likes to play dress up. I didn't break into her room to take anything . . . I really didn't . . . *I swear*.

"If I didn't know any better, I'd say you aren't having a good time," Jacob said, plopping down beside her.

She looked over at him and smiled a little, hardly hiding that she was happy to see him.

"What are you doing sitting on the couch? Aren't you, like, a really good dancer or something?"

"Or something," she said. "I'm dateless."

"Thought you were coming with Kyle?"

Sonny inhaled. “He’s sort of going through some things.” Then exhaled. “I think he wanted to come alone.”

“Man. If only I knew of a guy who wants to dance with you.” Jacob put his hands on his knees and pushed himself off the cushion. “Well. I’ll see ya.” He walked away.

Sonny’s mouth slowly opened, but quickly closed when he turned back around and beamed.

“You’re such an idiot,” she said.

“Come on.” Jacob held out his hand. “Let’s have some fun.”

“You should go,” I had told him. “It’ll be fun.”

“Who lied to you?” Guy asked. “School dances are Satan’s way of reminding us he exists, and it’s not even Halloween yet, so they’ve named this one the ‘fall dance.’ ”

“That’s not bad.”

“It’s not good.”

I listened to Guy tell me stories about Westcott for weeks. About the administration. The rules. The students. He told me stories about Sonny, and all of her friends, and all of their secrets. By the end of every coffee date, I could tell you what color socks they were wearing, down to who was hooking up with who behind whose back. He was almost obsessed with observing them—Sonny especially—and she quickly became his favorite thing to talk about. He loved to talk; all you had to do was listen. I was good at that. I learned if you remain calm, keep a pleasant enough face, and seem sincere, you can trick anyone into believing you're stable—even doctors.

"I'm sure Sonny will be at the dance," I said.

"I'm sure she will—but not with me."

"This Jacob kid doesn't seem like someone I'd be intimidated by. You're a catch, Guy Penn. She'd be crazy not to like you."

Guy's eyes drifted toward the corner of the room. "She won't like me once she realizes I'm the one who left the riddle for her friend JC. I wish I had known they were such close friends *before* I went and did all of this. I blew it."

"Look, you can't keep following her around, staring at her from a distance. If you like her, then talk to her. Shoot your shot."

"It's too late." He sipped his latte. "Watching from afar is fine with me."

Jacob waited for Sonny to grab his hand. Another slow song came on overhead—of course it did. Everything worked out for her.

She placed her fingers on his and pulled herself up, covering what she could of her leg—although, by the way he looked at her, I don't think he minded it was showing. Their hands grazing, he led her to the dance floor. I followed—I had to. Something told me there was lots to see there.

Jacob pulled her in. He cupped his hands on her lower back; her hands rested on his chest. They began swaying to the music; their eye contact was unreal.

"You look beautiful," he said, their faces close.

She stared at him without replying.

"This might not be the right time to bring it up, but I'm very sorry to hear about you and Dean." His grip tightened.

"Sort of knew it would happen."

"I hope not because of me."

"No," she replied as if the idea was idiotic. "Well, maybe a little."

Jacob dropped his head and let out a small laugh.

"It's not your fault," she continued.

He squinted and tilted his head.

"Okay . . . maybe it is a little."

Another small laugh escaped while the smile in both of their eyes dwindled.

"Your dad questioned me," Sonny said. "It was—"

"Yeah, hey, uh, can we maybe . . . *not* talk about that tonight?" She looked embarrassed, so he explained himself. "I want to hear all about it, I swear, but I was sort of hoping we could just enjoy each other's company for one evening without discussing the fire, or setups, or sorority-sister murders."

"Too heavy for a gala?"

"Especially heavy for a gala."

"Fair." She held back a smile. "Yeah, I guess things have been a little dark lately."

"That's all right. Not your fault."

"I don't know about that." She raised her brows. "There's a common denominator in all of this."

"Welcome mats?"

"Me," she replied, letting that smile go.

Jacob mirrored her. "I happen to think otherwise, Sonny Carter. You're perfect."

"You don't know me at all if you think I'm perfect."

"Oh yeah?"

"Yeah?" She squinted. "Besides, aren't you supposed to spend more than a couple of months with someone before determining whether or not they're worth such a profound adjective? Aren't we supposed to hang around each other long enough to know whether or not we're right about one another?"

"Probably." He stole her full attention. "Or maybe we'll just be the two people who change what falling in love is *supposed* to look like."

They stared at one another until his comment floated far away.

"About that," Sonny finally managed to say, her eyes making vertical lines on his face. "I got your note."

"Yeah?"

She nodded. "Do you really—?"

"Yes." They rocked back and forth; you could almost hear their heartbeats over the sad track. Jacob lifted his hand and slowly tucked her hair behind her ear; his fingers rested against her neck, his thumb on her cheek. "I really think I do."

"I . . . I, um . . ."

"It's okay." He rubbed his thumb against her face, staring into her eyes like it was his job. "I'll wait."

I took a deep breath and turned to the left so I wouldn't vomit. Ari caught my attention; she sat alone on a velvet couch. She looked sad, even sadder than when I left her. I didn't care for the girl, but I'm not a monster, and she looked like she needed a friend. I made my way toward her, attempting to come up with some quick Hallmark bullshit to brighten her mood. Maybe I'd have taken a page from Jacob's book, but fortunately for me, I didn't have to.

"Aren't you singing tonight?" Cliff stood in front of her.

Ari looked up, then down. Her brown eyes were leaking black. "Decided not to."

Cliff stood there, taut, his hands hiding in his suit pockets. He hesitated but eventually sat down on the couch. For minutes, he didn't say a word to Ari. Maybe he thought his company was enough because that's all he offered. He didn't touch her. He didn't wrap his arm around her. He even kept his distance.

But finally, he sparked a conversation. "You good?"

Ari immediately started laughing, her eyes squinted shut. "Yeah, Cliff. I'm good." She said she was, but her trembling body said otherwise.

I waited for him to embrace her, but he didn't move. It was almost like he recognized that a pass at her during a vulnerable moment was the last thing she needed. And that seemed pretty honorable to me. Then again, I wasn't the best judge of character.

"If you couldn't tell by the mascara on my chin, I'm not in the mood."

"Not in the mood for what?"

"Small talk," she replied. "For you. Honestly, Cliff, I just hugged the only guy who's ever loved me for the last time tonight. Can you please just . . . do what you're good at and disappear? Your Violet ass warming a seat next to me doesn't prove you care. I'm sorry if you thought it did."

Cliff stared ahead, nodding for no reason into the crowd. "Mascara's on your jumper too." He pushed himself off the couch and stood, the right side of his body facing her. "And Kyle's not the only guy who loves you." He tugged down on his suit, pausing for a brief second before walking off.

Before I could look at Ari, red roses caught my eye again; they floated through the crowd, pulling me in like a magnet. I followed Dean as he headed toward Sonny and Jacob, finding a nearby barrier I could hide behind. The anticipation was killing me. It was like watching a movie play out in real time, and I was determined to watch the entire thing—even if I had to do so from behind someone's overly broad shoulder.

"It hasn't even been a week, Harrison. Think you can keep it in your pants a few more days?" Dean approached them. He had the bluest eyes—and the cutest face. I couldn't understand why he wasn't enough for her, or why he wanted to be.

Sonny pulled away.

"Don't hold back for my sake," he said, chucking the flowers at her feet.

Jacob stepped forward. "Dude, what the hell is your problem?"

The crowd around us slowly formed a circle.

"You know the answer to that."

"We're friends," Jacob replied.

Dean laughed at how stupid he was. "Bullshit."

"Look, I don't owe you anything," Jacob said. "I've tried to be cool with you. I've taken your shit. I've overlooked your aggression toward me on the court. And I've respected Sonny's wishes and haven't pushed her to do anything with me. If you still have a problem, that's on you."

"My problem is with your good-guy act," Dean replied. "I don't like you, Harrison. I see right through it, and I can't explain how I know you're no good, or why I think that. It's just a feeling I have." He glared at him. "I know a piece of shit when I see one."

Jacob had enough. He lunged forward and grabbed Dean by his suit jacket.

I can't really explain what happened after that. People jumped all around me and blocked my view. It was clear the two were fighting by the way Sonny was yelling, but then, someone yelled for her.

"Sonny!" Cliff pushed through the masses. "Let's go!"

"But—"

"I'll handle it. Go!"

"Go ahead. Scroll." I handed Guy my cell phone, my photo album pulled up. The coffee shop was empty—it really was the perfect scene. No one was close enough to see the pictures. Nobody was in earshot of our conversation. And other than the nosey barista dozens of feet away, everyone was too preoccupied to care.

"What are these?" he asked, flipping through them. He seemed shocked by what he was looking at, but at the same time, he'd left a guy a riddle—so who was the crazy one?

I glanced toward the register, then back at Guy. "They're photos of Sonny."

Guy's dark eyes left the pictures and locked in with mine. "Why did you—?"

"You're going to do something for me."

He owed me. After all, I'd listened to him complain about his life for over a month. A life filled with secrets. Secrets which, should they have been leaked, could have ruined him. Thankfully, I didn't need to pull those cards; he agreed to help. He didn't even ask questions, other than the most important one: *why*? Why *did* I hate Sonny Carter? Why did I want to ruin her? Once I explained it, I think he understood. As much as one could understand my thought process. But our conversations took a turn when I realized the photo leak of her cuddling with a guy on his couch wasn't enough.

"Listen, maybe you should let this go." Guy leaned across the table in an attempt to sway me. "You really don't know who you're messing with. Those kids are smart. If you set her up, *however you do it*, they'll figure it out. And when they trace it back to you, believe me, they'll all pitch in to toss your ass in jail. You do something to her—you mess with Sonny Carter—you mess with all of them."

"Well, aren't you the pot *and* the kettle, Mr. Riddle?"

"I was playing around," he fired back. "That was a stupid game!"

"So consider this a game too," I replied, my voice deeper. "But in my game—Sonny Carter will lose."

And for the first time, underneath the clock on the coffee shop's wall, Guy saw me in a different light—the real one. But seeing the light isn't for everybody. I had a feeling Guy wasn't as tough as I initially hoped—I figured that out weeks prior. Call it an intuition—a lucky guess—but I just *knew* he'd eventually fizzle out. Which is why I also made friends with someone else in case he ever stopped being a resource for me.

"Thanks," she said, taking the paper bag from my hands underneath the streetlight. It wasn't easy breaking down her walls, but I eventually got to know her—every pretty and ugly part. And believe me, there were some pretty ugly parts.

"Of course," I replied. "Are they helping?"

She nodded, but I could tell she was embarrassed to admit it. I guess I would've been too.

"Let me know if you need anything else, okay?" I rubbed her arm. "I'm always here for you."

"Seems like you're the only one," she replied, tucking the bag underneath her shirt. "Back at you, though. Whatever you need."

Her words were meant to comfort me but I heard an opportunity instead. It seemed wrong involving her, it really did, but that night was our third exchange—so I figured it was probably time she came to the streetlight with something to offer me. It was only fair.

"Whatever I need?"

She nodded again, so I asked her for her help. She was hesitant at first, but I pressed her. "Listen, I wouldn't ask you for it if I didn't need to. I can't do this without it."

"You're underestimating—"

"No! You don't understand! I need your help."

"Well I can't give it to you," she replied, stepping away. "I can't. I—"

"I thought we were friends."

"We are," she shot back. "But think about what you're asking me to do. If anyone finds out—"

"They won't."

"You don't know that!"

"Look, you need my access and I need yours. I need a way in and you're the only chance I have at stepping foot on that campus."

"Fine," she yelled, looking side to side. "Just . . . keep me clean."

Sonny's eyes played tug-of-war with the scuffle and Cliff. "But—"

"I'll meet you there!" Cliff shouted, grabbing Dean's shoulders and pulling him away from Jacob. "Just go!"

Unfortunately for Sonny, she had to.

It was nine.

16 THE CHRISTMAS GALA: PART TWO

Christmas in Westcott—there's truly nothing like it. Holly is hung. Trees are up. Lights are wrapped around every square inch of every light post, home, and building. There's a certain calm in the air during the month of December—a blanket of peace, if you will. For one month, everyone's worries seem far away. Even while enduring endless hours of holiday baking, packed stores, and traffic jams that could make the sanest person lose it—there's a general consensus that things aren't so bad.

But that specific December had already proven otherwise for me, and by the end of the gala, my blanket of peace would be more like a wadded-up dirty tissue.

I dashed through the crowd, my leg peeking through my slit as I walked. I had to fight to stay focused; I couldn't stop thinking about what had just happened. But I didn't have time to worry about Jacob, or Dean, or the fact that they'd just laid hands on each other in the middle of our classy Christmas Gala. I had to hurry, even if that meant leaving my feelings scattered all over the dance floor like an overturned jar of marbles. My misty eyes searched for Buckets, but they landed on something much worse instead.

"What are you doing?!" I asked, running up behind Kyle and pulling him away from Norah's lips. "Are you crazy?"

He wiped his mouth, shamefully staring down at the floor. "Just having some fun."

"Fun?"

"Yes, fun, Sonny!" Kyle snapped back. "Ever heard of it?"

"What is your problem?"

He glanced at Norah, then at me. "Nothing," he said, fastening a button on his sleeve while walking away.

With a look of utter disgust, I turned to blame Norah. "Seriously?" Without giving her a chance to respond, I lifted my dress and walked off.

"You're welcome, by the way!"

Curiosity got the better of me; I twisted back around.

"I could've ruined you," she added, dragging her words a little. "I could've told Mr. Harrison everything. I could've told him you're the reason someone set the fire. That you and whatever enemy you made caused this to happen."

"So why didn't you, Norah? If you blame me for all of this then why didn't you just tell him?"

"I changed my mind."

Showy gowns and suits blocked my view of her as students passed by, but I rolled my eyes before leaving there—just in case she'd catch it. After taking a few steps, a bony hand grasped my forearm and spun me around. Norah was inches from my face. Her eyes were blacker than her dress; they were empty, yet somehow managed to convey pure hatred. "And I want you to owe me," she said, tightening her grip. I looked down at her hand just as she was letting go—one finger at a time. "I hope you enjoy the gala."

She took her insincere comment and drifted off. I watched, focusing on nothing but her as I rubbed my arm. There was no way I'd survive being indebted to Norah Soros, but after her dark statement, my only intention was to survive the rest of the night. I blinked myself out of my stupor, then bobbed my head from left to right until I managed to spot Kyle. Once I caught up with him, my fingers met his bicep.

He turned around, his black suit jacket brushing the front of my dress. "Please don't follow me."

His tone seemed serious, but following after people was what I did best. I caught up with him again, grabbing his arm once more. Kyle faced me; he looked like he'd gone through the wringer, and I wasn't around to see why.

"What's wrong? Is it Ari? Cliff?"

"Casey," he replied, giving in to the conversation. "I rode in on my trusty white horse and asked her to move in with me."

"You what?"

He grabbed a fistful of his dark hair. "I . . . I couldn't sit back and wait for Sawyer to decide whether or not he's going to help her. You know he's not going to. Not after I said no to his plan."

"So you asked her to live with you instead? Kyle—"

"Anything to get rid of him," he replied. "And I want her to. I want to help."

"Okay?" I crossed my arms. "Then what's wrong?"

"I ruined it, Sonny. I ruined everything. By the time I realized how stupid I was being for pushing her away, she finally opened up to me about the foster care stuff. Told me she was scared she'd have to leave Westcott." He chewed on the inside of his lip; his eyes moved to the side of the room. "What else was I supposed to do? I asked my mom if we could help them, and she agreed, but only after I promised her that we were just friends. She told me if she caught us doing anything, it'd be over. I can't ruin this opportunity for them."

"Ky." I sighed, his sweet soul softening my voice. "Why'd you do this?"

"Because it's the right thing to do."

"Yeah but now you can't be with her." I couldn't understand. "Why? Why not find another way?"

"Love is sacrifice, right?"

Our *Romeo and Juliet* debate came to mind, causing my heart to flutter. I wanted to reply—I tried to—but every time I opened my mouth to speak nothing came out. He'd just admitted to loving Casey, right in time for it to be too late.

Kyle turned around to escape the conversation—only to be greeted by Sawyer.

"What's up, buddy?" Sawyer's camel-colored suit made his green eyes pop, and his black bow tie matched his black soul. Behind him was Quinn Myers; behind Kyle was me. Sawyer really had the advantage.

"I heard you opened your home to Casey and her brothers." He tucked his hands into his suit pockets and pulled his shoulders back, puffing out his chest. "Why would you go and step on my father's toes like that?"

"Because your father's a slimy piece of shit." Kyle widened his stance, then planted his feet.

"He was helping them."

"No. He was helping you. You wanted me to turn on Cliff and Casey was leverage."

"Leverage is a good thing to have."

"Yeah, well, it looks like you don't have it anymore."

Sawyer looked behind him and shared a feigned laugh with Quinn. "Ahh, I don't know, man. I'll always have the showcase."

"If you want to take Cliff's spot, then why don't you just earn it?" Kyle asked. "On the field like men do."

"Oh, what, and Cliff's a man? I told you, buddy, he doesn't deserve to be on the team. Once his hobby is leaked—and it will be—I won't have to worry about earning his spot. He won't have it anymore." He leaned in closer. "I gave you a chance to jump ship and you spit in my face. Big mistake."

"Do whatever you have to do," Kyle replied. "But leave Casey out of it."

"You ought to be thanking me. We just paid her cell-phone bill so she could turn around and text you." He straightened his bow tie. "And I don't plan to leave her alone. I plan to knock on your bedroom door every time I pass your room on my way to hers—just so you'll know I'm there. I'm here, Kyle. I'm here to stay." He patted Kyle on his shoulder; Kyle clenched his jaw. "Have a good one, man." He took a few steps forward, then swung around with his finger pointed. "Oh, and what was it you told me?" He paused for a moment as if searching for the words in the sky. "Oh yeah. Fuck you."

"Sonny!" Cliff rushed to my side. "What are you still doing in here?"

"I got—" I glanced at Kyle; he was already three Christmas trees away from me. "I got sidetracked."

"What's going on?"

"Nothing." I shook my head. "We have to find Buckets."

"You haven't found him yet?"

"I told you! I got sidetracked!"

"Jesus, kid." Cliff peered over my head. "I'll find him. Just go."

With one quick nod, we agreed to move. He went left; I went right, lifting my dress and heading toward the side door. I placed my hand on the metal, looking back into the gala once more before the real event of the evening swept me away.

Pushing forward, I stepped into the hallway. It was dark, but I knew it would be. I'd walked through that black hall before, except that time I was with Kyle and wearing a mask. The clink of the door closing behind me sent a rush through my body; the sound it made caused echoes that had echoes. I released my dress and strolled as if a killer was in there.

Cliff and I apart weren't much, but if you put us together, you got superhuman brain waves. He was pessimistic, always thinking of the worst. I was cautious, always thinking of what could be, rather than what was. A thirty-minute conversation in his Mercedes and we figured it out. How did Principal Winchester know Kyle and I were walking through the halls on the night of the fall dance? Coincidence? Or cameras?

Principal Winchester wasn't a fan of Lana. To be fair, not

a lot of people were. But the moment she threatened to ruin the last of the Crescent, she made his list. And because we shared the same last name—so did I. He had his eye on me, and after I unraveled his secrets and practically broke every rule in the SCC—he likely felt justified in doing so. Sure, my friends were also aware of our principal's corruption, but most of them weren't investigative journalists like myself. I had the reason and ability to expose him with one anonymous paper to every news outlet in town, and honestly, who could write a paper like me? He knew I wasn't going to drop it—so he wanted to get rid of me. But how do you expel a straight-A Violet who's a Chosen Ten?

It's simple—you frame her for arson, collect the insurance money, and start over. Let a handful of Bella View kids slip in, temporarily relocate the rest, and rebuild a bigger and better left wing. Not only would that act of heroism prove Principal Winchester was the leader Westcott always needed, but it would also wash away any future accusations that he despised the entire student body. If he was watching me as I suspected, I was going to make sure he caught me on camera waltzing through a hallway I had no business being in, and into a parking lot where I had no reason to go. I just had to lure him there—the same way he tried luring me. But that time around, Jacob wouldn't be taking photos of Principal Winchester in a parking lot with a student—Buckets would be. And Cliff would be nearby recording our conversation—because we knew for a fact that

Principal Winchester wouldn't be dumb enough to leave the parking lot cameras on. Our plan? Get him to say something—anything—that would incriminate him in the slightest.

"Come on," I whispered, my eyes cutting above my head at the black circles in the corners. "Where are you?"

"Sonny!"

I jumped, whipping around to find Dean walking toward me. He had the roses in his hand, minus a dozen or so petals after they'd been trampled on. They drooped beside him.

"We need to talk."

"Not now, Dean."

"Here," he said, placing what was left of the bouquet against my chest. "I came to apologize for the other night. I didn't mean to kick you out of my driveway."

"Did you mean to fistfight Jacob in the middle of our gala?"

Dean rolled his shoulders back. "He swung first."

"You started it!"

"What are you? Three years old? He grabbed me!"

"Exhibit some self-control, would you? You're the captain of the basketball team. You're supposed to be a leader."

"Why are you sticking up for him? You two together?"

"Look, I can't do this with you right now." I looked up at the cameras. "I have to go."

"But we need to—"

I lifted my hand. "I can't. I can't right now."

"You're not serious." Dean rubbed his temples. "You can't seriously be choosing this guy over me."

I wasn't. I hadn't. I was still so in love with Dean it burned. But in a moment of weakness, I allowed an old ghost to resurface. "It hurts, huh?"

"Is that your way of throwing my relationship with Norah in my face again?" He laughed, but nothing was funny. "That's in the past!"

"Is it? Because you were really quick to jump to her defense the other day in Kyle's bedroom."

"Oh. Oh wow. You're really reaching with that one, Sonny. *Nothing* is going on between me and Norah. Nothing." He pinched his forehead. "I can't believe you're deflecting like this. I mean, what else do I have to do to prove myself to you? I made a mistake. I never should have left you. But Jesus, Sonny, I've all but thrown myself at your feet to get you back. What do you need from me?" He stared at me as if I were disappearing in front of his eyes. "What do you want?"

I wanted to tell him the truth. That I wanted the old Dean back. Before he lost his mom. Before he gave up on us. I wanted to rewind time and go back to the innocent nights we spent together—drinking those disgusting shakes and stretching nothing into hours' worth of conversations. I wanted to close my eyes and wake up in his bed, in his arms, and forget every bad thing that happened between us.

But that's just not how life works, it's just not how love goes, *is it*?

"I have to go," I whispered, making my escape toward the exit door as soon as he tucked his chin.

"He's going to hurt you!" Dean shouted.

As if a wall were in front of me, I stopped.

"I don't know when, or how, but he *will* hurt you."

After a few seconds, I dropped the roses and pushed the door open with my palm.

The cool air smacked against my body as I stepped into the night, and I allowed myself a moment to think. Dean's comment hit my mind like a cue ball, causing my thoughts to scatter, causing me to freeze on the other side of the door. But the distant sound of people talking in the hallway drew near. I pushed my dress behind me and ran toward the parking lot; the lace at the top pressed against my chest and held me together—and that was just about the only thing.

Balls were rolling around in my head, each one representing a different thought. Thoughts of Jacob. Of Dean. All I could see was their faces as they took turns punching me in the gut. I could feel Jacob's thumb on my cheek, his hand on my back. I could hear his words and the way he spoke them so effortlessly. I could feel Dean's roses hit my hand like a weight. I could feel his lips. I could smell his scent. Before long, I wasn't sure if I was running toward the parking lot or running away from my problems. But I couldn't stop. I was almost there. I saw the parking lot up ahead and ran a little faster. As soon as my feet touched the cement, I stopped and placed my hands on my knees so I wouldn't topple over.

"Carter!" The sound of Cliff's voice barely grazed my left eardrum. It was far away. Too far away.

Eventually, I saw him running toward me at full speed. He quickly got to the parking lot, his suit jacket nowhere in sight. "We have to bail."

Something was wrong. I could tell by the way he didn't acknowledge my sweaty, out-of-breath demeanor. "What's going on?"

"It's Ari," he blurted out. "She was just arrested."

Christmas. A time for family. A time for friends. A time to wrap presents, shamelessly stuff your face with sweets, and decorate gingerbread houses until your fingers are sore. But for Ari Ziegler, it was time to experience what it was like to ride in the back of a cop car—and I had a feeling that ride wouldn't come with a blanket of any kind.

17 DÉJÀ VU

Déjà vu. The feeling you're experiencing something for the second time. Like you've lived it before—seen it before—and everything seems to be moving in slow motion. Is it merely just a discrepancy in the memory system of the brain? A neurological anomaly? Most of the time, it's a fleeting feeling—gone before you know it.

But sometimes, things do happen twice. Best case, you'll enjoy the brief moment of familiarity it can bring. Worst case—and there's always a worst case—you'll be wishing your mind was playing tricks on you.

Leaving the frigid wind behind me on the empty sidewalk, I pulled open the heavy door of Laurel's Bakery the following morning. The wreath hanging center smacked against the glass as the door shut behind me, and the bell attached to the wreath rang loudly. It had been many weeks since I last entered their establishment, and I couldn't say much had changed in there. I walked to the counter, ordered two coffees, and then dragged my feet to the corner of the room. Glancing to the left, I saw the same man reading the paper. His wool sweater was brown—at least that much had changed. I sat down, placed the two piping hot cups on the table in front of me, and then peered out the window. Before long, Kyle walked by. I could tell he'd rolled out of bed by his wrinkled hoodie and half-opened eyes. He walked inside and fell into a seat.

"You look worse than I do," I told him.

"I was up all night."

"Have you heard any news?"

I didn't have to mention Ari; Kyle collapsed anyway, leaning forward and dropping his forehead on the table. My coffee rippled in its cup. "I haven't been able to get in touch with her."

"Me either." I pushed his coffee toward him.

"She didn't do it." Kyle lifted his head and grabbed it. "Why the hell was she arrested?"

My eyes ditched the conversation; I stared through the window in a trance. "I don't have a clue."

"And I don't know how much more I can take between the investigation, losing Ari, fighting with Cliff, and now this Casey stuff." He poured some milk into his cup. "I hope

I didn't make a mistake by asking her to live with us."

"You don't regret it, do you?"

"What would it matter if I did?"

I stared at him; he saw that I was staring.

"No. I don't regret it." He added some sugar. "It just put a target on my back for Ellington."

"Technically Cliff did that."

Kyle took a sip. He closed his eyes as he swallowed, the warmth bringing him some relief. "I didn't rat him out. I thought about it. . . . I just couldn't do it."

"I figured."

"And I won't." He leaned forward. "But someone needs to get through to him, Sonny. Cliff's on the fast-track to Cornell and he's risking it all by doing what he does."

"Don't look at me!"

"I'm looking at you."

"It's not that easy, Kyle. It's Cliff—he won't listen to a word I say."

"You don't know that. Try."

"Don't you think I have?"

"Well try again. I'm not going to have that hanging over our heads, and I'm definitely not taking shit from Sawyer as punishment for not turning on him." Kyle's mind commuted back to Cliff. "He doesn't even need anyone to ruin him, give him enough rope and he'll do it himself. I swear."

"Haven't you ever gotten caught up in the wrong things?"

"Not for two years."

I fell back in my seat and checked out.

"Speaking of *wrong things* . . . you and Jacob?"

"You know, it is so rich that you're team Dean all of a sudden. You spent months trying to convince me—"

"To be mindful," he interjected. "I may have said giving him another chance so soon was dumb, but I never said that Dean was wrong for you."

"And Jacob is?"

"I don't know, Sonny. I caught a glimpse of you two last night. The way he looked at you—the way he perfectly swiped your face at just the right speed—don't you think he's a little . . . too perfect?"

"Don't you think it's a little creepy you know the speed at which he swiped my face?"

"I'm serious," he replied, and he was. "It's something to think about."

I pulled dried mascara off my eyelashes. "Dean went nuts on me last night after seeing us dance."

"Do you blame him? He was scared."

"Of what?"

"Harrison!" Kyle added more sugar. "Any guy would have done the same thing. If the only thing Dean's guilty of is loving you too hard, I'd reconsider your stance on the situation."

"I love him too," I said, my mind bringing me back to the

note Jacob left on my pillow.

"But?"

"But Jacob." I rubbed my fingers together to remove the clumps. "What do I do, Ky?"

"When you're coming to me for dating advice, you've really reached rock bottom."

"I shouldn't have talked to Jacob when he came back. I shouldn't have gone to his house that night."

"You really think you were going to avoid a conversation with him? He would have found you."

"I should have switched schools."

"Now that's something I can get behind." He smiled a little, but just as quickly as it appeared, it went away. "I hope Ari is okay."

Before I could respond, my phone rang. I looked down at my lap and saw Cliff's name flash across my screen. Pressing down on the decline button, I looked back up. "Yeah . . . me too."

My phone rang again; I stared down at the screen. "I'll be right back," I told Kyle, pushing myself away from the table. I walked across the shop toward the bathroom. "Hello?" I answered, opening the heavy commercial door.

"Why didn't you answer your phone?" Cliff asked.

"Why didn't you take that as a hint?" I replied. "I'm with Kyle."

"And what? You can't talk to me?"

"What do you need, Cliff?" I asked, circling the small room. "Have you heard any news?"

"No. No one has heard from her."

I grabbed a paper towel and held it under the faucet, then stroked a small stain on my shirt. "Why was she arrested?"

"Maybe someone didn't stick to the story."

I looked up and stared into the brushed metal mirror, but I couldn't really see my reflection. I was focused on Cliff's statement and how certain he sounded when he said it.

"Can we really be sure of what everyone said during their interrogation? Think about it—a few days after we were questioned individually, the police took her downtown. Someone must have said something."

I turned away and tossed the wet paper towel into the trash can. "What in the world is going on in this town?"

"I don't know, but I don't know how much more I can take."

"Yeah," I mumbled. "I've heard that before. Look, let's not jump to conclusions before we've talked to her." I balanced the phone on my shoulder while I tucked my shirt into my jeans. "I have to go. Call me if you hear anything."

Cliff ended the call.

I took the phone and slid it back into my pocket, but just as my fingers left the device, it buzzed. I reached for it again, and seeing *Mom* slide across the screen, I pressed *decline,* grabbed the door handle, and walked back toward our table.

But something up ahead caused me to slow my pace.

Kyle wasn't alone. A girl stood on the opposite side of him. I was only staring at her back, but her body was a shell of someone I'd met before. I took baby steps toward them while I studied her from head to toe, making sure I was assiduous in my exam. Every piece of her wardrobe stood out. She wore overalls and a long-sleeved, tight black turtleneck. Her hair was piled on the top of her head in a bun, pieces falling down her neck.

But it wasn't until I was a few steps away when I recognized the most important part of her attire—her back pocket. As soon as my eyes landed there, fear pervaded my senses. I could still hear the espresso machine behind me, but barely. I could see the shape of Kyle's face, and there were two of them. Everything became cloudy, except for one thing. Sticking out of this stranger's pocket was my stolen flash drive.

My feet began to move as if the floor beneath me had become water and swept me away. I drifted toward her, getting closer and closer until I was one head roll away from seeing her face. I crept around her right shoulder, staring at the soft terra-cotta blush on her cheek.

"Sonny." Kyle's voice entered my ear, but it was muffled and slow, or perhaps my body was shutting down. "This is my new friend. . . . We met at the gala last night."

Her cheek disappeared, and her full face came forward.

"Brystol," she said, extending her arm toward me. "But most people call me BC."

I stared into her eyes; her beautiful thick brows were raised. Without realizing it, I'd reached for her hand. "We've met."

She smiled condescendingly, then squeezed my hand a little too tight before releasing it with a disingenuous laugh. "Oh my gosh." She grabbed her temples, then pointed at me. "You're . . ."

"Sonny."

"Sonny. Yes, yeah, yeah, we met at homecoming."

I wasn't sure which was more unsettling—her acting ability or knowing I was staring at the girl who was trying to ruin my entire life.

"I'm sorry," she said. "I'm so bad with names. It's unfair really. Mine's so easy to remember so no one ever forgets it, but I forget everyone else's."

"Nah, don't worry about it. I'm pretty bad with names myself." Kyle shrugged. "Had you told me yours last night, I wouldn't have remembered it just now."

"Well, it's Brystol Montgomery."

"Brystol Montgomery. Got it. I'll try to remember that."

She grinned. "I should get going. It was nice seeing you both again." Tucking her hands into her back pockets, she slid my butterfly flash drive deeper into the right one, then stepped onto the welcome mat.

Kyle stopped her. "Hey! What's the *C* stand for?"

She stood facing the door, her breath appearing and disappearing on the glass. "Oh, my middle initial. But only those closest to me get to call me by that name."

"So what is it?" he asked.

She turned around, her eyes immediately finding mine. "*Claire*."

The cool air she let into the bakery as she left swam around my ankles. I stared at the wreath, the bell, the girl on the other side of the glass who was casually strolling toward her car. At that moment, the town stood still—but I went on a long-distance run through my memory. *The beanbag chair, she died last year, the frame, distracted driver, most people call me BC, she loved to eat, the need for a fresh start, brownies, the flash drive, she was actually a lot like you, the butterfly effect, there are things I can't explain to you right now, colors, this could be the same person who took the photos of us, she was the first girl I've ever loved, let me look into this, you aren't just one—you're all of them, she was worth it, I think I love you, Sonny Carter.*

"Sonny!" Kyle's palm hit my shoulder. "Lana's on the phone."

At the mention of Lana, I blinked and rolled my head toward his. My eyes shifted to the phone in his left hand, but I couldn't say with confidence I knew what was happening. It was as if I'd switched to autopilot mode. I was there—but

I wasn't, and I didn't feel in control.

"Here," he said, lifting his cell to my face with a look of confusion.

I took it from his hands, staring into his eyes—but seeing something else. Everything else. "Hello?"

"God, why aren't you answering your phone?"

"I—"

"Remember when I told you I wanted to have a peaceful, no bullshit Christmas when I get back?"

"Y—yeah," I whispered, barely paying attention.

A door shut in the background and everything got louder, but she lowered her voice. "Then do you want to explain this letter to me?"

"Letter?"

" 'Meet me in parking lot C at midnight. We need to *freaking* talk?' Where did you get this?"

"I—"

"Did Dad see this?"

"No," I replied. "It was left on the porch. Look, I'll explain everything but I have to go. I—"

"Seriously, Sonny, if you didn't want me to see it, you could've at least hid it better. You knew I was coming to Dad's today." She opened and closed a drawer. "I know you don't exactly care for the guy—I don't either—but you should've told me about it."

I blinked again, and Kyle's full face appeared. "What?"

"The letter," she repeated. "You should have told me about the letter. You should have trusted me."

"What are you—"

"I wouldn't have gone."

"Gone where?"

"To meet Hill."

My mind took off running again. "*Mr. Hill*?"

"Yeah?" She started the bathwater. "The man's still folding his paper into triangles, I see. He used to do that to all our notes. You can barely open it, but he said it was his way of signing it without signing it. Kind of smart." She opened the towel cabinet. "Look, just don't tell Dad he tried to contact me. He'll kill him."

"The note was for you?" I whispered, my voice melting.

"When are you coming home?" Lana asked. "There are holiday movies to be watched and cookies to be baked. Oh, and I also bought us new pajamas for Christmas morning. Figured it's time we retire the candy canes."

The bell rang and Kyle looked toward the door; I did the same, turning my body around until I was blinded by the sunlight again. Kyle's phone dangling by my thigh, I watched Ron Harrison wipe his loafers across the mat. He corrected his posture and looked around the room, quickly finding who he was looking for. "Ms. Carter," he said, inching his way toward our table. "I think you need to come with me."

"What's going on?" Kyle stepped next to me, just an inch or two behind my right shoulder. Little by little, he lifted my cell phone out of my back pocket. My eyes cut beside me just in time to see him hide it behind his back.

"We'll talk," Ron said, attempting to assure me that everything was okay, but the officer standing outside on the sidewalk with my mom, Principal Clemmons, and Principal Winchester told me otherwise.

I could see Principal Winchester's age better on a Sunday morning. It was early—too early for a weekend—and the bags under his eyes were touching his cheekbones. Standing next to Principal Clemmons, he almost looked like a proud member of our society—but I could see the young man in him still yearning to return to Arizona. To Bella View Day. His forehead was filled with worry lines, but they were no match for mine when I finally got a full view of him. Hanging from his fingers was *the* manila envelope. "Where did you get that?" I asked Ron, but I didn't have to. The mixture of shock and confusion in my mom's eyes gave it away.

"Funny," Ron mumbled, lifting his chin. "I was about to ask you the same question."

ACKNOWLEDGMENTS

My family

My cast

My editor

…

Thank you!

ABOUT THE AUTHOR

Sarah Mello is the self-published author of the Westcott High series. After high school, she pursued her creative nature, which led her into the event industry. She opened a North Carolina wedding venue, which she managed for seven years. However, she never forgot the words of her twelfth-grade English teacher: "You're a writer." She published her first book, Westcott High, in July 2019.

Sarah was born in New York and spent her first five years on Long Island. When she was five, her family moved to Charlotte, NC, where she calls home.

"After writing Chapter Three of Westcott High, I remember thinking how real it felt—as if I were watching my favorite TV show." Sarah goes on to explain the project behind the book. "Bringing my book to life in the way that I did felt like a new concept. I had never seen another author do anything like that, and it was scary at times. But I think there's something to be said about pushing yourself to try new things." Sarah even tackled her own book marketing. "I hope I've shown that you don't necessarily need an abundance of resources to pursue a dream. Just imagine your characters, grab some models and a guy with a camera, and establish a presence on social media."

Made in the USA
Monee, IL
07 November 2021